To R...

May these words minister to your heart

BUSINESS UNUSUAL

A Novel

By

Linda F. Beed

John 15:16

Mama Linda

© 2007 by Linda F. Beed

Printed in the United States of America

Business Unusual is a work of fiction. Similarities to individuals or establishments are purely for the sake of lending authenticity to the story.

Library of Congress Control Number: 2006939253

1. Inspiration – Fiction. 2. Parenting – Fiction. 3. Single Living – Fiction. 4. Entrepreneurship – Fiction. 5. Domestic Violence – Fiction. 6. Romance – Fiction

Beed, Linda F.
Business Unusual: a novel – Linda F. Beed – 1ˢᵗ ed.
The Covenant Series #1

ISBN 0-9785890-0-9

Scripture is taken from the King James Version of the Bible.

ACKNOWLEDGEMENTS

It is with great reverence that I give all honor to my heavenly Father for the opportunity of being an instrument of His will. May I always listen for Your instruction and remain obedient to You.

To my parents **Addison and Dorothy Sawyer**. Ma and Daddy, thank you for the unconditional love you daily give. To our four blessings – **Ycedra, Maurice, Jeffrey and Aaris**. I have been blessed to have you as my children. To our godsons, **Michael Sanders, Solomon Johnson and Jerrell Mitchell** – delay is not denial. Do what you know to do. God will do the rest. To some fabulous women – **Rosetta Knight, Tanya Knight, Judith Pippens, Suzie S. Collier, Marie Stewart, Katherine Hooks, Zavonne Shareef, Renea Mitchell, Jamila and Yaminah Gardner** it is through all of you that God confirmed He had chosen me to write for Him. Thank you for the candor, critiques and insane actions I will not mention here. **The Pippen(s), Beed and Knight Family,** through your love and caring I have been blessed beyond measure. **Apostle Tony and Pastor Renee Morris,** thank you for being so vulnerable and providing avenues of growth for us in the Word and in self. Through watching the two of you I am fully able to comprehend the following: *Wherefore take unto you the whole armour of God, that ye may be able to withstand in the evil day, and having done all, to stand – Stand.* **Minister Karen Wells**, I treasure who you are and all that you have poured into me. To all of my **New Covenant Christian Center Family**, for your prayers I am grateful. **Special shout out to our Youth Ministry – M.A.P.P.** You guys have only touched the surface of the greatness that lies within. Allow nothing to detour you from the purpose God has preordained for your lives. **Prophet James Giles,** it seemed that every time I had grave concerns about writing you were there to encourage me to go forth. **Bishop A. L. and Dr. Gladys Hardy**, thank you for all that you do for the sake of the Kingdom. **Maurice M. Gray, Jr.**, what can I say except – thank you. You are the consummate mentor and I thank you for your unselfishness in sharing. **Jacquelin Thomas, Rosalind Stormer, Jeanette Hill,** I am blessed by your friendship. **Lynel Johnson Washington, Pittershawn Palmer and Idrissa Uqdah,** you three have been such a blessing.

This Book Is Dedicated To

BERNARD BEED — Husband of mine, our life together has not been what anyone would call storybook. It is however, one dedicated to standing in the face of adversity that comes our way. From inception to completion you have dealt with all the crazy that came with the process of writing and publishing this book. Thank you for being the man I needed by understanding and supporting the purpose God has for our life together. Without trepidation you provided the support necessary to bring this book to fruition. I like, love, honor and cherish you.

And if it seem evil unto you to serve the LORD, choose you this day whom ye will serve; whether the gods which your fathers served on the other side of the flood, or the gods of the Amorites, in whose land ye dwell: but as for me and my house, we will serve the LORD. **Joshua 24::15**

CHAPTER 1

Bernadette's arrival at her place of business heightens a sense of accomplishment within her. She can barely get two steps inside the door of 303 Covenant Place without drawing attention to herself. "Good morning Ms. Lewis."

A hearty smile revealing professionally cleaned teeth greets the head of security's welcome. Morning greetings ring out three more times as she waits for the elevator.

Confidently, she emerges from the stainless steel transport knowing that she is more than able to handle her business. Rays, streaming in through a domed skylight, shower her with warmth from sunshine not ordinarily present this early in the year.

"Good morning Ms. Lewis," greets Bernadette, as she nods toward her assistant.

Hand-sponged rose walls intermittently dressed with several rare pieces of artwork welcome their owner as she makes her way down the corridor. Her favorite piece, Lois Jones' Les Fetiches, stares at her from its place of honor. As she stares back, the imagery of the five masks seems to discern her spirit.

She moves on to her office door. 'Bernadette Lewis – President', engraved upon a radiant brass nameplate, serves as a daily reminder of her fourteen-year-old bedside pledge to be a responsible, servant leader.

As she steps through the door, the sun peeking through a gap in ceiling to floor blinds catches her attention. Hand over hand motions move them away from the windows like hands over eyes in a game of peek-a-boo. The morning sun floods the room, causing slivers of silver woven into lavender, silk wall coverings to sparkle like diamonds.

Living up to her position of power, Bernadette's everyday goal is to plunge head first into those necessary tasks associated with staying ahead of the competition. However, business as usual for Bernadette is far from the norm among her peers. The manner in which she lives her life and runs her business affairs indicates that she will never be anything but unusual in the eyes of the uninformed.

Often, those who are trying to help offer her ideas touting so-called proven methods guaranteed to get her to the top in a short period of time. Her courteous refusal to accept such suggestions lead people to believe that her prosperity will be short lived.

Her purpose, long ago understood and accepted, energizes her each day just like a cup of Cuban coffee. Wisdom beyond her years is not arrogance, but rather falls in line with her constant desire for self-improvement.

Recognizing a need Bernadette walks into her private quarters, stretches long, toned arms upward and begins to pray. "Father I worship and adore You for who You are. I give You praise for all that You have entrusted me with. I am mindful that without You I can do nothing." With utmost humility, she bends her knees, bringing them to rest upon lush carpet. "Please hear the prayer of Your servant, for my desire is to do Your will and honor You with a lifestyle of truth. I yield to Your command and pray daily for You to reveal through Your Spirit how I am to handle Your business. Amen."

Bernadette raises from her kneeling position, smoothes her dress and then heads toward the bathroom. Her reflection, in the six-foot horizontal mirror surrounded by Hollywood lights, makes her laugh. Several braids upon her head have taken a detour from their original pattern. She adjusts the wayward strands before returning to her office.

Habitually she reaches for the daily schedule her assistant, Mrs. Bell always has ready for her review. Following a morning meeting with her Chief Financial Officer, she is free to work on a few contracts and a training manual for a local daycare collective.

As the owner and president of B. L. Lewis Enterprises, a privately held consulting, software development and personnel training service, careful planning and strategic implementation have brought her to a place within the business community that have left others curious to know her 'secret'.

Words of encouragement engraved in marble rest upon her desk – 'Yesterday's ceiling is today's floor'. In order to remove the 'ceiling' blocking her path to the next level, she opens yesterday's unfinished document. A review of what has been formatted thus far yields a few concerns.

Thoughts of Falimah Meyer interrupt her research flow. Following their initial interview, nine months earlier, the decision of whether or not to employ her as the company's financial officer challenged her usually keen, discerning spirit. While everything on Falimah's resume indicated that she would be a valuable asset, their first encounter left Bernadette slightly cautious.

Falimah arrived fifteen minutes early for the interview, self-assured and dressed in a kiwi green, double-breasted power suit that fit like butter. Their first verbal exchange revealed her high confidence level, which was necessary for the position. Falimah showcased her competency by remedying an off-the-cuff financial crisis thrown her way. Not only did she solve the problem, but she also presented a strategy to offset the loss and prevent a re-occurrence.

Bernadette was impressed, but still on guard. Her apprehension rose out of concern for what Falimah's personal agenda might be. Contents of her resume disclosed that her education and previous work experiences more than qualified her for positions that would pay much more than B. L. Lewis could currently afford.

Bernadette's prayer had been that the Lord would send her quality people who would not only see her vision, but also relish being capstones for building a company with a reputation of integrity.

Regardless of her misgivings, something deep within Bernadette told her that Falimah would indeed be an asset to her company.

Vibration from Bernadette's preset watch brings her back to the present. Today's preparation included a half-hour review of monthly balance sheets before her meeting with Falimah.

While heading to the meeting, she prays as she walks. "Father open my eyes, ears and spirit to what You may have for me today. Show me how to handle all things pertaining to Your business, Your way…thy will be done."

Treva Scott, bold, accomplished and well suited to be Falimah's assistant, stands to greet Bernadette when she enters the junior executive suite. Treva's exaggerated turn opens her tea-length wrap skirt enough to expose shapely legs. The sheer, long-sleeve burgundy blouse over a spaghetti strap camisole leaves little to the imagination. Treva's distinctive style would raise questions in most executive offices, this one included. Ordinarily, Bernadette has no qualms with her uniqueness, but there have been days when she thought she might need to converse with Treva regarding a more appropriate dress code.

Taking her seat, Treva tells Bernadette that Falimah is on the phone.

"I'm a little early. I can wait until she's finished." Bernadette spins quickly towards a chair, transforming her tunic into a billowing cloud of color.

A burst of shrill laughter diverts the attention of both Bernadette and Treva toward Falimah's slightly opened door.

"I am being real. Every time my eyes fall on our Ms. Lewis, I have to remember where I am. Until I see the pedigree on this filly, I'm sticking to my original belief."

As unflattering words speed through the air insulting Bernadette, Treva redirects her attention to a miscellaneous task in an attempt to look busy.

"I'll tell you once again; there is nothing real on her except the designer clothes on her back. And stop trying to defend her like Treva does, the facts speak for themselves. When have you ever seen a sista that dark with gray eyes and that much hair? You know those are contacts and a well-maintained weave. And from the expense put into this building, I can guarantee you she has a very, very white boy tucked away who's financing this operation."

Treva risks a peek from beneath her mascara-laden lashes. Coldness crosses Bernadette's face before she bows her head and prays.

Confident that she is collected enough; Bernadette stands, knocks, and enters Falimah's office. Falimah's almond-shaped eyes become enlarged, then return to their natural state as the phone is hung up. Lips perfectly covered with hibiscus colored lipstick open and then shut with no sound from a somewhat disheveled Falimah.

"Good morning."

Falimah responds to Bernadette's greeting by extending the expected quarterly report to her. It is quickly scanned then placed under her arm.

Tension in the room is so prevalent it has become tangible.

Falimah's discomfort is easily read. The silence is finally broken when Bernadette inquires about Falimah's afternoon schedule, which she happens to know is full.

"Since you're busy today, I'm going to postpone this meeting. My assistant will email you my address. We'll meet at my house tomorrow around eleven." Without waiting for a response Bernadette exits the room.

Falimah falls into her seat from overwhelming fatigue. As anxiety dissipates, she considers the possibilities. An invitation to Bernadette's home surely means that she did not overhear her phone conversation. As her fatigue begins to wane, Falimah is filled with the realization of her near fatal mistake. Olympic-fast feet carry her to the reception area.

"Treva!"

I gotta go Daddy," she whispers into the receiver before abruptly hanging up. "Yes Falimah?" Treva sweetly replies.

Falimah's ongoing love affair with the authority afforded by her executive position inserts condescension into her tone, "I pay you to take care of my business. Why didn't you?"

Rapidly moving lips allow no room for Treva to respond. In an effort to assert more self-importance Falimah demands that a report with an original end-of-the-day deadline be on her desk by noon.

Without missing a beat, Treva hands the perfectly prepared report encased in the company's customized folder to Falimah. Rather than thanking her, Falimah barks out a long list of orders.

"You need me to repeat any of this, Treva?" she snaps when she realizes Treva is writing nothing down.

Treva's expression remains neutral. "No."

Falimah's eyes narrow.

"I'm good at what I do. If I wasn't, you wouldn't have hired me, and that report you don't need until tomorrow afternoon wouldn't be in your hands right now."

Heat rises in Falimah's medium-brown face. "You might want to rethink how you address me. I'm the one who decides whether you'll be in that chair from 9- to-5."

"Yeah, but Ms. Lewis decides where your butt parks." Treva leans forward. "And for the record I'll give you some free advice. Work on timing and voice control before your back-biting tongue gets you put out on the street."

Crimson creeps up Falimah's neck. "You just make sure you get your work taken care of and don't let what happened today happen again."

Instead of a humble reply, Treva's response is a confident chuckle.

Falimah's body language stiffens indicating her intent as she takes a step forward. Treva stands. Falimah stops herself and then adjusts the hem of her tailored suit with her manicured hands.

"I'll remind you one more time. This is a place of business. Your job is to take care of my needs and those of this company. Calls to your daddy don't come from here."

If looks could kill, there would be an immediate opening for Falimah's position.

***

"Good morning and thank you for calling B. L. Lewis Enterprises. How may I help you?"

"Good morning. Is Bernadette Lewis available?"

"Ms. Lewis will be available after eleven. May I have her return your call or would you prefer to leave a message?"

"Please tell her Hayes Davis called."

***

Facial warfare between Falimah and Treva continues all morning. Falimah's weapon of choice is a frosty stare, which proves useless against Treva's shield, a mirthful smile. Their nonverbal squabble carries into the employee lounge, and is very obvious to other employees. Falimah tosses one last scowl at Treva before leaving the break area. It is repelled by soft laughter.

Brian Chin moves to Treva's table. "What's going on with you two?"

Using intricately painted burgundy and gold nails, Treva finger combs her shoulder length hair. "Falimah's been hitting the witch's brew a little too hard lately. She thinks she can send her evil my way without response because…"

Brian laughs aloud as Treva continues her tirade. His laugh turns into a low-toned warning for her to lower her voice.

"Don't shush me, boy. I don't care who hears me. I'll tell her to her face she ain't…"

"She ain't what?"

Falimah's reappearance, though surprising, does not unnerve Treva. Brian makes no pretense about being interested in whatever is about to transpire.

Falimah stares with eyes turned to daggers at Treva before walking away.

Secure behind a locked door, Falimah rants out loud. "I gave Treva this job to tide her over till she decides what she really wants to do. I hope she's made a decision, because her time here is up."

***

Long before darkened skies receive the sun's morning kiss, motivation has already risen.

Motivation to surpass goals obtained the day before, and above all, to obey Divine instruction, catapults a body with less than six hours of sleep from its resting place into action.

Bernadette lies flat on carpet as soft as spun lamb's wool and the color of August ripened plums, to enter into solitary time with the One she loves with joy and humility.

With the sweetest embrace, the Spirit of peace overtakes her, and complete awareness of self is lost in the ministry of love.

Time spent in meditation reveal what must transpire between her and Falimah at their luncheon meeting. While Bernadette could remain there forever, her emergence from this holy place is a must.

Wrought iron and electronics separates the public from the private residence of Bernadette Lewis.

Awaiting permission to enter, Falimah reads the words 'WELCOME TO THE PLANTATION', embedded in the stone pillar attached to the gate.

Falimah receives admittance and instructions to drive to the rear of the property. She maneuvers her matador red hardtop convertible Lexus/SC forward. Slowly she drives past enormous dogwood trees and rose bushes that will soon blossom into a multitude of colors.

The rolling form of comfort comes to a halt in front of a beautifully kept guesthouse approximately forty yards beyond the formal residence. Lilac bushes yet to offer their fragrance to the world line the circular driveway.

Bernadette waves. She is striking in a bright tangerine print dress with its hemline tied just above the knee, giving it an asymmetric look.

The words 'SLAVE QUARTERS' engraved over the doorway catch Falimah's attention as she climbs the steps of the enormous porch.

"Welcome," Bernadette says leading the way inside.

Falimah surveys the tasteful surroundings while Bernadette takes a visual inventory of her guest. Falimah's sleeveless white rayon three quarter length top marginally conceals the scanty gold top beneath it. The modest outer garment compliments matching Capri's, and accentuates her defined calves. Gold painted fingernails match her toenails, sandals, purse, and sunglasses atop her head.

"This is a beautiful house Ms. Lewis," Falimah comments as her eyes survey the room.

Office politics come to the forefront of Bernadette's mind. She moves a few steps closer to Falimah. "Professional courtesy is appreciated. You can call me Bernadette while you're here. But don't ever call me Bernie because I hate that."

Since there is time before lunch is ready, Bernadette offers Falimah a tour of the house.

"Tell me about the Plantation sign," Falimah says while examining a quilt mounted over the fireplace in the great room that depicts a slave auction.

"It's a family tradition too long to go into."

Falimah's attention moves from the quilt to the seating area. Flowing antique gold sheers flank each side of arched windows behind a uniquely patterned sofa in tones of red, gold and purple.

"Is this a real mud cloth couch? Where did you find it in this combination of colors?"

"Excuse me Ms. Lewis." Turning her attention to the doorway, Bernadette acknowledges her housekeeper.

"Lunch is ready."

"Thank you. We'll eat now."

Falimah follows Bernadette to the dining room while continuing to take in as much of the house as possible.

For all guests, the dining room becomes the focus of conversation in this luxurious home. Traditional southern décor merges with African accents to make the room exquisite.

Craftsmanship far superior to anything Falimah has seen roots her before the showcase of the room. Hands in various sizes and conditions are carved into the wood frame of the mirror above the buffet. Old hands, young hands, hands balled into fists, clasped together, bound by chains, ropes and hopelessness all have a story to tell. Gnarled and disfigured hands reveal the result of forced slavery. All appear to be reaching for the liberty of freedom - freedom that was denied repeatedly to slaves. Hands rising from empty Motherland thrones literally implore all to never forget the African Maafa (holocaust).

Bernadette points to a pair whose index fingers are missing. "These are the hands of my great-great-great-great-great grandmother. She was a house slave who gave two pieces of fruit from a kitchen bowl to her hungry children. Her punishment for her actions was the amputation of two fingers and the selling of those two children. This frame was made to honor her and to remind us to be thankful for the hands that prepare our meals."

Jambalaya over steamed brown rice with a compliment of Jalapeno bread overrides each woman's resolve to only have one helping. Their taste buds overrule their second determination not to have dessert when a fresh blackberry cobbler and homemade vanilla ice cream is placed before them.

Following the meal, Bernadette motions toward an exit on the opposite side of the room. Falimah follows her into an impressive home office. Bernadette offers her a seat in one of the leather chairs before an acacia wood desk.

Sparing no time Bernadette gets straight to the point. "We've been working together a while, so you know I'm a straight-to-the-point type of woman."

Bernadette pauses allowing her words to sink in before pulling one of many braids on her head forward. While maintaining eye contact with her guest the braid is undone. Using the comb at her side, Bernadette begins at her scalp to comb through the lock reaching below her shoulder.

Falimah's eyes widen.

Bernadette vigorously rubs her eyes.

Falimah stares, but does not speak.

Bernadette swaggers to a closet.

The force in which the door is pulled open startles Falimah. Bernadette laughs, then points inside a closet filled with winter coats, hats and forgotten items. "There's no white boy in here. There's not a black, purple or yellow one in here either."

Blood drains from Falimah's face.

A master at doing what it takes to get and/or retain what she needs, Falimah speaks candidly. "You heard me on the phone, didn't you, Bernadette?"

"Yes, and to be perfectly honest with you, you should know you used the last of your nine lives under my employ."

"Are you firing me?"

Bernadette looks her in the eye. "There is nothing average about me or my company, including my employees. If you were average, you wouldn't be sitting in that chair right now."

Bernadette is at Falimah's side almost before Falimah registers her movements. "I have what I have because of who I am. Everything about me is authentic, Falimah." Bernadette pauses in order to squelch the unprofessional language threatening to take over the conversation.

"Before I go any further, I need to know we're speaking the same language, Falimah. I speak truth at all times. I need that to be your first language in my place of business."

Falimah quickly assures Bernadette that she will abide by this.

Bernadette nods, then continues. "In addition to that I need to know you have my back and I can trust you with my friendship and my business. If I can't trust you, I will let you go."

Falimah apologizes for her words and assures Bernadette she can be trusted.

Silence accompanies the two to the front door where Falimah's exit is acknowledged only by Bernadette's slight nod.

Bernadette remains on the porch until the car disappears. Whether Falimah will ever cross her threshold again is uncertain at this time. Although all the right things were said, her performance does not fool Bernadette into believing she will change overnight, if at all. She walks down the hallway praying.

"Father, You told me I am required to minister to those You bring to Covenant Place. Even though I really want to fire her, I thank You Holy Spirit for guiding me today. Father help me to continue to seek You for what You intend to accomplish through those you bring through the doors of Your workplace…"

***

Careful planning has always been the key to opening windows of opportunity for Falimah Meyer. Carelessness caused her to play the loose lip card that was soundly trumped by Bernadette's ownership hold card.

A single knock interrupts Falimah's mental vacation. Treva enters. The two women lock eyes.

"You wanted to see me?"

Falimah's hand extends toward a comfortable chair in front of her desk. Treva sits.

"First off all I need to apologize. I had no right to talk to you the way I did the other day."

Treva's mouth slightly opens, but she does not speak.

Falimah perches theatrically on the edge of her desk and drones on and on about needing to work together as a team.

Totally oblivious to the fact that she lost Treva after the second sentence, Falimah mercifully reaches the end of her monologue. "…I also need to know you have my back and I can trust you with my friendship and my business."

Without removing her eyes from Falimah, Treva stands and adjusts her slightly snug skirt and top.

"Treva?"

Treva's stare is hard; her words are blunt and without pretense. "You talk a good game Falimah, but you forget I've been privy to the real you longer than we've worked together. The issue isn't whether or not you can trust me. It's really about whether I can trust you."

CHAPTER 2

Knowing that Hayes called lights Bernadette's face like the sun at high noon. The light is quickly overshadowed because he did not leave a return phone number.

In an effort to find his number, she pours out the contents of her large purse onto her desk. She intensely examines every scrap of paper she finds, which yields much anxiety but not Hayes' telephone number.

'Jesus Loves Me' coming from her specially programmed cell phone, halts Bernadette's search. "What do you want, Miss Terry?" she sings to her older sister.

"What did you get me for my birthday?"

"You'll find out when I get there."

"Then you need to get here soon, Twinkle," she says calling Bernadette by her nickname. "Your crazy sister, Zavonne flew in this morning, and she's already been in my closet stealing."

Determination to remain on task wanes. Bernadette's linen covered legs cross then uncross then cross again. Weeks ago when she learned they would celebrate Terry's birthday in Chicago due to her theatrical commitment, she began visualizing trips to establishments to seek out items not available locally. Additionally, she would be able to partake of a meal at a restaurant that a college friend recently opened.

Numerous ways of how to spend time in one of her favorite cities provokes, taunts and outright dares Bernadette to yield to spontaneity.

"Where's your mind, Twinkle?"

"On your husband. Make sure Kentucky Boyd has my money ready when I land. I don't want no stuff. I have Daddy's number on speed dial. One push of the button will seal your man's doom."

Laughter dismisses Bernadette's playful extortion attempt.

"I'm serious, Terry."

"I know you are, but you're five years and three children too late for that."

"No, I'm not. Kentucky promised me a million bucks to keep Daddy occupied while you two slipped off to Catalina. I plan to collect every dime."

Sisterly banter moves from humor to a more interesting subject. "Tell me if you've given any serious consideration to what's-his-name."

Bernadette's imagination places Hayes Davis before her very eyes. She leans back. The coolness of her glove leather chair cools the heat creeping up her neck. Contoured chair arms are caressed as if they are human flesh.

"Talk to me, Twinkle."

Bernadette presses the conference button to allow her freedom to resume her search. "Nothing's going on", she says rifling through her wallet for the coveted number. "We've been back and forth. I gave him my number and he called while I was out."

"And?"

"He didn't leave a number and I can't find the one he gave me. What if he doesn't call again?"

"Mmm hmm. I thought he was just an acquaintance. From the tone of your voice I'd say he might be a bit more than you're letting on." Terry replies.

Bernadette does not respond.

"Talk to me, sis."

"Okay…but only if you keep this confidential. I don't want your relatives turning my business into a fact-finding mission."

"Don't make me say it again. Talk to me!"

Bernadette picks up the receiver pressing her lips close as if whispering a secret. "This may sound odd, but I believe Hayes and I have a future beyond friendship."

Tonight's revised script abruptly lands on the seat beside Terry.

"Hayes must have something strong going for him for you to say that. Is he that fine?"

"Physically, yes. We haven't really had a chance to get real deep into conversation yet, so I don't know if he really is fine or not. I just have a feeling about him."

"When you get here I want you to promise to talk seriously with me."

Bernadette makes the promise before hanging up.

Terry stares at the phone long after her conversation has ended. Her instincts say there is more to what Bernadette hasn't said than what she has. As accomplished as Bernadette is in business, her experience with men is limited and very few are aware of this.

Terry moves from the comfort of the plush chaise and kneels. "Father, show me how to be the sister Twinkle needs as she steps into…"

***

"What you mullin' over, man?"

Roosevelt Hillis' query receives a vague response.

"What?"

"I asked who or what are you concentrating on? Your mouth is movin', but I'm not hearin' ya."

Hayes Davis' history with Roosevelt brings life to the phrase 'closer than a brother'. As he ponders a response, a diversion presents itself. A plump woman seated several tables away winks at Hayes. His eyes quickly assess her outward trappings. The woman has large, inviting bright eyes, and dark brown skin with a natural glow. Bright tones of red, yellow and purple scream loudly upon her caftan accessorized with gaudy jewelry that falsely enlarges the size of her head.

His nod acknowledges receipt of her wink. Her grin reveals a wide space where two front upper and three lower teeth should be. The emptiness of the black hole draws Hayes into her mouth. Her tongue wags at him like the tail of a lion inside a cage. He turns his attention back to his luncheon guest.

"Do you recall the woman I met at the Saving Grace auction?"

Roosevelt leans back, neither acknowledging nor denying the memory.

Hayes, the master at getting what he wants, presses ahead with words he knows will provoke a response from Roosevelt. "I admire your dedication to your wife by pleading ignorance. Perhaps this will jog your fading memory. It was my Queen who made every woman displaying her attributes appear as desert dust as she defined the power of the simple black dress."

Eloquence from a man of many words is an expectation from those who have held any lengthy conversation with Hayes Davis. Without failure, his diction and command of the English language demands attention, regardless of the subject matter.

"It wasn't the dress, or what she was working with underneath it. It was her virtue that reached out and touched ya," Roosevelt responds before placing a large portion of Fajita into his mouth.

"Attempts for further interaction have been futile."

"Good, 'cause you already have a woman. You do remember the one you've been stringing along for the last year or so?"

"We are no more."

Roosevelt downs the remains of his raspberry lemonade. "Okay Hayes, start at the beginning and go slow."

It is only to this man that Hayes would acknowledge severing a relationship rather than cheating in order to have what he considers the absolute best.

"After I won the bid for the book I sought, she attempted to purchase it from me. Small talk revealed she owns Covenant Place where the auction was held."

Roosevelt's expression shows signs of interest in Hayes' conversation.

Hayes' nod certifies his positive impression of the woman who now holds his interest. "Yes, we are both business owners with similar worldviews and interests. She gave me her cell number. We have only marginally conversed. Business and my involvement with the stage production I'm in, has kept us from getting any deeper."

"That's a start."

"So I thought, Brown Man. The last we spoke she gave me her office number. She was not available."

Pride goeth before the fall, Roosevelt muses inwardly. *This girl has bruised Hayes' ego and now he's sulkin' 'cause he doesn't know what to do. I don't plan on spendin' the afternoon with him bellyaching, so let me bite the bait then cut the line.* "You gonna call her again?"

"No."

"Then I don't wanna hear nothin' else about this girl."

Hayes concedes with a nod before taking a huge bite of his roast beef sandwich. As he wipes his mouth, his eyes again meet those of the tongue-wagging woman. He resumes eating his meal. When he finishes he pushes his empty plate aside, wipes his mouth then removes a second napkin from the collar of his custom made indigo and pomegranate patterned linen tunic. His smile reveals the dimple in his left cheek. "I will call her tomorrow."

Roosevelt's dark brown pupils stare at Hayes. Hayes' black pupils return the stare. Roosevelt leans back, runs a manicured fingertip over the top of his wedding ring, then leans forward and nods. Hayes rubs his chin with the tip of his left index finger.

The wagging-tongue-woman's melon-sized breasts rest heavily upon the table before her. She looks around the room. She, like many others, has centered her attention on the animated men.

Roosevelt's pressed lips holds onto his laughter as he watches Hayes make eye contact with the many solo female diners paying more attention to the two of them than to their own meals. He turns again to see Hayes' rotund admirer looking his way.

"You notice the direct looks of interest given to us my friend?" Hayes says more as a comment than a question. "I believe more than a few would allow me into their beds within weeks if not days after our first encounter. Today I have no interest in a short-term conquest."

Roosevelt remains quiet.

"My words may sound odd to you my brother, but I feel something different since I encountered Bernadette Lewis. Is that presumptuous, given the fact that we have just met?"

"Well…you've always presumed your agenda will be met, but this sounds different."

"I feel it is. It is as though I've been taken captive."

Roosevelt's raspy chuckling sounds like a low growl. "You are a captive – to your libido. I saw that girl and I know you. You've been getting to know her for a little over a month. The fact that you ain't had her yet got you going crazy. I'm just wondering why you're still interested. What insecurity does she have that you'll use as the key to opening her treasure chest?"

Hayes' relaxed body language becomes rigid.

"Your change-up ain't stoppin' nothin' from my mouth, brotha man."

"There is nothing wrong with her," Hayes defensively replies.

"How would you know? You don't' know her yet."

Amusement turns the corners of Hayes' mouth upward. "Man of intense passion. Are you saying you do not believe in the possibility of love at first sight?"

"If you're trippin' the way you say, love ain't nowhere in the neighborhood you tryin' to move to."

Hayes leans forward. Arrogantly he proclaims, "I may be moving soon."

Hayes kisses two fingers then extends them toward Roosevelt. "Enlighten me. What made you know Nee Nee was meant to be your wife?"

Roosevelt places two large hands over his own heart. Hayes does the same.

"Let me go to the Men's room. When I come back we'll talk seriously."

Hayes watches Roosevelt exit the room. Despite the personal nature of the pending conversation, Roosevelt is the only person that he would discuss this matter with. His confidant's personality prepares him for brutal honesty. It is their honesty with one another that drew them together and has kept them hip-tight since college.

Hayes and Roosevelt were not a pair anyone who knew them from their Morehouse College days would have bet on becoming lifelong friends. Roosevelt arrived on campus from Philadelphia with a partial scholarship and a work-study job to finance his education. Hayes stepped off the plane from

Seattle with all expenses paid in full and a large check to deposit into his bank account.

The financial divide did not hinder what was meant to be, and neither did the fact that Roosevelt insisted Hayes check his arrogance at the door of their shared dorm room. Hayes is indeed a man with a high opinion of himself. Truth be told, Roosevelt is somewhat arrogant as well, but insisted that his personality stemmed from a godly boldness.

Outwardly, the two friends are different, but share many inner commonalities. Both men are avid readers and have a strong passion for music. Their shared determination to succeed in a world that frowns upon them by virtue of ethnicity led them to seek business degrees. Hayes minored in English while Roosevelt chose a minor in Education. Both men are loyal to whom they love. Their roads forked on the Sabbath day. Roosevelt went searching for a church home as soon as he unpacked. Hayes went with him on occasions, but usually reserved Sundays for serious studying.

During their four years as roommates there was only one physical altercation.

Lack of interest in the women who literally threw themselves at Roosevelt's feet caused Hayes to question his roommate's sexual preference.

When he bluntly asked, Roosevelt's response was a quick right to the jaw. Roosevelt helped Hayes up from the floor and apologized before he could catch his breath.

Roosevelt's pain at being asked such a question turned to hysterical laughter when Hayes shared the reason for the inquiry. Laughter gave way to a lengthy discussion.

Roosevelt posed the question of why men were viewed as some form of oddity if they had not slept with five or six women before marriage.

Hayes felt it his personal obligation to enlighten his seemingly ignorant friend. He enthusiastically shared learned lessons from his father. In his father's opinion men who are men, will be men. In doing so it taught them how to identify women who are for playing and those who are worthy of marriage. When Hayes factored in the increasing number of available women created by the rising gay population, he saw an abundant crop waiting to be harvested.

Roosevelt donned his armor and countered Hayes' assertions with a swift rebuttal.

Hayes ignored his words by proclaiming that as long as no woman was forced to engage in sexual activity, men were well within their rights to harvest the abundant crop.

Roosevelt dismissed that point of view by rebuking what he saw as irresponsibility.

Hayes responded with words from his father instructing him on how to take precautions in order to ward off the possibility of fathering an unwanted child, or receiving gifts requiring prescriptions to get rid of such gifts.

Every tested instruction from Hayes' personal value pack was dismissed like children anticipating the recess bell by Roosevelt's opinions rooted in his strong religious beliefs.

As Hayes persisted, Roosevelt became blunt. "Say you sleep with every woman breathing, and then you find the one you think is the marrying kind, but she busts your bubble once you get the ring on her finger. This happens 'cause she won't bend over backwards ta make ya holla the way the others did. How long before you go down memory lane, then back to your old ways?"

Hayes brags about the length of his parent's marriage as truth for all he had been taught.

Roosevelt's disbelief in such logic took him to a higher level of boldness. He asked if the length of their marriage included fidelity.

Crazy will take over when you have nowhere to run in a verbal scrimmage. Hayes shouted out his father's love for his mother.

Just as Hayes was about to enter another round of lunacy, Roosevelt halted it by raising his large hand. He told Hayes that it represented morality and encouraged him to grasp it.

The essence of Roosevelt Hillis sprang forth with compassion, yet his words cut deep as they reminded Hayes of the women left behind like crumbs on a trail by his cold-hearted ways. Razor sharp words drew blood when Hayes was told that there was one way to find out if all that his father advocates is truth – and that was to ask if his father had been unfaithful to his mother.

Before he blew up, Hayes walked away to nurse his gushing wound.

Later, Roosevelt revealed what he shared with no one other than his father. He led a life of abstinence because of a personal pledge. He pledged to God that on his wedding night his wife would have something no other woman would ever have – him.

Hayes' laughter was followed by words ridiculing Roosevelt for being weak.

Roosevelt's response caused Hayes to consider looking for blood donors. Those donors were needed to replace blood spurting from the artery punctured when Roosevelt boldly stated that the only weakness in him would be in not publicly standing for the godly convictions he cherished.

Wagging Tongue Woman moves from her seat and blocks Roosevelt's path when he returns to the dining area. His cold stare halts her intent to grasp his arm. Regrouping, she offers him a business card. It is refused.

Roosevelt retakes his seat and resumes eating. Hayes' stare reveals his irritation as he impatiently waits. He waits, knowing his friend will answer his question in his own time. Unfortunately, depending on his mood that time could be now, tomorrow or the day after.

"When I wanted to marry Nee Nee, I put myself before the Father because I needed to know if I had the right to ask anyone to marry me. Then I asked if she was supposed to be my wife. I needed to know if she'd back me in what God's plan is for me and vice versa. If I went left, I had to know she was the one who wouldn't rest till she prayed me back to holy. I had to be equipped to do the same for her 'cause if she went crazy on the honeymoon, she'd still be my wife."

Puzzlement possesses Hayes' face.

"You're sittin' there lookin' null and void 'cause you don't have that relationship, son."

"I'm a believer."

"Yes you are, Hayes, and that's the problem. You believe in who God is, but you don't believe Him. That's why you treat Him like the string of women you continually mess over. You go to church pretty regularly, you date pretty regularly. You hang out with your flavor of the month callin' whatever y'all do a relationship. When you get what you want you drop her then move on. You come to church, get a need met through a couple of messages and/or marginal involvement with various functions and you equate that with Christianity. In both cases you're wrong. It's about commitment to the relationship, a matter you have neglected with your women and with God because it's still all about you."

Hayes frowns at the weight of words he does not care to hear. "No time for one of your lengthy sermons today."

"No time like the present, my fearful friend."

"Answer my question, Ro."

"Prayer will give you the answer you need."

***

Bernadette logs onto the Internet.

One of her favorite songs plays in the background as she searches for her site of choice – Chicago Daily.com.

Teeth made straight by the aid of a three-year relationship with an orthodontist appear while reading of Terry's theatrical success. Joy turns to a slow burn as she reads further - *The sensational musical, 'I Just Can't Take It No More', starring Terry Boyd will reach new heights when she is joined by the first lady of the African-American silver screen – Eleanor Burton.*

Bernadette utilizes her trusty speed-dial to call her sister. Terry's husky voice answers after the second ring.

"Hello."

"Terry Josephine Lewis Boyd!"

Terry snaps to attention at the mention of every legal name she has possessed.

"Twinkle?"

"Yes, it's Twinkle!"

"What's wrong? You sound upset."

"I'm not upset. *I'm mad!* You thought I wouldn't find out until it was too late!"

"Come on, Twinkle," Terry says after an uncomfortable pause. "Would it kill you to say hello? It's been three years."

"Don't start, Terry," Bernadette warns. "I'm still coming, but you make sure you keep distance between me and her."

Dial tone ends the conversation.

Anger prevents Bernadette from focusing upon business. She opens one of several personal photo files. She scrolls from Terry's wedding to Zavonne holding the deed of her first property acquisition to the one photo that hardens her; the one of her maternal grandmother, Eleanor Burton.

Despite inward resolve, Bernadette loses the battle to control her tears. Streaked mascara across the back of her hand when she wipes her face heightens her anger.

Her stinging eyes blur her vision causing her to stumble to the bathroom. Before the mirror she frowns at her makeup stained reflection.

She soaks a towel and begins the process of stripping away the remaining makeup. Staring into the mirror she studies her steel gray eyes that have been the genetic marker for generations of members of her maternal family. Those eyes forever connect her to a grandmother she prefers to erase from memory. It is this grandmother, who through her high profile career, guaranteed that the lives of her loved ones would not be ordinary.

Eugene and Eleanor Burton were screen and stage actors during a time when people of color primarily received demeaning roles. Determination enabled them to break through glass ceilings in order to portray characters of dignity. They used their growing influence to open doors for others to walk through with pride. To this day they are highly esteemed for their tireless contribution to the arts.

Bernadette returns to her desk. She stares at the image on her screen then speaks as though her grandmother were sitting before her. "I don't understand you Bunky, but you are going to understand that I'm my own woman."

CHAPTER 3

The song "Surrender" melodically serenades Bernadette and fills her with warmth.

"Yes I packed extra undies and have them and toiletries carefully tucked away in my carry on bag Mrs. Lewis," Bernadette sings into the phone then bursts into laughter.

"Good morning to you too, Ms. Twinkle."

"Where are you, Mama?"

"I'm on my way to the airport."

Memories of rash words spoken to Terry drain the warmth from Bernadette's disposition and bring her face to face with her options. She can either apologize for hanging up on Terry and in the process remove storm clouds hovering over them, or rain on a rare weekend with her mother and sisters by behaving like a spoiled brat.

"Mama. Terry and I had a few words."

Tightness in Addie Lewis' voice reveals her displeasure. "You're angry because your grandmother is going to be there, aren't you?"

Deep breaths become Bernadette's control mechanism. Avoiding this conversation is of utmost importance to keep her secret locked behind the door to her past.

"I know you and your grandmother haven't been close."

Bernadette's efforts to conceal emotions, that maternal instincts can detect from anywhere in the universe, fails.

"Don't start crying, Twinkle."

Bernadette asks that they drop the subject. Addie agrees to table the conversation until they are face to face.

Despite the comfort of a first class seat on a nonstop flight from Seattle to Chicago, Bernadette cannot escape unpleasant memories. Memories of a grandmother who caused scales to fall from semi-naïve eyes on Bernadette's sixteenth birthday remain as bitter as brine water.

What should have been a solitary birthday celebration was merged with an awards ceremony honoring her grandparents in Chicago. A private showing and selection of new dresses from the exclusive couture house, Marabel's, was the salve needed to heal hurt feelings.

Hours spent with her grandmother's best friend, a very small woman simply known as Ms. Marabel, left a lasting impression upon Bernadette.

Throughout her fitting, Bernadette was reminded that she was a seed from extraordinary lineage. For that reason alone, she had the responsibility of setting and maintaining a certain standard. That standard included never succumbing to what the world thought of her or what it told her she should be. She remembers the woman's wise words spoken with a hint of a lisp to this day.

Her father reinforced the value of who she was that evening when he arrived for their exclusive catered dinner in her suite.

Joseph Lewis appeared as the prince of her dreams standing before her in a custom made tuxedo. His heavenly white teeth set in a face the color of charcoal briquettes made Bernadette feel like the princess he had always proclaimed her to be. He heightened that feeling by presenting her with white roses signifying her purity and innocence. The coy expression she practiced for weeks gave way to a wide-eyed grin when he bowed before her.

Joseph had long ago removed constraints of inhibition between the two. On this evening, he ushered Bernadette across a threshold into new heights of maturity and self-respect.

Their main entrée that consisted of her favorite foods, mustard greens with a hint of pepper sauce, hot water cornbread and a medley of okra, corn and tomatoes, was accompanied by Joseph's dissertation on hormonally driven males. He placed special emphasis on lines that guys used to get next to women. His execution was so polished Bernadette wondered if he had used any of them on her mother prior to marriage.

Tenderly he cautioned his daughter about casual kissing and touching. Wise words relayed how kissing often led to petting, which in turn stirred emotions that led to a quest for sexual release.

Although at times Bernadette was clearly uncomfortable discussing such matters with her father, Joseph's demeanor remained somber as he explained why sexual intercourse between a man and woman was restricted to the marriage bed.

His deliberate words answered her unspoken questions. If she ever had to weigh the option of whether or not to surrender her virginity to someone who was not her husband, the simple answer was no.

The answer to her second unasked question quickly followed. Joseph spoke of the godly standards set for her from the day of her birth. Emphatically, he declared that because he knew how to love his wife and daughters he would never consider asking them to lower standards set for them by God. He also stated that any man asking her to do so did not truly love her.

Joseph's speech peaked with the serving of her favorite dessert, peach cobbler. He reiterated how she was expected to carry herself as a woman of God. He also impressed upon Bernadette that prayer would reveal the true spirit of a person.

Overwhelming love moved Joseph from his chair to kneel before his daughter. To him, she was perfect in every way.

Hands roughened by weekend tasks reached into an inner pocket. From it he drew a two-carat diamond ring. The inscription inside the band read, "I promise until I wed". Without hesitation, Bernadette accepted the ring and pledged to God before Joseph to remain a virgin until she married.

What should have been a memorable weekend filled only with sweetness turned into a nightmare.

Dressed in lavender satin pajamas Bernadette made her way to her grandparent's suite to thank them for her experience at Marabel's.

Shouts of anger met her in the corridor. Her pace slowed as her sensitive ears were assaulted by words that penetrated cherry wood doors. With lightning speed, harsh words sliced through the air hitting an unintentional mark. The force of their impact destroyed innocence, replacing it with a spirit of rejection that has been guarded closely by an impenetrable wall ever since.

"Ladies and gentlemen, please fasten your seatbelts and prepare for landing."

The instructions given to the passengers, jar Bernadette out of her daydream. She gazes out the window. *Why did I have to talk crazy to Terry? With running my business, I can't just hop on a plane and meet up with her or Zavonne for a little sisterly fun and power shopping anytime I want. This is a rare opportunity, and I want us to have a good time. Let me just swallow my pride and do whatever it takes to keep everything light and fun for Terry's birthday.*

Making her way through throngs of travelers pushing their way toward their destinations irritates her.

Traveling these days is crazy, she inwardly murmurs. *I should bill Terry for the two hours of idle time I spent at SeaTac trying to look like the all American girl to keep security from pulling me out of line for a random body check.*

"Hey lady, can I buy ya a drink or something?"

Café au lait and honey-bronzed faces stare at Bernadette. Hypnotic gray eyes, often described as seductive, welcome their baby sister. She sprints into their outstretched arms.

"I'm sorry I talked crazy to you, Terry."

"I know you are Ms. Twinkle, and you'll have a chance to prove it by buying me many presents. I left my lovely daughters with Mama and Bunky, so there are no distractions. You can start buying me stuff now." Terry laughs.

Extending her long arm with an open palm Bernadette demands her hush money.

Terry places a crisp five-dollar bill with a note from her husband pleading for an extension due to having to fulfill the extravagant needs of a spoiled wife into Bernadette's hand.

"How come your husband doesn't give me money?" Zavonne demands to know.

Terry laughs, "Because unlike your evil sister, you have nothing on him."

Bernadette looks down and notices a pair of her sandals on Zavonne's feet.

Zavonne pretends not to notice. "You can lapse off into fantasy land if you want, but if you have to walk barefoot, you're coming out of my kicks, girl."

Zavonne starts to say something, but is interrupted by Bernadette. "Just take me to Marabel's and buy me some clothes and shoes to compensate me for your theft."

"I didn't get these from you," she laughs holding up one foot. "Direct your words to Terry. I took these from her house six months ago."

Bernadette glances at Terry. "I'm gonna work your husband's wallet hard while I'm here."

Marabel's – located at One Magnificent Mile in Chicago, Illinois is the sisters' destination. Today they will preview ensembles that will only be available at Marabel's. However, it is the unique line of shoes they are most interested in.

Bernadette and Zavonne spring from the car before it comes to a full stop, then race toward the canopied entrance.

Fred Flintstone style brakes prevent the two from crashing head first into the back wall of the open elevator. Bernadette formulates her game plan while they are in the glass elevator.

Like a WNBA guard, Bernadette moves past Zavonne when the elevator door opens. An equally skillful Zavonne snatches the back of Bernadette's blouse. Fumbling forward, the two arrive at the door of their favorite suite.

"RESERVED."

Two sets of eyes narrow at the sight of the lighted sign.

"Terry!"

Shrill laughter is the response of the cunning woman whose goal is always to work smarter rather than harder. Instead of joining the foot race, Terry reserved the showing suite by calling from her cell phone.

Terry checks her watch. "I hold the keys to this shoe kingdom." She checks her watch a second time. "I have a show to put on tonight, so time is of the essence."

"I love you, Terry," Bernadette purrs.

"I know you do. As a matter of fact, you love me so much you're going to spend every dime you extorted from my husband over the years on me. Ms. Zavonne will spend an equal amount to show her undying love for her big sister."

Anticipation of attending the show is well worth groveling and keeping forced expressions of affection upon their faces.

"You guys gonna spend a lot of money on me?"

"Yes ma'am."

"Then you may enter with the queen, but make sure you stay a few paces behind."

Terry takes full advantage of her position of power. She commands her perturbed siblings to sit a row behind her, so that they do not obstruct her view with what she refers to as their rather large heads.

Satisfied with her view, Terry leisurely sips herbal tea from a gold gilded demitasse cup. Exaggerated moans escape into the air each time she samples a succulent piece of fruit. She deliberately makes no request for the suite attendant to serve the agitated women behind her.

The exclusive showing of the latest trend in footwear is impressive right along with the number of shoes on Terry's 'to purchase' list.

The final pair of shoes modeled leaves them breathless. Upon the model's feet is a pair of jeweled shoes with three inch, fourteen-karat gold-plated heels. The narrow strip that fits over the top of the foot and ankle strap are encrusted with tiny diamonds.

A magnetic force pulls all three women to the runway. Bernadette immediately takes mental inventory of her shoe collection, then whispers to Zavonne. "Row six, center. No, I think these deserve a special place of honor. They'll reside next to my Etu Evans collection. They'll look good there, huh Zavonne?"

Zavonne tightens her grip on her Yellowstone leather purse.

"You make more money than the law allows. Buy me those shoes," Bernadette hisses.

Zavonne's rare refusal of any of her requests infuriates the somewhat spoiled woman.

Their sniping at one another continues throughout the purchasing of an array of designer clothing. To add fuel to Bernadette's fire, Zavonne taunts her with pictures of two pairs of shoes she will return for later in the afternoon.

The sisters load the packages into Terry's car and then walk from Marabel's to Eli's The Steak Place for lunch to be followed by exceptional cheesecake.

At Terry's request the bickering duo agree to a truce for the duration of lunch. With the heat reduced under their simmering kettle of crazy, Terry shares her news.

"Bunky has agreed to move in with us to help with the girls."

Bernadette stabs an innocent table napkin as if it threatened her.

"She's not the same person she was when we were younger, Twinkle," Terry offers. "Plus, she's all the family we have in Los Angeles now."

A roll on Bernadette's plate meets the same fate as her napkin.

Their entrees arrive. After it is blessed, Bernadette shoves her plate aside.

Rather than give in to Bernadette's juvenile behavior Terry changes the subject. "How are your wedding plans, Ms. Zavonne?"

The most dramatic of the Lewis sisters predictably takes them on a scenic tour of what she wants to say before actually answering the question.

"With Daddy's help, my real estate investments have turned into gold. Next year, I'm adding on to Saving Grace." Zavonne pauses to take a sip from her glass. "I'm adding two more houses and a skills center. Adding to my staff will allow me time to perform in a few plays and to travel with my honey."

"As long as that traveling doesn't include you and your husband living in and out of my house the way you currently do, I'm cool with it." Bernadette quips.

"Last I knew your name was not on the deed to the Plantation, Twinkle. It's a family residence for a particular reason." Zavonne shoots back.

"But?" Terry interjects in an effort to ward off crazy words between Zavonne and Bernadette.

"But we need to get through the wedding," Zavonne sighs. "Much as I miss Mommy, I'm hanging in the streets with you guys to get away from Bunky and her grandiose plans for a wedding and reception we don't want."

Bernadette's teeth work their way through the top layer of her lip. She takes a mental vacation from the conversation in order to remain civil. Her return is prompted with the mention of Hayes' name. Her involuntary smile triggers inherent traits. Terry and Zavonne simultaneously lean their heads to the side and then wrinkle their noses, a habit inherited from their mother and grandmother.

"Has Hayes gotten through to you yet?" Zavonne queries.

"We'll get together," Bernadette says.

Zavonne laughs, "Didn't you guys meet a couple of months back? How slow is the boy?"

Bernadette's dessert fork becomes a potential weapon.

Their laughter draws unwanted attention. Recognizing Terry, theatre fans make their way to the table in hopes of getting an autograph. Zavonne positions herself to become a buffer between Terry and a possible overzealous fan.

Bernadette recognizes opportunity. She pays the bill and then heads toward the door.

"Where you going?" Zavonne calls out.

"To Marabel's to pick up my shoes."

Terry laughs so hard she can barely sign the paper in her hand. "She got you good, girl."

"Oh, you just wait; I've got something for little Miss Goody Two Shoes."

"She knows that. That's why she's on her way to get *your* two shoes right now."

Silence is an unfamiliar presence in the kitchen where Eleanor and Addie are preparing the evening meal.

Cornmeal, baking powder, flour, oil and sugar go into a large bowl for mixing. An egg cracked on the side of the bowl is the only audible sound in the room. Eleanor's reflection in the window allows Addie to study her distant gaze.

"What is it, Mother?" Addie finally asks.

"Are your girls angry with me?"

Respect for her mother cushions Addie's response. "Zavonne's not angry, Mother. She is agitated. We all know you love her and will provide the best money can buy for her. You just need to let the wedding and reception be what she wants."

Eleanor's waving hand dismisses advice often tendered, but rarely heeded.

"Your daughter is too young to understand what must be for a woman in her position. Your father and I worked hard to establish ourselves at the top of our professions. Your husband is sought after as advisor and confidant to powerful men. Your singing career and evangelistic prowess has made your name internationally known. We have a social responsibility to set examples for others."

Addie rolls her eyes at the familiar spiel from a woman dedicated to protocol.

"What about Twinkle? How is she doing?"

Pride momentarily has its way. "Twinkle's a lot like her daddy when it comes to business. She's already moved far beyond her first year's projections."

Eleanor's perfectly rose-painted lips separate to expose professionally capped teeth. She glances out the window. Softly spoken words reveal vulnerability. "Does she ever talk about me, Addie?"

Negative words are spoken kindly. "No, she doesn't."

Cornmeal batter is beaten like a recaptured slave. Tears cause Eleanor's eyes to sparkle. As discretely as she can, she wipes them away.

"Mother, what's wrong with you and Twinkle?"

"We're two women who are more alike than we're willing to admit."
Pounding feet, screams of glee, unexpected pranks and retaliation followed by hysterical laughter have ruled Terry's temporary home nonstop for the past thirty-six hours. Though they are supposed to be dressing for a formal portrait to be taken in less than two hours, three little girls and three grown women continue to frolic about in loungewear. Magnificent manes crinkled, braided and bone straight flutter through the air like Superman's cape in flight as merriment abounds.

Eleanor ends their little party when she demands that they be ready for inspection in less than one hour.

Within forty-five minutes five females are assembled and awaiting Eleanor's inspection. Bernadette strolls in ten minutes later wrapped in purple, gold and red fabric. Her enormous Afro is one that would rival that of Angela Davis in her prime. Holding her hand is her youngest niece who is dramatically wrapped in the same fabric with her hair standing as big and proud as the African Princess Bernadette tells her she is.

Terry and Zavonne swallow hard as they watch Eleanor's eyes sweep over the two. They let out a sigh of relief when she does not comment.

The photographer's arrival sets off another round of merriment between the sisters and the little ones. Eleanor sternly commands them to mind their manners.

"The little girls are awfully cute, Mrs. Burton," the photographer remarks to Eleanor.

A wide smile puffs Eleanor's lightly powdered cheeks.

"They look like they're pretty close in age too, if you don't mind my saying so."

"They're triplets."

The family's amusement at the photographer's reaction does not stem from the fact that the girls are triplets, but rather from their varying skin color. The family joke is that Terry gave birth to Addie's children. The oldest is fair skinned (high-yellow) with long (what people consider good) hair, just like Terry. The second born has the same bronze colored skin as Zavonne and long hair that is tamed with oil, a comb and a brush. The youngest triplet with her dark, dark skin is often mistaken to be Bernadette's daughter when they are together. Like her sisters, she has very long hair which Terry hot combs for more control. All three have the infamous Burton gray eyes.

Alone in her room Eleanor pulls a picture from her wallet. It is of Bernadette at age twenty-one sitting in her late grandfather's lap.

Deep pain moves upward. It is a pain so immense it often causes Eleanor to hold nightly conversations with photographs of her estranged granddaughter. Tears pelting the photo are wiped away. She falls asleep praying for forgiveness.

Bernadette fluffs her pillow and leans back in her seat with a wide smile. Thoughts shifting to Eleanor turn it upside down.

Despite her initial apprehension, exposure to her grandmother was not as unpleasant as she had imagined.

When she found out that her granddaughters had plans to eat at Bernadette's friend's restaurant, Eleanor called some of her industry friends and arranged for them to join them. That call was followed with one to an executive friend at a local news station. The result was media exposure for Terry and her play as well as unprecedented exposure for the restaurant.

The food was so delicious the five women placed orders to go. A majority of Eleanor's friends followed suit. Two of the departing diners gave the proprietress their card and asked her to call regarding future catering opportunities.

Terry made it a point to whisper Eleanor's support of her friend's endeavors into Bernadette's uncaring ear. Her one-woman campaign at reconciling the two was unending. So bold was her crusade that she went so far as to suggest Bernadette invite Eleanor to Seattle for a visit.

Bernadette punches her now tear-soaked pillow. *The only way she'll get in my house, is if someone lets her in before I get there to block her.*

CHAPTER 4

Growth is rarely experienced without a measure of discomfort.

In Treva's case, growth, in the form of independence and comfort in who she is, has her emotions spiraling. Desire to own her own business stems from a need to be as financially independent as possible. Right now, the discomfort in her life is rooted in the attitude of a green-eyed monster named Falimah Meyer.

Their last sparring round forces her to reexamine what true friendship really is.

Refusal of a dinner date with one of Falimah's male friends was regarded as treason. Falimah retaliated by standing Treva up for their lunch and shopping date. Rather than changing plans, Treva keeps the date with herself.

What should have been a relaxing drive to the restaurant becomes aggravating. Rainbow-dressed cyclists, in a world of their own, slow down traffic considerably. Ten riders in single file speed up and then slow down at will. Quick reflexes prevent Treva from striking a straggler when the group comes to a sudden halt.

"If you can't ride them things, get off the road!"

The straggler extends the international finger to Treva.

She laughs at the gesture like she would laugh at a clumsy pick-up line.

Ten minutes later she reaches her destination. Her short skirt covering little more than her firm derriere is quickly adjusted when she steps from her car. Extra sway in her hips garners attention from men strolling and jogging past the Blu Water Leschi Café.

She pauses just inside the wooden floor establishment to inspect her appearance in one of the two large fish tanks. Her burgundy-rinsed hair pinned up in a gold clamp is neat. The semi-snug tangerine shell, above the waistband of her jean skirt, meets her approval.

The thirty-something hostess escorts Treva to a table with a great view. She can see cruising vessels and everyone entering and exiting the restaurant.

After ten minutes spent perusing the menu, Treva is faced with a tough menu choice. Only her determination to maintain her health and physical fitness stifles a rash decision to order crab cakes and the Cobb salad.

A smile appears across her face when Bernadette and several others enter the dining area. They exchange nods of greeting.

Toned legs extending from mid-thigh jean shorts carry Bernadette toward Treva's table while drawing sly and overt gazes from young and old male patrons alike. A swift kick brings one particularly observant man's attention back to his companion.

"Are you waiting for someone?" Bernadette asks as she gives Treva a hug.

"No. I'm dating myself today. I'm headed out to do a little shopping after this."

Treva accepts Bernadette's invitation to join her and her friends for lunch and a little shopping.

Four women filled with gourmet delights make their way to downtown Seattle. Inside Nubia's on First Avenue, the new clothing arrivals heighten their euphoria. The purchase of two dresses, three tops and a variety of accessories bring Treva to her spending limit.

From Nubia's the foursome journey to Carol's Essentials in the Central District for a book signing by a local author. Their next destination is Joy Unlimited to check out the latest in gospel music, videos and books. Ms. Kay, an angel on earth and shop proprietress, scolds Bernadette for not stopping by to see her sooner.

The decision to unwind at Bernadette's house over a light meal is unanimous. The proposed simple meal becomes an elaborate sit down affair. Conversation flows over plates filled with braised lamb shanks, steamed asparagus, new potatoes and a mixed salad. From a small covered dish Bernadette takes a serving of mustard greens then replaces the lid without offering some to anyone. Words from the wise caution Treva not to ask for any.

Strong opinions regarding the arts and its influence upon the youth float around the dinner table. At times, their verbal exchanges become heated.

Not one to back away from expressing herself, Treva voices her views and supports them with examples of life application.

Saturday night turns into Sunday morning before Treva departs with an extended invitation to stop by anytime.

***

Treva presses the send button to transmit Falimah's weekly calendar to her computer file.

She takes a sip of her tea then sets it aside. Her attention goes to Falimah. After being stood up, Treva refused to return the ten calls she placed to her home and cell phone.

Falimah's calls were not unexpected, but definitely unwanted. For years responses to what she considered a slight by Treva, ranged from disappearing acts to verbal tirades. When she would calm down she would call or come by, offer no apology and act as if all was well between them.

Anticipation rides to work with Falimah. Working for B.L. Lewis has been a plus in more ways than one. The trust Bernadette has placed in her has allowed Falimah to represent her boss at many prominent affairs throughout the greater Seattle area. Mingling with the big guns has placed her in an enviable position amongst her peers.

Unabashed speech announces Falimah's mood when she reaches the landing of the junior executive suite. "Girl, where have you been? I couldn't stalk you down anywhere this weekend."

Treva responds without looking up from her computer screen.
"Good morning to you too. And for your information, Ms. Thang, I was preoccupied."

Falimah takes in the unfamiliar appearance of her long-time friend. "Whoever occupied you must have the magic touch. You have a new look. Stand up."

Treva goes into model mode to show off her new outfit, hair and nails. Coral and gold hand-painted upon a rayon shift with a respectful side split, delicately showcase her assets. Lucite mules with a modest two-inch heel expose a fresh pedicure with coral and gold polish matching her fingernails. Burgundy rinsed hair has been replaced by Treva's own dark brown tresses with chestnut highlights.

"You look great. Why the sudden change?"

"Just testing the waters."

Falimah's one hundred twenty pounds lean against the door. Her firm backside does not allow her to be flush with the wood. Healthy breasts strain to escape the push-up bra beneath a low-cut silk shell. "Who's testing your water?"

Falimah deflects a wad of paper aimed at her head as she disappears into her office.

Summer weather usually comes to Seattle on the fifth of July. The date is also a signal for the sun deprived citizens to don their shorts and tank tops. When the mercury reaches mid-70's or above, fashion folly abounds as the fit and unfit slip into clothing revealing more than the public should ever be privy to.

This summer has been an exception to the rule. Temperatures have remained in the 80's since mid-June. The beautiful weather adds to the gaiety of annual festivities for native Seattleites and tourists.

During July and August the city buzzes with preparations for the season of Seafair activities. Milk box flotillas and pageants make for high spirits. Many will turn out for Central Area and International District's festivities, and a host of other events associated with the season.

There are three events truly synonymous with Seafair tradition. Arrival of the Seafair Pirates at Elliott Bay is a delight for the young and old. When the Blue Angels thunder overhead, normal activity ceases in order to watch brilliant blue and gold F-18 fighter planes practice ear-splitting, precision stunts.

The third exciting event is the arrival of hydroplanes at Stan Sayres Pit on Lake Washington. Spectators will park as far away as the Rainier Valley then hike to the beach days in advance to stake out prime viewing territory. Innovative children use water from garden hoses to power their Styrofoam prototypes during serious neighborhood competitions.

It is a hectic time. It is an exciting and noisy time. It is Seattle at its summer's best.

This Monday morning, as well as days during renovations, area drivers slow down to get a better view of a once decaying Seattle landmark now known as Covenant Place.

Months of work have turned a once dark and ostentatious estate into a warm and inviting business center.

To accommodate her needs, Bernadette added several thousand square feet to the building. The new addition included the crown jewel of the edifice – the executive suite referred to as The Penthouse.

Pleasant thoughts of today's carefully planned luncheon fill Bernadette's mind as she drives toward Covenant Place. Business associates view the frequent perks she awards her employees as an unnecessary gesture. To her, they go hand in hand with building relationships.

Loud singing and her speeding rate keep pace with the tempo of the music blasting from her car speakers. Several times she checks her speed, knowing that without divine intervention, any policeman stopping her would indeed cite her for speeding.

After parking in her reserved spot, Bernadette leisurely gathers her attaché and Kate Spade bag. Her entrance into the Penthouse brings a loud sigh of relief from her assistant.

Assured that all is well for this morning's meeting, Bernadette strolls to her office. Habitually she pauses outside the door. French tipped nails trace the engraving upon the name plate.

With little time to waste, Bernadette deposits accessories then picks up notes for the meeting from her desk. She offers a brief prayer before leaving. "Father, I pray You will go before me. I ask that You would please bless those among us who need a blessing today."

She moves quickly down the hall. Anticipation accompanies her into the elevator. To Bernadette's surprise, red roses greet her when the doors open.

"These just arrived for you," Mrs. Bell announces, handing Bernadette the card that accompanied the bouquet. "You get to the meeting. I'll put these in water."

Warmth creeps into Bernadette's face as she reads: *Attempts to reach you by phone have been futile. Perhaps these roses will* speak *what I have yet to verbally transmit. My desire is to escort you to breakfast, lunch and dinner, Monday, Tuesday, Wednesday, Thursday, Friday, Saturday or Sunday. The choice is yours. I await your response. Home 206 772..., Office 206 860..., Cell Phone 206 271..., Hayes K. B. Davis.*

Lips, turned up into a smile, stretch the width of Bernadette's face as she races to the terrace where her employees await her.

Purple and gold fabric fashioned into a flowing ankle length dress enhances her regal gait. Braids, dramatically fashioned, serve as her crown. Feet inside gold sandals secretly removed from Zavonne's suitcase and gold earrings recaptured from Terry complete her look.

"Good morning ladies and gentlemen," Bernadette begins. "I'm not going to bog our session down with the regular syrupy things you thought I'd deal with today. The purpose of our quarterly luncheon is my way of showing you how much I appreciate the hard work you do." Looking into a sea of curious faces, Bernadette continues, "At the last meeting I promised to give you a little more insight into who I am."

She reveals that she migrated to Seattle from Los Angeles to attend the University of Washington, where she earned degrees in business and education. To lighten the mood even more, she hints that gifts of ethnic jewelry and size twelve shoes will keep them on her good side. She gives them all permission to call her Bernadette, and strongly emphasizes her aversion to the tag of Bernie.

To everyone's surprise, the conclusion of office business kicks off unexpected pleasure. Winners of several games receive certificates for box lunches from That Brown Girl Catering.

The grand prize, an all expense paid weekend for two to Chicago and two outfits of their choice from Marabel's is won by the luck of the draw. It goes to one of the housekeeping staff.

The man is so overwhelmed by emotion he cannot speak. When he regains his composure, he reveals how he has been scrimping to send his wife to her sister's wedding. The wedding is in two months in Chicago.

Centrifugal force is what keeps Bernadette on her feet. Silently she gives thanks for the blessing of someone in need.

***

Time, once lost, can never be recaptured. Hoping to turn back the hands of time only fools one into believing what has slipped away can be recaptured.

Refusal to accept the fact that their affair has ended, keeps a stream of unwanted calls, flowing to Hayes' home, cell and office phones. His negative response to a demand that they meet provokes the undesirable caller into shrieking obscenities into the receiver. One click disconnects foul language from uncaring ears.

Hayes' arrogance pities the dismissed caller, while caressing his huge ego.

Vibration from his watch indicates it is 6 P.M. Nine hours since the roses were delivered to Bernadette. Pride reins in a burning desire to call her while his imagination conjures visions of what he hopes to partake of in the near future.

Rather than linger in the realm of possibilities, he changes into running attire. Two hours later, a winded Hayes returns to his home.

The red light flashing on his bedside phone indicate missed calls. The first message is from a cast member reminding him of dress rehearsal for the production he is performing in. The second is from Bernadette thanking him for the flowers. He cannot dial her number fast enough.

Three rings suggest the phone will not be answered, but her jolly hello quells his anxiety.

"Ms. Lewis. This is your florist. I presume the roses met your satisfaction?"

"Yellow roses would have been more than sufficient."

Hayes removes silk pajama bottoms from a drawer. "Are you offended?"

"Any florist I interact with needs to understand what is appropriate for all occasions. Red roses signify love at first sight. Yellow roses are indicative of *friendship* and *respect*."

Bernadette's words leave Hayes no room for misinterpretation. He tosses his pajamas into a nearby chair.

Determination to complete a home project prevents her from accepting his invitation to catch a late movie. His obligation to a dress rehearsal negates them from connecting at a time Bernadette is available. They soon find themselves playing calendar roulette. Bernadette suggests a Sunday phone date, but Hayes talks her into a personal encounter.

An unfamiliar eagerness has Hayes standing outside The Wellington fifteen minutes early. His erect posture inside a Tabasco hued short sleeve shirt over cargo shorts draws the attention of those walking and driving by.

A blur of black catches his eye as it speeds around the corner. The driver maneuvers the Infiniti Q45 into a tight spot across the street from the restaurant with the skill of a veteran stunt driver. From the driver's side, amethyst covered legs seem as if they will never stop coming from the car. Hayes' raven colored eyes remain fixed upon Bernadette's every move.

She smiles mischievously. "Why are you staring at me? Do I have a boogie in my nose?"

Hayes' response is the offering of a single yellow rose.

CHAPTER 5

Bernadette picks up a strawberry yogurt then returns it to the shelf. Her pledge to lose five pounds wills her to pick it up again. "I promise I'll eat you tomorrow." Believing her words, she feels free of guilt.

She picks up her carry bag and purse and then heads to the door. Her departure is delayed when she catches sight of herself in the hallway mirror. Soft palms slide down her mid-section. Tautness of her flat abdomen is pleasing. Although her exercise routine has lessened since returning from Chicago she is in great shape. Sideways vision brings about laughter. If these hind-quarters get any firmer, this dress and a few others will be on their way to someone else's house soon.

She chuckles as she heads to her grandparents house.

As she makes her way she leisurely sniffs the budding flowers. Everywhere the eye can see her grandmother's award winning red, yellow, white, pink, and hybrid roses stand tall and full. Fragrant lilac bushes burdened with rich blooms of white and purple nestled among dogwood trees look so comfortable, one might believe that they sprang from the same roots.

"One, two, three...fifteen...twenty-six." Bernadette counts the plants blooming everywhere space permits inside the glass-enclosed atrium leading to her grandmother's kitchen. As she steps through a door that is never locked, familiar smells caress her nostrils giving comfort one only equates with home.

"Good morning Ms. Twinkle," her grandmother calls out as Bernadette merrily skips into the kitchen. "You've been so busy lately, I was wondering when you would drop in for a meal with us simple folk."

Bernadette immediately processes the word simple – *having or composed of only one thing, element, or part. Not involved or complicated. Being without additions or modifications. Having little or no ornamentation; not embellished or adorned. These people are not simple. They are complicated. They have made many modifications to their lives and mine. Neither one of them will leave this house until their wardrobe adornments are perfect.*

"Some new people up in here? Last I knew y'all were still living high on the hog."

"You want this food girl or do I need to put you out?"

Eyes that have melted her grandmother's heart since birth plead for mercy. Together they move about the kitchen putting finishing touches on the meal.

"Tell me how you're managing, Twinkle?"

The simple question sets off a red flag. *Somebody leaked something and it's about to hit public airwaves.* Knowing her grandmother is far too wise to be put off by surface words, Bernadette remains silent.

Julia Lewis presses for what she seeks as she places golden brown biscuits into a linen-lined basket. "How do you manage all you have to do and find time for your new beau?"

In lieu of a verbal response, Bernadette folds napkins monogrammed with the family crest then sets them on the table.

The entrance of her grandfather carrying his bible sends Bernadette into his outstretched arms. Her embrace lingers as she whispers, "Help me Papa. Nana's on a hunt."

Holding his head upward he softly replies, "Just tell her everything now, so we can get to church on time."

Will escorts Bernadette to her place at the table. He leaves her standing until he seats his wife.

Rather than avoiding the inevitable, Bernadette speaks. "What do you want to know about Hayes, Nana?"

"*Everything.* With your parents living in Alabama it's me and your granddaddy's responsibility to know what's going on."

"Mama already knows that I've been spending a little time with Hayes," Bernadette responds in hopes of appeasing Julia's curiosity.

"What does that mean these days?"

"Our work commitments and social schedules don't leave much time for personal interaction, but we've managed to share a few meals. Most of the time we talk on the phone."

"How do you feel about him, baby?"

"So far I like him."

"And?"

"It's not that deep, Nana."

"But you'll see him again?" she is asked.

"Yes ma'am."

Bernadette fills in a few pertinent blanks for Julia by telling her that Hayes is a Morehouse graduate. He received his MBA from Temple University. He travels abroad often, and has an astounding grasp of African culture. He's fluent in Spanish, French, and the Bantu dialects of Shona and Ndebele.

Her unnecessary trip to the sink for water brings a temporary lull to the conversation. Upon her return Bernadette resumes eating her food as if there is no expectancy for her to continue.

"Stop playing around, girl." Julia warns.

"Hayes and his family are members of Zion Faith Temple. He owns two bookstores. One is in Seattle. The other is in Tacoma. He's never been married and he has no children in his arms or in gestation."

Julia's sideways glance warns Bernadette not to get too smart with her responses.

Will grasps Bernadette's hand. "You say he attends Zion Faith Temple. I know the pastors. They're good word teachin' and livin' people. Do your young man and the Lord know each other?"

Bernadette's gaze travels from the dark serious face of her grandfather to the light brown face of her grandmother. "We've talked about different activities at our respective churches but we haven't gotten deep into our individual walks."

Julia places her napkin over her unfinished food, and then pushes the plate aside. "Tell me something, Twinkle," she softly says, "how long have you been keeping time with Hayes?"

"About three months."

Julia's placid expression is far too familiar. Bernadette braces for her response.

"Think on this Twinkle. Three months you been sizin' up this boy, but you still don't know about his walk with God. Now, say you spend another three months going out with him before you find out he just goes to church and doesn't really know the Lord. That's six months wasted on second or maybe even third best when the prize that was meant for you may be getting away. Where do you go from there?"

Since there are no words to respond with, that would not be attached to a lie, Bernadette chooses silence. In silence, she examines the ageless wonders known simply as Papa and Nana. At seventy-five years of age they are as in tune to the evolution of the culture their grandchildren are exposed to as they were to the trends of their own youth. Their knack for effortlessly pulling truth out of the air, at times has caused Bernadette and her siblings to confess to disobedient actions before the subject is even brought up.

Will enters the conversation. His focus is upon his wife's face, but his words speak directly to Bernadette. "What we're saying, Twinkle, is that you've been raised up with Jesus values. Ain't nothin' the Lord gave you worth givin' up for any man. If you got a hankerin' for this here boy you go to God and ask Him to show you who he really is." He taps Julia's hand. "It's time for you to bring that boy 'round here so we can see him."

Bernadette shivers as she awaits words that are a family mantra.

"He needs to know you got value and you come from people who come from somebody," he says patting the bible resting near his left hand. Will leans back in his chair with a bit of a distant look. "You know Papa been prayin', baby. You bring that boy 'round here so I can get a good whiff of who he really is."

Julia rises from the table and heads toward the exit. A lifetime of cohabitation has conditioned Bernadette to respond to Julia's non-verbal commands. She follows obediently.

The soft rustling of Julia's baby blue and white satin dressing gown is savored. As a child, the sound alerted Bernadette to Julia's presence. To save herself from the switch, she quickly ceased any disobedient behavior. This sound of softness also calmed her anxiety as it signified protection was near.

Swishing sounds now accompanied by the clicking of wedge-heeled slippers carry Julia across the glistening linoleum of her quilting room. From a drawer in her desk she removes a worn journal, then extends it to Bernadette.

She grins widely as she accepts the forgotten treasure with the words "GOD'S PURPOSE FOR MY LIFE" printed across the front.

"We need to get ready for service, Twinkle. I want you to take that home, read it, then think about what we talked about today."

She promises to do so, then returns to the kitchen to gather her belongings before setting out for church.

Will's small, sturdy hands grasp the sink in order not to disturb any of Julia's African violets lining the windowsill. His gaze remains upon Bernadette's car until it disappears from sight. He returns to tidying up the recently remodeled kitchen. Enormous roses in a crystal vase placed in the center of the six-foot table signify that all is in order. Time waiting for his wife is spent reminiscing.

Fifty-eight years of marriage has literally blended the minds of Will and Julia into one. They are so in tune with one another that whether seen or unseen, one can sense the presence of the other. He turns to acknowledge his wife's presence.

Julia's discerning spirit speaks to her husband's thoughts. "We can talk about this in the car, Will. We need to get to church."

Julia takes the extended arm of her husband and walks as proudly today as she did when they marched down the aisle following their wedding ceremony.

"You were thinking about Joe and Addie weren't you?" Julia softly says as Will maneuvers their midnight blue Cadillac towards church. "I know about the dream Joe shared with you just before he proposed to Addie. I had the same one a few days before he told you about his."

Will cocks his head to the side, but says nothing.

"It's as clear to me now as it was then," Julia continues softly. "In the dream I saw him and Addie and three babies. Some type of light rocked two of the babies. Whenever it came near the third baby it turned dark. The baby was pitched into the air. When it fell, it was caught by something sent to protect it."

Will's unspoken question fills Julia's spirit. "I'm telling you this now, because now is the time. Twinkle's got more of a fire for this boy than she wants us to know. If they move too fast it will hinder both their purposes."

"Because?"

"I been prayin', Will. This boy doesn't know God."

"And?"

"Today we gave Twinkle something to think about, but she's the only one who can make the right decision."

Will parks in a space close to the entry of the church. Gently, he brings Julia's hands to his lips and kisses them. The glimmer in his eyes causes her heart to accelerate the way it did the first time she laid eyes upon him. "Are you worried?"

"Why would I worry about tomorrow when I can pray *today*?"

Sight trained upon upraised fists immobilizes tyranny about to rain down on a helpless victim. The culprit's statue-like posture allows the innocent to run for shelter behind her Shero – Sister Bernadette.

Now that his initial plans have been sabotaged, the pudgy student peripherally searches for a substitute victim. He finds one. Bernadette's will power is tested when he takes two steps to the left. His tightly balled fingers relax then return to defense position. Another carefully taken step moves the stocky predator closer to his unsuspecting target. His fists unclench then clench several more times, daring classroom authority to challenge him.

As he smirks, his facial features twist making his reflection look like he is standing before a funhouse mirror. In a split second, the chair before him is grasped and then thrown towards a group at play. Bernadette's lightning fast reflexes catch the chair with one hand and the fleeing assailant with the other.

"What are you doing to my baby?"

An obese woman draped in pink polyester lopes to the aid of the tantrum-throwing child struggling to free himself from Bernadette's grasp. Her overrun mules clap like an audience with each step.

Dramatic wailing and kicking eventually work to the child's advantage granting him a sudden release. Bernadette's foot and his butt, which is almost as round as hers, cushion his fall to the floor. Pain shooting through her bunion makes her want to kick the child. Instead she works hard to remove it as he gleefully applies weight to her throbbing foot.

Bernadette hobbles over to the group of wide-eyed children stunned into silence by the event. The mother needlessly fusses over her one hundred twenty pound, nine-year-old now drawn into the fetal position and wailing at the top of his lungs.

Arriving parents are immune to the performance between the two. Past history has taught them not to listen to the false accusations being made against Bernadette.

"We'll see what Pastor has to say about this, Sister Lewis…"

Bernadette's number two pencil points to several cameras strategically set about the room. Mother and son waddle away knowing they have been defeated.

"Thank goodness for nanny cams," Bernadette sighs. Due to their presence this particular student has been shown to be the perpetrator of many classroom outbursts. Unfortunately, today's conflict means extra time spent filling out an incident report.

Being forty minutes late for her luncheon date adds to the irritation of Bernadette's day. So does six hours inside two-hour shoes.

Of all the places she and Zavonne have dined, The Marina is by far a favorite of the sisters. Aside from the fantastic food, the popular draw of The Marina is its dockside dining for seafaring clientele. Split-level outdoor seating is at a premium during the summer months. Regular maintenance keeps the wooden pier shiny. Picnic tables with green and sand colored umbrellas can accommodate parties anywhere from two to ten. Fabric covered chairs in the same hues of the umbrellas complete the inviting motif.

In order to stave off Zavonne's comments about her tardiness Bernadette tries to hasten her pace. Doing so on sore feet makes her look like she is walking barefoot across hot coals.

"If you'd quit wearing runway shoes while you're chasing after children you wouldn't have to walk like Jenny pimpin' harder than any." Zavonne laughs aloud.

Bernadette ignores her as she removes her swollen feet from the exquisite shoes. Her release from shoe captivity does little to relax her aching toes. "I will never wear these shoes again."

"You were the one coveting." Zavonne taunts pointing to the shoes that were given to Bernadette rather than to her.

"Let me permanently close your mouth about these shoes. With all the pain I've been in since wearing them I've figured it out. These are not a gift. They're payback for working Terry's nerves when we were in Chicago. Trust me, when she least expects it I will pay her back."

After ceasing conversation to order lunch, Zavonne abruptly asks about the status of Hayes. Bernadette ignores her question while fumbling through her purse.

Zavonne's jeweled hand moves toward a water glass.

Bernadette's eyes turn menacing. Her promise of public retaliation should water fly dismisses Zavonne's plan of an aquatic assault.

Zavonne's hands move slowly to the table's edge. Her fingertips erratically tap out a beat then stop just as suddenly as they began.

"Are you on a hunt for Nana?" Bernadette asks.

"No."

Zavonne's hand is lightly tapped with one of Bernadette's bronze colored fingernails. "This is sister talk Z. I'll know if you set me up. To answer your question, I'm taking my time with Hayes."

Zavonne's somber expression announces the seriousness of her train of thought. "Time is a precious commodity that can't be redeemed, Twinkle. Do you think he's worth it?"

Past experience with the family sleuth and self-appointed gatekeeper tells Bernadette to tread lightly. She sighs wondering if she should have said anything. Since she has, she prepares for the possible battle of opinions. *Better put on my leather glove before the beast in her jumps out when I feed her this next tidbit of information.*

"When we first met, I was caught up in his looks because the boy is fine enough to turn Mama's head."

Zavonne's relaxed posture becomes erect as she moves to the edge of her seat.

The silent beast is stirring. Let me see how much she can handle before I have to render her unconscious. "Hear me out Z. It took a minute before we had a chance to get beyond the surface stuff." Infatuation takes control of Bernadette's words. "We have a lot in common. Our conversations...um...," she says while rolling her eyes upward. "Our conversations and unspoken communication are very natural. Just after we met Terry asked if he was fine. He really is."

Bernadette casually sips lemonade before details worth hearing continue. Zavonne listens intently. The conversation is interrupted when the waiter offers them a vacated deck table.

Zavonne cuts her eyes at Bernadette to show disapproval of her barefoot sibling traipsing amongst diners. In order to press Zavonne's button Bernadette waves the expensive shoes at patrons like a flag on a blustery day.

Rather than feeding into Bernadette's immature act with a few choice words, Zavonne steers the conversation back to civility once they are seated. "Whatcha gonna do with them kicks?"

"Why?" Bernadette asks dangling them from her index and middle fingers.

"If you're not going to wear them again, I can put them into next year's auction catalog for Saving Grace. When word gets out that Terry owned them, the price will skyrocket."

After a deal for a pair of shoes in exchange is made, Bernadette surrenders the tortuous footwear to Zavonne then excuses herself to change her clothes. Home training has taught the sisters to always be prepared for emergencies. There are two sets of clothes inside a monogrammed garment bag in the trunk of Bernadette's car.

Solitary waiting time allows Zavonne to focus upon the flotilla of boats bobbing about upon glassy green water. Her attention goes to a twenty-seven foot cruiser headed toward a slip reserved for the restaurant's sailing clientele. Her Ray Ban sunglass-covered eyes light up at the name of the vessel – the U.S.S. Anointed.

She repositions her seat in order to get a good view of the passengers when they disembark.

Close-cropped hair, moustache and an expertly trimmed beard give intensity to the face of the first mariner stepping forward. Defined biceps and strong calves exposed by a sleeveless shirt and knee-length shorts turn casual glances by some women into outright stares.

Her own regular heartbeat becomes erratic when his companion comes into full view.

His twisted hair cascades downward when released from the hold of a red print scarf. Developed pectoral muscles, lightly sprinkled with hair, remind male patrons of unfulfilled resolutions to visit the gym. Around his waist fire truck red and golden yellow Kikoi cloth, strategically wrapped, stops just above bare feet. Its softness provocatively outlines strong hindquarters when he stoops to retrieve wire rim glasses that have fallen from his face. How quickly they secure the vessel indicates they are not nautical novices.

What seems to be an intense conversation abruptly halts when the bespectacled gentleman's attention is diverted. His previously passive expression evolves into a sultry gaze. Zavonne follows his stare like directions on a map. Those directions lead to Bernadette standing a short distance behind her.

Her firm, high hips, wrapped in a red and white sarong gently sway with each forward motion she takes on bare feet. Braids fall like vines of black licorice when the bobby pins holding her French roll are removed.

Without removing her fixed view from one who can be described as an African Prince Bernadette saunters to her table. Placement of her hand upon her hips with meaning hold his attention.

Majestic strides place the intriguing male within inches of Bernadette. His spearmint breath cools flirtatious words petitioning the honor of providing lunch. Her sideways glance at Zavonne indicates she is not alone.

Full lips part bringing even teeth into view while his enamored expression remains steadfast. From the pouch dangling from his shoulder, a money clip is drawn. From it he removes two one hundred dollar bills. With the care of one handling a fragile keepsake, they are placed into Bernadette's soft hands.

"Is my request granted?

"Yes."

Zavonne scrutinizes every move he makes.

He respectfully escorts Bernadette to her seat. His manicured hands gently support her arched back. Affectionately he strokes Bernadette's hand without opposition.

Not so tactfully Zavonne whispers a warning for Bernadette to figure out how to remove this man's hand from her before she does.

Bernadette's laugh infuriates Zavonne.

"I'm not playing with you," Zavonne warns.

Knowing Zavonne to be a woman of her word, Bernadette helps her out. "It's okay sis. This is Hayes."

Hayes does not sequester his amusement while beckoning his friend to join them.

"We need to break man?" Roosevelt inquires from a respectable distance.

"An exit is not necessary, my friend. This is Bernadette. The one you gave such a glowing dissertation of how her virtue reaches out to touch others. Is she touching you now, my brotha?"

Roosevelt's sneers at Hayes, then turns his attention to the ladies. His disarming smile brings grins as wide as a Cheshire cat to their faces. "I really have been tryin' to train the boy. As you can see he's kinda slow. That's why he didn't introduce us like normal people would. My name is Roosevelt Hillis. I'm glad to finally meet you," he says to Bernadette.

"According to Hayes, my virtue and you have previously met. Thank you for the compliment, Mr. Hillis."

Her bold words make Roosevelt grin like a schoolboy with his first crush. It remains during introductions to Zavonne.

Light conversation between the quartet continues until the lady's entrees arrive. Bernadette places one of the bills on the tray to cover the meal. The second is returned to Hayes. He gives her a nod and a wink, then walks away with Roosevelt like a king headed to his throne.

"Twinkle-Twinkle-little-star-brotha's-fine-from-near-or-far," Zavonne sings as soon as she feels Hayes is out of hearing range.

"Yes he is, my sista. Yes he is."

Deep-seated concern crosses Zavonne's face. Her freshly manicured fingers rapidly tap her knee.

Bernadette nonchalantly sips from her fast warming beverage. The half empty glass is returned to the table without a word offered.

"I know why you've been holding out on me, Twinkle?"

Bernadette ignores Zavonne's words.

"Since you've never known me to be shy, let's get down to it. You've been undercover because you knew when I met Hayes I could read him. Something about him ain't quite right. What is it?"

Bernadette snaps a response to Zavonne's assertive words. "Don't go getting all holy on me."

Zavonne pushes past the point where Bernadette hoped her offhand remark would have stopped her. "Holy is exactly the ground you need to be standing on. You make sure you know what you really need to know about Hayes. Take it slow, and make sure you keep your testimony."

"Why are you going there?"

"Because there is where we need to go!" Zavonne shoots back.

Uninhibited, Zavonne speaks the truth. "I need to be straight with you, Twinkle 'cause from what I can see there's something strong between the two of you already."

Bernadette blesses her food, then begins to eat allowing her mind to wander while Zavonne speaks her mind.

"Hayes is a gorgeous colored boy. He's so physically fine, comatose women will rise up and follow him when he passes by. I have a feeling he's used to getting what he wants and you definitely possess what he wants. You don't have time for games or settling for anything less than the best. And I have no desire to fend off Mommy and Daddy because they expect me to be your babysitter."

"You don't need to be tripping about me and Hayes. As a matter of fact, if you've been praying for me the way you should..."

Crazy blinks across Zavonne's forehead like a neon sign. Her sharp response cuts deep. "It's just a little too blissful in that world you've moved to since you met Hayes. Since your mind is needed in the land of the thinking, I'm giving you a passport back to reality. You ain't prayed about this boy 'cause your mind is on his conversation and his body. Now you have the audacity to pretend it's my job to do your praying for you. If that's the case I'll just date him for you, so I can tell you what's really up."

CHAPTER 6

Falimah's irritation at being second on Treva's social list has had her in a foul mood. For days, her angry flame has been fanned when obvious hints do not result in an invitation to Bernadette and Treva's monthly book club and dinner meeting.

By Friday, those flames reach upward and scorch the foundation of Falimah's common sense.

Explosive energy seeks a means of release. Inside the first floor lavatory of her home, porcelain facilities endure lethal doses of disinfectant. She uses double-handed strokes upon bended knees to scrub an already glistening floor. The process is so severe that if the floor could speak it would beg for mercy.

Falimah marches toward the kitchen. Each step she takes down the Brazilian cherry wood corridor sounds as if it belongs to one weighing at least two hundred pounds.

Her eyes dart about the kitchen seeking a way to expend her pent up frustration. Smudges detected on the stainless steel refrigerator become her innocent victim.

Confident in her ability to handle tasks efficiently, she mixes unknown amounts of ammonia and water. With one clean jerk, she rips several paper towels from a nearby roll. Within moments the surface of the refrigerator is shining.

Falimah's agenda for whom Treva should socialize with is moving very close to Treva's limit of understanding.

Of late, the two have argued more than Treva can remember in all the years that they've known each other. Her patience was stretched to the limit when Falimah curtly stated that she, not Bernadette, has always been her friend and that true friendship is hard to come by. The need to process internal feelings prevents Treva from picking up the phone whenever Falimah calls.

At this point, reality dictates that she take stock of the quality of her life in order for her to attain recently set personal and business goals.

Lying upon her back, Treva stares into darkness. Reuniting with friends, who were set aside to appease Falimah's narcissistic personality, has not been as smooth a process as she would have liked. But it is a decision that she is glad to have made.

Building a friendship with Bernadette has also been good. The two have much in common and are able to interact without the stigma of employer/employee apprehension.

In a moment of boldness, she took Bernadette with her to inspect a piece of property she has been eyeing for months. When she revealed she has been considering it as an investment for income property, Bernadette encouraged her to make the dream reality and offered the number of her real estate appraiser.

Once a month a core group consisting of Bernadette, two of her friends, Treva and one of her reacquainted friends gather to whip up meals and discuss books and other interests.

Occasionally, Treva has been asked to join a couple of them for church. She politely declined. However, there was something so genuine in Bernadette's invitation that she accepted.

***

The U.S.S. Anointed glistens under rays of a red orange sun. Before disappearing for the evening, the coveted sight kisses the western   shores of Alki Beach and other Washington coastlines where throngs of people leisurely frolic beneath summer's gift.

In no hurry to arrive at their final destination, Roosevelt jovially prods Hayes for more details about Bernadette. "Man, you told me your girl was fine. After that little time spent with her the other day, I got a feelin' she really is. Tell me who she is."

"My lady friend is exquisite. Contrary to popular belief, your wife is not in a class of her own."

Roosevelt's dark eyes flash. "Yes she is! Can't nobody compare to my woman, boy! My only question is how did you get Bernadette to be interested in you?"

Hayes' responds confidently. His impromptu body-builder posing places emphasis on his well-maintained body. "Have you forgotten that aside from my exceptional looks, I am extraordinary company?"

"Now, tell me the truth."

Hayes' dimple is exposed along with his wide toothy grin. "The way Bernadette penetrated the concrete wall in front of your emotions speaks to her abundance of charm."

"Is that so?" Roosevelt chortles.

"She has touched a place that no other woman has. Intelligence is a trait I require for longevity with any woman. Her honesty, which challenged my manhood, is not," Hayes says while watching Roosevelt maneuver their vessel toward its resting place at the covered dock that the two built together on the shore of Hayes' Lake Washington property.

"I will give an example of her straight-forwardness. Last week my storyteller voided his contract. Bernadette demanded to know why I would stress over seeking a replacement when I know how to read. She hit me hard in the ego, but had me thanking her for the force of the blow. That night on the floor with the children changed me. I will take over the story hour at the first of the new year."

Further conversation reveals that Hayes and Zavonne have agreed upon the days he will provide story telling for the children transitioning through Saving Grace.

His soft ramblings reveal specifics to his trusted confidant.

Rather than pressing for a point to be made, Hayes is allowed to ramble on. Thirty minutes later their vessel is in its resting place. The two work in silence to secure their large investment.

In silence, they walk the boardwalk. As they near Hayes' home the almond mocha fudge and butter pecan colored men dash the length of the dock. They run across grass, then through the door leading into a glass enclosed Florida room. A fantastic leap lands Hayes in the comfortable lounger accessorized with heat and massage features. Roosevelt plants his two hundred fifty-five pound frame on top of him. He playfully rubs as much perspiration as possible across Hayes' face before he is pushed to the floor.

Roosevelt inspects a home as familiar to him as his own. Intermittent items dot the sparsely furnished room of the two-year-old structure. With the exception of a furnished bedroom, kitchen and home office, this is the only other furnished room in a 6,000 square foot house with endless decorating possibilities.

"Seven digits, Hayes."

"Not in the mood, Brown Man."

"You're payin' seven digits for this timber, but you won't dress it up. What's wrong with you?" Roosevelt snarls.

Hayes moves from the throne to the floor. From his back, he launches into dialogue that is not in the air. "What you observed about Bernadette is true. She is definitely a woman of virtue."

Roosevelt challenges Hayes opinion. "She looks good, and seems to have charm. The only thing I don't know about her, that's on your standard list of prerequisites, is gainful employment and promiscuity. Does she work? Are you trying to work your way into her bed because you need to prove you can wear down what appears to be a virtuous woman?"

Hayes does not answer.

Without thought, Roosevelt rests his size fifteen sandals upon Hayes bare chest. "Tell me what's up."

An inward glow gives Hayes as much warmth as the sun shining through the glass ceiling. Pushing Roosevelt's heavy feet from his body, he rolls to his stomach. He writes Bernadette's name upon the hardwood floor with his left index finger. A heart is drawn around it. His downward palm makes erasing motions as if his finger movements had actually produced something legible. "I am in a predicament."

"Why?"

"She is different. I have had associations with many women pretending they are preserving their treasure for marriage. Within a week or two of our first encounter, all that I desire is deliciously served on a platter garnished with promises to fulfill my every whim."

Roosevelt Hillis rocks with enthusiastic laughter. "She laid her cards on the table and now she's got you hungry as a three hundred pound man at a weight-loss convention, huh?"

"You say this because?"

"Because sooner or later we meet the women who are gonna challenge who we are. I had to deal with that when I was tryin' to hang on to Nee Nee. It wasn't her intent to make me squirm. It's who she is that made me check myself. What's Bernadette doin' that's blowin' your mind?"

Hayes divulges personal information knowing it will go no farther than the wife that Roosevelt keeps no secrets from. "I played my 'I will make you mine' card."

Roosevelt stifles laughter.

"I asked if she could handle meeting the needs of a real man." Hayes pauses as he mentally relives the pivotal moment he assumed would be business as usual. "Her sincere response rocked me hard. She stepped into my soul when she told me a real man has no need to pose such a question. She clarified by stating if he were with a real woman, his needs would be met when the real need arose."

"Ooooh boy. Sounds like she's been taking lessons from my wife. How you dealin'?"

"Foreign approach. Her lack of inhibition allows us to talk candidly regarding our feelings toward one another." Hayes pauses.

"And?" Roosevelt asks.

"She believes solitary time spent with a man is only extended to one with possibilities of becoming a life mate."

"And?"

"Those words from anyone else would have led me to deposit them onto the next available corner."

"But?"

"Not her."

Roosevelt leans forward, planting his feet firmly on the floor near Hayes' head.

"Physical attraction between us is magnetic, yet has been polarized by a need for something much deeper. That depth has led me to revelations regarding the women and habits of my past. At our next encounter, I provided her with evidence of my health status."

"Why?"

"Security. She must know I am drug and disease free."

Roosevelt reserves further comment on this subject by walking another road. "What'd she tell you 'bout herself?"

Hayes' full lips form into a broad grin. His eyes momentarily close then reopen. "We share many similarities. From what I've gathered from some of our conversations, she has a good head for business. She is an avid shopper, loves the theatre, reading, song writing and gardening. She has another sibling who seems to be rather intellectual."

Roosevelt's thick eyebrows arch.

"Bernadette refers to the thought process of her sister as one within another dimension. From what I gather, she is a woman ahead of her time with confidence and ability that perplexes the ordinary mind." Mirth crosses Hayes' face. "Actually, you and your wife greatly admire her."

Hayes allows Roosevelt's curiosity to languish in the realm of possibilities until his shadowy eyes demand an explanation. He wanders out of the room. Roosevelt follows him to his elaborately decorated home office. Hayes stands before a massive wrap around walnut desk filled with orderly stacks of paper, books and a variety of expensive writing tools in a specially crafted holder.

Without seating himself, he logs onto the Internet. Several strokes bring him to his desired site. Two fingers summon his curious friend.

From over Hayes' shoulder, Roosevelt views a dove descending from the upper left portion of the screen. From beneath its wings the words 'Three Praises Productions' appear. Selecting the enter option brings the second screen into view. Billowing clouds frame the faces of Bernadette Lewis, Zavonne Lewis and Terry Boyd.

Hayes is vigorously shoved aside. Quickly Roosevelt reads vertically and horizontally. Twenty minutes spent checking offered options and links answers his inquisitiveness. "You mean to tell me your girl and Terry Boyd are sisters? I heard that her play is so hot folk been standin' three deep in line for hours to get tickets! On top of that, they run that slammin' production company in L.A.?" His huge hands move up then outward. "I don't know what to say. Bernadette's got all this goin' for her and she wants you?"

"Your words are not humorous," Hayes says while throwing a playful punch.

Roosevelt goes to the kitchen to heat whatever leftovers Hayes may have in his refrigerator.

Hayes sets the table and then sits.

Roosevelt examines the man whose moods he can read as easily as an elementary textbook. "What do you want to ask me?"

Hayes rubs his chin with his index finger and thumb. "It's more of what I need from you."

It is their vulnerability in one another's presence that has formed a bond far beyond the limits of what most consider manly. Unknown to Hayes it is his openness that led Roosevelt and his wife to make the conscious decision not to disassociate themselves from him. While others scolded and rebuked his lifestyle, Roosevelt and his wife committed to daily intercession on Hayes' behalf.

"I purchased last week's service CD. I have not been able to remove the scripture from my mind."

Roosevelt searches his memory bank. Slowly he recites Mark 8:36-38. "For what shall it profit a man, if he shall gain the whole world, and lose his own soul? Or what shall a man give in exchange for his soul? Whosoever therefore shall be ashamed of me and of my words in this adulterous and sinful generation; of him also shall the Son of man be ashamed, when he cometh in the glory of his Father with the holy angels."

Hayes' head moves vertically throughout the recitation. "I am faced with reality. God has blessed me with literally all things I have asked for. In return for His favor, I have only given lip service to what He expects from me."

Anguish covers Hayes' face. "The Word says, '*If ye love me, keep my commandments*'. I thought I loved God. That scripture continuously whispering to me confirms that I do not."

Hayes grasps both of Roosevelt's hands. His soul deep gaze opens dialogue that has been prayed about for years. "I do not want Him to turn His face away from me. I want you to help me become a disciple of Christ."

Joy envelops the gigantic Roosevelt Hillis. He watches Hayes' lips move. All he can hear is what he perceives to be a heavenly choir. Hayes keeps talking about wanting to fully surrender to Christ while angels continue to sing.

A man perceived to always be in control of his emotions falls to the floor. Through tears he openly worships and gives thanks for the choice of his friend while heavenly rejoicing continues.

When Roosevelt rises, he instructs Hayes to go get his bible. While Hayes is out of the room, Roosevelt phones his wife.

"Hello."

"Hey baby, I'm gonna spend the night with Hayes."

"Is anything wrong?"

"No. Everything's right. He wants to surrender totally to the Lord."

Screams of hallelujah can be heard clearly even though Nee Nee has dropped the phone. Roosevelt hangs up knowing that once she stops praising she'll go into immediate intercession for their friend.

CHAPTER 7

Falimah's excessive cleaning regime has every piece of wooden furniture in her home and hardwood floors glistening. Anything that could be bleached has been disinfected inside the four thousand square feet of her house. What has been referred to as an obsessive-compulsive need to clean, this time, has gone a little too far. To keep the combination of pine-scented cleanser, wood polish, ammonia and chlorine from asphyxiating her, she heads to the safety of the second floor.

Walking through her sleeping suite, Falimah comes to grips with the fact that she is lonely. This emotion is repulsive to her. *How could this be? I am desirable.* Pausing before a mirrored wall inside her immense walk in closet, Falimah studies her image. She knows from a male perspective her body rates between an 8 and 10.

Genetics and the consumption of gallons of purified water has blessed her with flawless skin. Coarse hair with nappy edges that required daily touchups during her juvenile years has evolved. Now corn rolls, twists, Afros, plaits and mini dreads, alternately crown a head brimming with intellect.

Dedication to daily workouts keeps her lean, curvaceous body in top physical shape. Her hands and feet receive weekly professional care that leaves them baby soft.

Slowly she outlines her upper torso with her slender finger. She feels good to herself, but not about herself. Another night spent alone adds to her secret feelings of inadequacy.

Water turned on in a sunken tub breaks the din of overwhelming silence. From glass shelves above a granite vanity she selects several apothecary bottles. With the skill of a chemist, wild clove and mint oil are carefully blended to create the desired fragrance. Her perfectly blended ingredients mixed with water yields aromatic pleasure. The scent is so pleasing the idea of marketing it becomes more than a fleeting thought.

Submerging herself into fragrant waters brings about a sense of serenity. Tranquility lifts her clouded mind above chaotic thoughts. Upon the plateau of calm, anger begins to retreat.

"Hello."

"Hi Treva, it's Bernadette. What are you up to?"

Treva sits down with a doll she is considering for a makeover. "Just playing with the children."

"What?"

"Restoring dolls is a hobby of mine. I'm studying one of them."

Bernadette rolls to her side atop her bed. "What's the dilemma?"

"Haven't discovered who she is yet."

Bernadette's laugh is loud. "I know what you mean, girl. When I'm working with the kids at church, I study them hard. I can't teach effectively if I don't know who they are."

Their conversation is interrupted by an incoming call. "Hold on a minute Bernadette, my other line is ringing."

"Hello."

"Treva, what are you doing?" Falimah yells into the phone.

"I'm talking shop. Do you need something or can I call you back?"

Falimah rambles on about nothing in particular.

"I have Bernadette hanging on the other line, Falimah. Let me call you back."

Falimah slams the phone down hard. It rings within seconds. She snatches it from the base. Unkind words are snarled into the receiver in hopes of hurting Treva for being short with her.

"Does your tone indicate a foul mood?"

"I'm working through it." She replies in a more civil tone once she realizes who it is.

"That means you need my special care. May I come by to help relieve your stress?"

"Yeah. Come on over."

***

Bernadette's surveillance of Falimah Meyer provides her with more information than words ever could.

Her straight-no-chaser business style has produced the type of results Bernadette demands of her personnel. With contract negotiations she can hold her own. Financial creativity and her knack for simplifying the seemingly overwhelming have increased the company's client base.

Despite an underlying feeling that Falimah is not happy with her budding friendship with Treva, Bernadette is pleased that she has not expressed it in the workplace. In fact, their darkness and light business approach has moved the company's financial projections far beyond Bernadette's timeline. She and Falimah mesh so well as a business team that Bernadette invites Falimah to accompany her to a luncheon at the Seattle Guild of Businessmen.

Change has slowly infiltrated decades of tradition embraced by the Seattle Guild of Businessmen.

Monthly gatherings of the previously male only fraternity is now sprinkled with what all know are token women attendees.

From her table Bernadette watches accomplished women force their way into conversations only to be dismissed with words synonymous to a pat on the rear end. Those same women, when inquiring about her livelihood, respond with a mixture of feigned interest and indifference.

Less than receptive responses to the uniqueness of her integrity and accomplishments lost its sting years ago. At the tender age of nineteen, she sat at the head of the negotiating table warring with the agent of a singing talent she desperately wanted to bring into Three Praises. Her refusal to meet frivolous diva demands brought forth words from the 'saint' that would offend one making a living by using profane words. She learned two things from that verbal assault. The first was to know all there is to know about anyone seeking to do business with you or to know your business. The second was to place her personal feelings in her pocket before sitting at any negotiation table.

Despite being the novelty amongst old school mindsets and being recipients of less than cordial treatment from female peers, Bernadette and Falimah believe they have made a favorable impression. That belief is confirmed when a 6-foot, strongly built thirty-something male dressed in a St. John's suit makes his way toward them. His green eyes set in a tanning booth baked face lights up as he nears their table. "Ms. Lewis?" he inquires of Bernadette.

His body language and broad smile suggests the possibility of them being time-separated colleagues reuniting. Being recognized by someone she does not know puts her on alert.

His grasping of her hand is annoying. Annoyance turns to outrage when he takes the liberty of calling her Bernie and then sits without invitation.

She takes control of the conversation by instructing him to refer to her as Bernadette or Ms. Lewis.

Being put in check for offensive behavior would have caused color to rush into the face of a modest man.

Her inquiry as to what she can do for him opens the door to explore what game this bodacious man is playing.

"It's what I can do for *you*," he says while eyeing Falimah. In the manner of a used car salesman, he tenders tidbits of what he believes he knows about Bernadette's business. His offer to become her mentor in order to help her keep her head above water reeks of an attempt to overthrow her.

Bernadette's curt refusal brings about his real agenda. "Let me tell you what I know about you," he says just above a whisper.

Falimah leans in.

"You probably have a friend in a high position giving you occasional tips that you have the guts to follow through on."

"Really?" Bernadette responds without any indication of whether his words intimidate or offend her.

"Yes, really. It's the only way you could have accomplished what you have thus far. Plus, we both know that a woman, and if you don't mind my saying so, a woman of color, needs a front man. You probably have already tried the *brother* road and found out that the glass ceiling over your heads will send you both to the poor house."

The intentional insult does not change Bernadette's expression.

His words clearly laced with self-importance continue. "I will be very candid with you. You have what I want and I have what you need."

"Just for the record, tell me what that is," Bernadette says without emotion.

"Talk has it that for a small company you have potential. You're actually sitting on a goldmine, but you need the proper tools to mine the ore."

Falimah presses her lips tightly together.

"And *you* have the equipment?" Bernadette asks looking him directly in the eye.

His obvious disrespect for her is shown as he runs his tongue around his lips then remarks, "Oh, I have all that you need and more."

Both Bernadette and Falimah laugh at his gesture. His discomfort is evident when he coughs then adjusts his tie.

"I don't take you to be a beat-around-the-bush type of woman, so I'll lay it on the line for you. First of all, for a small business, you're too pricey. This indicates you need help with your marketing skills. You won't last long if you don't lower your fees." He pauses to tap his Rolex. "Let me rephrase that. You won't last long if you don't lower your fees as a solo act without marketing appeal, if you know what I mean."

Falimah grinds her teeth, but remains silent.

Bernadette clearly understands his game plan and forces herself to hear every crazy word he has to say, before responding.

"The second thing you have to face, but don't see as a liability is your attitude. Like most second generation African American shop owners, you have the, 'I don't need affirmative action syndrome'. You do, Bernie. As long as you live in America, you'll always need someone like me to open the door for you."

His spiel ends when he places an expensive business card before Bernadette. It announces his position as junior executive at what she knows is a sinking consulting firm. "What do you think about us joining forces? We could go really far together." Looking at Falimah, he arrogantly states he can help her too.

If I were the fool of the week, I wouldn't let this man in the back door of my company. It's time to put this boy in check so I don't go crazy and mess up my business rep. Scripture - I need a scripture! The LORD is my light and my salvation; whom shall I fear? The LORD is the strength of my life; of whom shall I be afraid? When the wicked, even mine enemies and my foes, came upon me to eat up my flesh, they stumbled and fell.

Slight nods indicate Bernadette and Falimah are in sync. Bernadette's second nod invites Falimah into the conversation.

Falimah's fingers rhythmically drum upon the linen covered table. With her left hand, she reaches into her leather attaché. From it she removes a company brochure. It is intentionally slapped on top of his business card like a domino upon a game table. "Now that you've told us why you strolled over, let me enlighten you about B. L. Lewis."

The previously relaxed man becomes rigid at her boldness. Falimah moves the brochure closer to his now clenched hand. Tapping the glossy advertisement, she says with force, "This is who we are. We're about taking businesses where they have never been before. Your obvious recognition of our success and self-invitation to this table speaks volumes. You realize you need B. L. Lewis in order to reach your projected goals. You have a personnel challenge. We can help you. You desire specific software. We can develop it. Technical surveillance, Internet filtration with perpetual upgrading is all in a day's work for us."

Falimah's confidence causes the cocky male to spew rage-laden words. "I don't need *you people* to do anything for me! It's all about what I can do for you! If you want in on the big leagues, you need to have friends in high places."

"My goodness," Falimah coos, "the use of the words *you people* sounds very condescending coming from your mouth. Was that your intent, or am I imagining things?"

To Bernadette's disbelief, the natural color of embarrassment actually makes its way into the offender's face.

Falimah moves in like a shark drawn to blood. "I understand how fragile the male ego can be, so I'll help you over the rough spots. I sense you were sent as a scout. We have no time to waste with those lacking authority." Deliberately she places her business card atop his still clenched hand. "Take this and our brochure back to your superiors. If you find your budget too meager for our non-negotiable fees, we'll direct you to a smaller company better suited to your financial constraints."

The card is flicked aside as if it were a feasting mosquito.

Bernadette rises. Falimah does the same. Their femininity dripping with confidence is a formidable duo before the previously overconfident messenger. Attempts to express his rebuttal are dismissed by the raising of Bernadette's hand. "The rancid odor of your assumed superiority arrived at my table before you did. Just so you know; I always take garbage out rather than allowing it to contaminate my environment. And just for the record, I'll have you know I excel at what I do because I have a 'Friend in the Highest Place'. You go work your con man tactics on someone who doesn't know who you *aren't*."

The defeated man is left alone muttering obscenities at their departing backs.

***

Five calls, within six hours, to Hayes' place of business demanding a meeting for closure's sake receive the same response – disconnection.

He considers changing his personal telephone numbers to end Renata's unwanted calls. This would help to a degree, but it is necessary to maintain current numbers for business purposes.

Hayes' annoyance with the persistent calls has him in a surly mood. Within the quiet of his office, he seeks solitude and the opportunity to refocus. Pen and paper become an outlet for private thoughts. *Within the depths of the inner man is a place that can be touched only by the one intended by our Creator. Substitutes are futile attempts at fulfillment which lessens the value of a holy place. How does one recognize when his soul mate has graced his presence? When there is no room to receive anything else. My soul is filled with your essence leaving no desire to receive from contaminated wells. Thirst can only be quenched from waters of the blessed fountain...*

Penmanship with a distinctive flourish produces page after page of endearments revealing what no woman has ever stirred in Hayes before. Pleasurable thoughts of Bernadette evoke more than words upon paper. He urgently presses his speed dial button.

Bernadette's melodious singing is a welcomed surprise greeting Hayes. "I see you have lyrical appeal."

"I can hold my own, Mr. Davis."

"Did you receive what you sought today?"

Memories of an interesting day turn Bernadette's merriment to contemplation.

"Share with me?" Hayes coaxes.

Healthy legs retract to compact her seventy-inch body. With a free hand she pulls her deep plum throw upward. Without misgivings, Bernadette shares her private thoughts without fear of them being divulged to anyone.

His response challenges without offense. "Surely you expected some type of adversity to your presence."

"Disrespect is never an expectation, Hayes."

"But?"

"I'm tired of disdain for my success being dispensed like something on someone's 'to do' list."

"But you understand why?"

"Yes. I'm a woman. But more importantly, I'm a woman achieving more than anyone other than God and my family expects."

"Their deepest fear is not a belief in our inadequacies, but the knowledge of our power. It is our light, not their illusion of our darkness that they fear." Hayes pauses then proceeds to explain. "Those words are a variation on a theme taken from the works of Marianne Williamson. Often I speak them to myself when I address adversity in the business realm."

His deep bravado shushes her attempted response then like a balm, he soothes her exposed feelings. Passion poured into every syllable from Hayes' mouth extracts tension from Bernadette's body and mind.

"I need to tell you something," he whispers following a brief lull.

With a need to drink up Hayes' every word, she presses the receiver firmly to her ear.

"People talk. I make it my business to listen. You have made a name for yourself in this town. Very few attended that luncheon without knowledge of your accomplishments. Their intentional insults were meant to lower you to a level they deem suitable. From what you say, you handled yourself well. But be careful."

"Why?"

"A man's ego is a huge part of who he is. That bruised ego will seek opportunity to defame you for the sake of nursing a war wound. It will not be long before we hear words he will plant in an attempt to tarnish your reputation."

Silence.

"Are you concerned?"

Soft sighing is her response.

Hayes' gentle words usher Bernadette into a realm of vulnerability she has not experienced with any man unrelated to her. "How others treat you based upon rumor will tell you more about them than they anticipate."

Wisdom from Hayes certifies words impressed upon her long ago by her father. It is Joseph Lewis who cautioned his daughter to understand that one cannot stop people from lying on you, however, you can make sure their words remain a lie by the way you carry yourself.

Their ongoing conversation reveals a lot about one another. Most endearing to Bernadette is Hayes' genuine interest in her goals. His offering of business advice interwoven with humorous dialogue ignites a passion she has never known. Three hours pass before common sense dictates the need to end what Bernadette wishes would go on forever.

In an effort to extend their time, Hayes requests and is granted the opportunity to read a passage to her. "It is seen out the corner of your eye. Its brilliance is initially small, but has lasting effect. Daily, the need to become vulnerable in the presence of twinkling serenity grows…"

His words become hypnotic, carrying Bernadette's mind to an oasis of contentment. Beneath the borderless sky, red and blue brightness dance with total abandonment. Deep vibrato spoken with care becomes melodic inspiration. Two independent, yet interdependent hues circle, bow and mesh, becoming one. They become a royal, rich, protective purple melded upon an isle with no constraints.

With the tenderness of a goodnight kiss shared between first loves, Hayes' tender words end. Bernadette does not try to conceal her schoolgirl gushing. "That was beautiful. I'm not familiar with the author. Is the work from a rare collection?"

"The works are from the collection of a relatively unknown. With permission, I would like to share more at our next encounter."

Discernment clearly recognizes Hayes as the unknown. The fact that he has invited her into the privacy of his gift indicates him opening himself to her. Sincere thanks for listening and the extension of sound advice is given.

Bernadette opens up to Hayes and ends the conversation by telling him that she considers him a friend, and her friends call her Twinkle.

Hayes leans back and smiles.

Sitting cross-legged in the midst of her bed, Bernadette relaxes as she free-falls backwards. Mounds of down pillows swathed in varying hues of purple cushion her landing.

Thoughts of today's meeting are again processed, and Falimah's face flashes before her. *Lord, I know why you wouldn't let me fire her. She's Your diamond in the rough. Help me to maintain Your standards while You do what it is You plan for her.*

Thoughts move from Falimah to Treva. *Lord, I really like Treva. I feel like she's somebody I can trust with my friendship and my business. I need You to show me if this is a relationship I should continue.* Falimah's face again appears before her. *Show me how to not be a problem between Falimah and Treva. If it is Your will, allow me to be Your instrument that will lead them toward the Cross. Above all, grant me wisdom in how to proceed so that Your name will be given the glory.*

Bernadette moves to the edge of her bed. Her soft feet swing to and fro. Leisurely, she assesses her room.

Contents of the antique desk once belonging to her great grandmother are neatly arranged. Bernadette moves from her bed to the padded desk chair. An engraved fountain pen is taken from a holder. Its stem is rubbed between her thumb and forefinger for several moments before beginning to write urgently.

Purple, written with romantic flair across the top of the page set the tone of words to follow. *Purple - the most precious dye of the ancients. An ounce of its existence came with the sacrifice of no less than 250,000 mollusks. So esteemed, it resided in the Tabernacle and Temple in the presence of the living God. Its majestic color was reserved for the robes of royalty. Purple evokes a sense of passion, confidence and commands respect. I identify with all that purple is. It is precious. It is royal. It is passionate and confident. I am purple.*

***

Treva's preset watch alarm beeps. Eager to back out of a revised document, she presses the wrong button. Angst lifts her to a standing position. In an effort to maintain her balance, her size eight feet become tangled with the computer's power cord detaching it from the electrical outlet. Treva presses her palm against her mouth in an effort to keep her scream from escaping into the air. The only recourse she can think of is calling Brian Chin.

She quickly dials his number.

"This is Brian Chin."

"Save me now and I'll take you wherever you choose for lunch."

Lightning fast steps place Brian before Treva instantly. Rapid-fire language explains her dilemma. Brian's hilarious remarks regarding her predicament as he leaves the room pulls Treva behind him like a toy on a string.

Computers hum at every station lining the path to Brian's lower-level sanctuary where Treva finds him already at work. Several strokes upon his keyboard log him into the office server. "What's the name of the file?" he asks.

"Negotiations."

In a matter of moments the file is found, transported to his queue, saved, and then printed.

At this moment Brian, looks good enough to eat. They head out to lunch.

During the rather expensive meal, Brian goads Treva into revealing the root of her near disaster. Sheepishly she admits she wanted to go to lunch before Falimah returned to the office.

Rather than remark, Brian steers the conversation to Treva's cars and when he can drive them. Treva's 1958 Ford Fairlaine and 1964 Ford Mustang are as precious to her as a first-born child is to a new mother. Brian's persistent requests are rejected.

***

"This is Bernadette Lewis. I'm calling to see if you were able to get my name on the list for my shoes."

"You're on the list but you know this particular designer only makes a dozen pair of her shoes. Two of the twelve are already sold and there are thirty people in the bidding war for the remaining ten."

Defeat is not a word in Bernadette's vocabulary. She is determined to employ all tactics necessary to have what she seeks – the $2,500 shoes from Marabel's.

Bernadette's next call is to Treva.

"Hello."

"Hey Treva it's Bernadette. My oldest sister lives in Los Angeles. I have a video created by her personal shopper. There are a couple of pieces in the collection calling your name. I'll bring it to your house tomorrow night if you promise to feed me."

"Sounds like a deal. While you're here I need to talk some business with you. I'm considering making an offer on that property we looked at."

***

Hayes' orange linen pants and shirt compete with the brilliance of the setting sun. Today his hair is brushed backwards, creating a sea of waves that flow to the nape of his neck. The excess has been gathered into a single braid concealed beneath a dramatically twisted tamarisk scarf.

The fact that he is already five minutes late meeting Bernadette increases his impatience at missing the light.

The pedestrian to his left begins to cross. Lengthy, exaggerated strides likened to that of a runway model, bring the single ambler in tight jeans across the intersection to stand at his side. Hayes' peripheral vision and sense of smell detect the eclectic person beside him. The cheap perfume and designer bag are as ill-matched as Rush Limbaugh and Louis Farrakhan would be as roommates.

Perfectly shadowed eyes beneath pencil drawn eyebrows and drugstore lashes hone in on Hayes. Without looking, Hayes can sense he is being watched.

The crass walker rudely stares while licking thickly painted lips, smearing pink, oily dime store lipstick.

"Ah uhm."

Hayes ignores the attempt to get his attention.

"Excuse me, 'Mr. Man."

No response.

Physical contact is attempted.

Hayes' muscled arms assume a defense position.

Offended by Hayes' stance, the man stomps away yelling profanities at drivers jamming on brakes in an attempt not to run him down.

At the corner of First and Main, Hayes finds Bernadette waiting for him in front of Elliott Bay Book Company. She is not surprised when he pulls her inside. If there is a bookstore anywhere near, Hayes must check it out. Following a whirlwind tour, they head out the door.

As they stroll arm in arm, a woman and an adolescent guarding a tattered garbage bag distract Bernadette.

Downcast heads, harsh words and people stating that they have no change to spare reveal the heartlessness of those in a hurry to move past the two who look like chimney sweeps. Pain inside Bernadette's heart deepens with each rejection of their pleas for help.

Bernadette's preoccupation prevents her from responding when Hayes asks where her thoughts are. Instead, she pulls him behind her until they are within inches of the curbside pleaders. Shivers visibly shake her body when the woman dares to brave another possible affront to her pride. "Excuse me. Could you spare some change?" she asks jutting her hand toward Bernadette.

Hayes places his body between Bernadette and the unknown woman. Breath so foul it feels as if it is singeing his eyebrows halts his response.

Bernadette's empathy with the situation moves her from behind Hayes. "I have change Miss," she declares. "More than that I have time. Would you and the young man join me for dinner?"

"We can get by with a little change if you have some," she responds while looking downward.

Compassionate words from Bernadette raise her bent head. "God never meant for you to just get by. Will you join me?" Bernadette inquires a second time.

A big grin that reveals dark yellow teeth replaces the look of shame that covered her dirty face moments earlier.

"You want us to eat with you?"

"Yes. Will you accept my invitation, Miss?"

"My name is Dinah. This is my son, Blaine."

"Hello young man."

The boy leans closer turning his head from Bernadette to his mother.

"He can't hear you, but it would be nice to have a hot meal."

Bernadette grabs the disintegrating garbage bags and thrust them into

Hayes' fastidiously clean hands. The distance already placed between him and the departed trio silences his protest.

All but Hayes orders from the menu offering hearty portions to its diners.

Conversation at the table reveals that the two have been on the streets since Dinah lost her job and apartment two years ago. Bernadette listens intently before excusing herself.

During her absence Hayes watches the mother and son devour food like a pack of wolves.

Unidentifiable flakes shower the boy's dingy tee shirt, the table and his plate each time he scratches his head. Hayes quickly covers Bernadette's entrée when a bug, falling from the young man's hair onto the table, hops toward it.

Bernadette returns, blesses her food, then shares what she believes is great news. She spoke with the leaders of her church's outreach ministry. If Dinah is in agreement, they will meet them at the restaurant. "We will provide a safe place for you to stay until you can get on your feet. Is that okay with you, Dinah?"

"Yeah."

Bernadette places a large portion of veal Parmesan onto her fork. Before it reaches her mouth, a purposely clumsy move by Hayes causes him to hit her elbow sending the fork flying. A second premeditated motion overturns his water glass spilling the contents over Bernadette's food.

"You cannot eat this. I will order you another." Hayes offers.

When the church van arrives Bernadette senses Dinah's apprehension. "Would you like me to go with you?"

"No, we'll be okay. But could you come see about me tomorrow?"

"Yes."

Bernadette whispers to Dinah before she boards the van. "God will never stop loving you because you will always be worth loving."

Turning to Hayes, Dinah smiles broadly. "I know you didn't like being around us much, but you didn't stop your wife from helping us. Thanks mister."

Hayes and Bernadette watch until the van fades from their sight.

Hayes pulls Bernadette near. Concern for her safety is expressed in his words. "You must exercise caution. Too many people out here are dangerous."

Softly, she whispers into his ear, "Come, follow me, Jesus said, and I will make you fishers of men." Emphatic words punctuate her position. "I'm committed to living for Him. I will follow and do whatever the Spirit of God commands of me."

Before meeting with Dinah, Bernadette makes her way to a few stores. When she arrives at the shelter, her arms are full of garment and shopping bags.

Dinah's transformation changes her appearance to the point that Bernadette bypasses her sitting in the dormitory lounge.

Her freshly washed shoulder-length blond hair, is pulled back into a neat ponytail. Freckles previously hidden by layers of grim are now visible.

Dinah's squeals of delight permeate the air when item after item are pulled from Macys, Nordstrom, Talbots and Victoria's Secret bags. Tears flow when all five pairs of shoes selected with care, fit.

Dinah pulls a few items from Eddie Bauer, Gap and Foot Locker bags awaiting the sleeping Blaine. "How did you know what size to get?"

"I pray you come to know how powerful God's spirit is. When you allow yourself to be led by Him, wonderful things happen."

Bernadette prays with Dinah and promises to remain in touch.

CHAPTER 8

Contents of conversations with Bernadette mingled with events of their street corner encounter presents Hayes with an epiphany. Callous indifference toward the less fortunate is a trait he must remove from his personality.

Throughout his restless night, Bernadette's words of commitment inhabit his thoughts. *Come, follow me, Jesus said, and I will make you fishers of men. I will follow and do whatever the Spirit of God commands of me.*

Crimson sheets upon his king-sized bed softly rustle as Hayes' right hand seeks the bible that has become his nightly companion. With his left hand he turns on the bedside lamp. Thumbing through pages, he is not sure what he should read. The book of Matthew catches his eye. Gently pages are turned. Chapter four – *And he saith unto them, Follow me, and I will make you fishers of men. And they straightway left their nets, and followed him.*

Hayes moves forward. He pauses at chapter sixteen. *Then said Jesus unto his disciples, If any man will come after me, let him deny himself, and take up his cross, and follow me.* Bernadette's words fill his head again. *I will follow and do whatever the Spirit of God commands of me.*

Night turns to day with Hayes seeking Divine direction. Soft tones from his security system disturb his concentration and alerts Hayes to the fact that someone has entered his home. He rises to check the monitor.

A man whose housekeeping regime can withstand the scrutiny of most grandmothers, watches Roosevelt Hillis remove his shoes before venturing from the parquet entry onto the expensive mulberry carpet.

Two at a time, he bounds up stairs. Turning left on a reflective hardwood landing points Roosevelt in the direction of Hayes' palatial sleeping suite. He enters the double doors without knocking.

Hayes' slight nod acknowledges his guest. He turns to the window then softly asks Roosevelt, "Have you ever been in a place so good and so foreign it terrifies and excites you all at the same time?"

Roosevelt's lack of response diverts Hayes' attention from the view. Internal cues bring each man to Hayes' freshly made bed. They sit crossed-leg, facing one another. Simultaneously, their massive hands touch the heart of the other.

"I recognize your mood. It's how I felt when I knew Nee Nee was the one for me. You can't let it scare you. Fear is the enemy of growth."

From their resting place upon deep red and gold covered pillow shams, Hayes lifts sheaves of ivory parchment. One upward motion sets them to flight. They appear as floating feathers above their heads during downward descent.

Hayes' index finger touches his own temple. Roosevelt's own finger taps his temple, moves downward to linger just beneath his breastbone, then reaches out to gather several scattered papers. The rapid reader consumes two pages of privacy. Snap action flicks his wrist. "Pssh. *You're whipped.*"

"Her essence is one with my soul. But there is more," Hayes admits. He eloquently shares details of the previous evening and a drive to understand just what is being required of him.

"Listen to the words, man," Roosevelt says touching his own ears. "Come, follow me, Jesus said, and I will make you fishers of men…I will follow and do whatever the Spirit of God commands of me. Last night you got practical application of what discipleship really is. Your girl's obedience blessed that woman and spoke to your spirit at the same time."

Perplexity appears on the face of Hayes Davis. "I was amazed at her actions. All I desired was distance between us and the repulsive smelling woman."

Love for his growing friend is evident on Roosevelt's face. "Justice," Roosevelt softly whispers.

Hayes' unrestrained hair falls to the left brushing his bare shoulder.

"Justice man. Bernadette knows the difference between charity and justice. Charity gives handouts but keeps people in need. Justice looks for ways to teach the needy without steppin' on dignity."

Clarity has such magnitude it thrusts Hayes into a growth spurt not unlike that of a genetically altered mutant. An insatiable need for total comprehension keep the two side-by-side reading the scriptures, talking and praying the remainder of the day.

***

Falimah's plan for successful living has few flaws.

Top high school grades earned her a full scholarship to Stanford University. From there she excelled in her graduate studies at Wharton University of Pennsylvania. Possession of intellect and aptitude were the combination that helped her win a coveted internship on Wall Street. Her quest to obtain financial independence drove her to parlay what she has learned into an investment club.

Savvy strategy earns her elite clientele substantial returns on their investments. Shrewd business tactics and handsome commissions keep her financial accounts as full as the breasts of a nursing mother. Financial expertise has sheltered her funds in a way that guarantees a healthy retirement as well as income to live a lifestyle envied by many.

Employment at B. L. Lewis perplexes many of her corporate driven associates. For her the choice is strictly for the purpose of self-gratification. Wall Street gave her a rush she believed no drug could ever induce. However, it was not her goal to burn out like so many of her power drunk peers. At B. L. Lewis she has been given leeway to apply creative strategies to her daily tasks inside a relatively stress free environment.

What she has taught Treva and a few other friends about their finances has helped them to prosper. She is actually considering developing a financial course for high school students.

Financial stability has led Falimah to believe she is ready for a mate. Pride refuses to allow her to acknowledge that the need has been accelerated by Treva's seemingly pulling away.

***

Exposure to people such as those at the Businessmen's Luncheon fuels Bernadette's desire for success.

Leaning back in her chair she seeks solitude behind closed eyes. *Lord I will continue to do Your will regardless of what others assume. Thank You Holy Spirit for guiding my words and my actions.*

Her need to remain on task returns her concentration to the training manual she is developing to accompany newly developed educational software. This is the part of the job Bernadette loves. Often she is so engrossed with the development of the curriculum that the end of the day she looked forward to at 6 a.m. arrives without notice.

The ringing telephone is an unwelcome interruption. "Yes."

"I have your grandmother on the line."

"Put her through please."

"Hi Nana."

"Twinkle?"

"Bunky?"

"How are you dear? Did I catch you at a bad time?"

Her cheerful words do little to elevate Bernadette's plummeting spirits.

"You were on my mind so I thought I'd give you a call."

Pleasant conversation becomes an echo in the cavern of Bernadette's detachment. The conference button is pressed, so that she can return to the keyboard. Occasional 'yes ma'am's' keep this from being a one-sided conversation.

"It sounds like you're overwhelmed with running that business of yours. I just wanted to say hello. I love you."

"Goodbye Bunky."

***

Brian's pursuit of information regarding the fleet of classic cars Treva is rumored to own is hilarious. In an effort to persuade her into divulging her secret, he takes her to lunch and then asks question after question about what she might own. Regardless of the appealing method used to persuade her into giving him what he seeks, he is kept at bay.

As mysterious as Treva tries to be, Brian likes what he already knows about her. She has a sense of humor as bold as his. Her ability to take a joke as well as to dish one out has created a great bond between them. By the end of the meal he learns that spending time in the garage with her auto mechanic father taught her a lot about cars.

The downside of her personality is her intense perfectionism. She will not end a task until it is completed to her satisfaction. Suggestions have been made that she lighten up. Regardless, Brian's thoughts are beginning to linger on more than Treva's cars.

The fact that she is a woman of strength and intellect makes him wonder about her level of security. One trait he desires in a woman is her sense of wholeness.

***

Seeds of insecurity watered with the pain of being motherless, has produced a garden of masked insecurity inside Treva Scott. This garden is usually closely guarded.

Over the years, Treva had used her overachieving personality and continuous extreme clothing and hair makeovers as tools to remove weeds seeking to stunt her emotional growth. To her dismay, these acts only created more despair. The aching woman/child longed to know how her deceased mother would have responded to her life choices.

The lack of a mother to teach her family traditions, share feminine secrets, and mold her into one that people recognized as 'her mama's girl' turned her pain into anger stronger than gale force winds. Those potentially destructive winds lashed out at a father who did the best that he could for his only child.

A void as deep as the Grand Canyon has left Treva searching for something to numb her internal pain. Unfortunately, her need to belong has turned a blind eye and deaf ear to less than respectful treatment from Falimah Meyer.

Today is another attempt to find peace. Trinity Christian Center is larger than Treva expects. Instead of looking for Bernadette, she chooses a seat in the rear of the balcony. Rising heat, crying babies and cranky toddlers cause her to rue the decision.

The few times she attended church were very different from what she is experiencing this morning. An earlier intercessory prayer service ushers attendees into the praise and worship service that is pleasing to her.

Offering time – Treva's shoulders tighten then relax when the process is not prolonged by an obstinate parishioner holding up the line while demanding change for their five-dollar bill.

When a woman dressed in white is escorted to the platform, Treva leans forward like a flower in a brisk wind. The soloist's low tones of humming escalate then taper. The first verse of the song 'Surrender', sang a cappella, brings Treva to her feet. Something in the delivery causes her to jot a few of the words down on the back of her bulletin.

Following the song, many remain on their feet openly sobbing. An usher offers tissue for Treva's tears. She sobs as she remembers. Past experiences remind her that words from the pulpit will do nothing to extinguish her anger.

She is angry with God for allowing her to be motherless, and worse, a motherless child conveniently tortured by the whims of one professing to be a sister.

Unexpected change for Treva begins the moment Pastor Filmore opens his mouth. He speaks of how many do not come to Jesus, who is waiting for all to surrender their will to Him. Impassioned words punctuate examples given of how crucial opportunities to win souls are missed. Missed opportunities are summed up as oversights because most are concentrating on the obviously rebellious. The congregation is reminded that they may be related to or work with people who will go to hell.

Anointing hits many marks.

"People, who don't rob, steal, murder, so on and so forth, the ones we classify as nice people, are in just as much danger as the outwardly sinful. They may be going to hell in droves because they have not surrendered to

God. Why? Several answers. We are not adhering to the command of the Great Commission. We rarely ask people if they would like to join us on a Wednesday or Sunday or whatever. We go about our day and never mention Jesus' name until we get around the saints. Even worse, we act like anything, but a saint until we hit the sanctuary door. So many people have seen your sermon that they can't hear the one you try to preach. Sometimes it isn't us. It's their refusal to accept an invitation to church."

An audible gasp escapes from Treva. The times she has refused invitations to attend a service or church activity are too numerous for her to tally.

"Don't give up on the person. Continue to love them and extending invitations to join you." Pastor Filmore pauses briefly then continues. "Keep in mind that you can disciple through a refused invitation. What is discipling? A lifestyle. Outside of a general invitation *have you taken personal time to show someone the way to Jesus by exuding Christ-like characteristics?*"

***

"Have you no pride, woman? We are no more. You are to cease from calling my numbers."

Irritated by yet another one of Renata's persistent calls, Hayes disconnects himself from what he expects will be the last call from his former love interest. His facial features prune as he reflects upon her many displays of lost dignity. His reflection in a nearby mirror confirms what his father has told him to accept as the Davis legacy – they are desirable men.

Narcissism like that of an over-indulged celebrity draws Hayes closer to the mirror. He makes several facial expressions ranging from teasing to pouting then to sultry. For years each seemingly innocent look has been perfected and used cleverly on unsuspecting women. Many have been left heartbroken by his gradual or abrupt dismissal. Despite the parting circumstances, the majority accept reality and move on. A few; however, do not. His ego rationalizes that his exceptional intellect, wealth and sexual prowess are so intoxicating that women just need more.

On many occasions, women seeking reconciliation with no strings attached were used for sexual gratification then disposed of like two-week-old egg salad.

Half-closed eyelids and lips slightly upturned at the corners, is a look women have fallen for time and time again. It exudes a challenge to trust him with promises of taking them beyond what they have ever experienced.

Suddenly Hayes' breaks into a wide grin with a hint of mischief reflecting through his eyes. It is this combination that makes him appear vulnerable and sincere. It is what touches the soul of Bernadette Lewis.

Hayes removes his shoes. Methodically, he finds space to place his feet atop a desk forever covered with business materials.

The image of Bernadette appearing before his eyes sweeps away the unpleasantness of Renata. His refreshed thoughts seek an outlet. Donning a headset, Hayes leans back ready to release the creativity filling his head. His imagination sets a stage casting Bernadette as the star of the show. He speaks with unrestrained ardor. "Fiery. Intense. Impassioned, yet reserved. Foreplay without intent subdues lust yet heightens intrigue. Wit dry as French claret disarms without offense. Never common. Without pretense femininity declares her strength, value and expectancy to be handled with care. She makes me as giddy as a freshman romantic. Being in her presence is glorious and encourages inner growth. In her company I explode releasing crimson, blush, cerise, rubicund and simply red. My eyes turn as red as a drunkard as I drink her essence. Red, it is the color of blood necessary for sustaining life. She makes me feel like red."

Words of adoration are saved to a file titled "Queen". In the seclusion of his majestic master suite, Hayes will transfer them onto scented paper.

***

Sunshine streaming through the skylight above Falimah's bed bathes her with warmth.

Exhaustion brought on by a very late night entices her to snuggle beneath her sheets. But dedication to taking care of business wills her to the edge of her bed. She runs a hand over hair that is matted and will require a lot of moisturizing and creative styling this morning. Stretching brings pain to her left shoulder.

Emergence from the mistress suite with revitalized hair, flawless makeup and a knockout suit helps Falimah forget about her aches as she heads to the garage. The doorbell reroutes her steps. The security camera showcases the image of the unexpected visitor. Despite misgivings she answers the nonstop ring. "What are you doing here?"

Stepping through the door as if invited, her surprise guest reacts as if she was awaiting his presence. He pulls her near. "You can skip work today."

"I don't skip out on work."

"Fine. You can go in later," he growls.

***

Bernadette happily exchanges business attire for worn jeans and a white sleeveless top. Over it she places a Seattle Storm jersey with the number of her favorite player and the team's championship MVP, Betty Lennox.

A dab of perfume behind her ears and on her wrists is just enough to leave a lingering memory for one person in particular.

Her reflection in the mirror does not quite please her.

Quickly, she carefully removes her makeup exposing her natural beauty to the world. Next, she puts her hair into a braid that hangs slightly below her shoulders.

Bernadette waits outside Covenant Place for Hayes. She steps to the curb as he approaches in his beet red Hummer H2. He looks as though he does not recognize her as he passes her by. Slowly the car backs up, then halts in front of Bernadette. "Twinkle is that you? Forgive me. My vision was obstructed by that foolish jersey."

The two, WNBA fanatics, go to war over their favorite players. Their hearty bantering continues until Bernadette shifts gears. "Your ignorance is dense, but I hope you are able to receive vital instructions. You are meeting my grandparents tonight. I guarantee you my grandfather will ask you to get things for him from places he believes you should not know about in my house. It's a set up to find out how familiar you may be with my home."

Hayes' eyes squint. "Just do what I ask Hayes. It'll make life much simpler for you."

Roosevelt backs his black Hummer H2 out of the driveway of his Beacon Hill home when Hayes and Bernadette pull up. Their similar taste in vehicles and a cell phone conversation held between the men during the short ride to Bernadette's Seward Park home piques her curiosity about how close the two really are.

Nee Nee takes her time walking from the car to the porch after they arrive at Bernadette's home. Roosevelt greets Bernadette with a big squeeze and peck on the cheek.

Roosevelt's demeanor alerts Hayes to what is on the horizon. The rubbing of the wedding finger by Hayes is reciprocated by Roosevelt's slight tilting of his head to the left. Bernadette glances from one man to the other as they carry on their mysterious motions.

Nee Nee takes her aside. In a low voice she explains. "They couldn't be any closer than if they were co-joined twins. Their soul tie developed long before I met Roosevelt." She blows Roosevelt a kiss then returns her attention to Bernadette. "You see how fine they are. People, women in particular, strain to get into their business. Their special communication was born out a need for privacy."

Bernadette nods then links her arm inside Nee Nee's. A tour of her home is offered and accepted.

Left on their own Hayes, and Roosevelt set out on a tour of their own.

Tantalizing aromas draw the two into the kitchen. Hearty greetings are extended to Zavonne. They both momentarily loose the power of speech when their eyes fall upon Eleanor Burton.

Without looking up from the pot of greens she is stirring, Eleanor inquires about which man has an interest in Bernadette.

Hayes steps forward. "I have been seeing Bernadette. My name is Hayes Davis. This is my brother/friend Roosevelt Hillis."

"Zavonne escort Mr. Hillis to the parlor while Mr. Davis and I speak in private."

Hayes walks to Eleanor's side, extends an arm, then escorts her to the padded chair that she points to. Request for a refill of her tea is silently fulfilled. Exceptional manners prompt Hayes to remain standing at a respectable distance after placing the cup before her.

On no one's timetable, Eleanor daintily sips the steamy tea while appraising the image of the man before her. A single braid reaching just above his shoulder blades does not detract from his masculinity. His mauve and crème ethnic pattern shirt over lightly starched crème shorts meets Eleanor's approval. Hayes' manicured fingernails and fresh pedicure speaks to his attention to detail.

Eleanor's hand, turned golden with the passing of time, taps the seat beside her. Hayes sits. His slight tentativeness does not go unnoticed. "Relax young man. I won't bite unless you give me just cause."

Hayes remains silent before Eleanor, who is used to getting her way. Her soft hands grasp his large firm ones. Her eyes seem to look into his soul.

"You need to understand how much I love my granddaughter," Eleanor says in a tone that clearly defines her mood. "The fact that she has invited you into her home says you are a man of possibilities."

"Thank you, ma'am."

"Don't thank me yet. When I'm finished you might not like me."

Sitting up a little straighter in her chair Eleanor releases Hayes, then touches her snow white hair that is never out of place. "I've been around a long time, young man. Looking at you I can tell you've been intimate with a woman or two. Is that an expectation you have of my granddaughter?"

"Ma'am?" is all he manages to say.

"I'm not a shy woman. If your intentions aren't honorable concerning my granddaughter you are to walk away from her today. Bernadette is a woman with high standards. She doesn't have time to waste on second or third best and this family will not appreciate you wasting her time."

The appearance of Zavonne and Roosevelt without Hayes is puzzling to Bernadette.

Zavonne's mocha frosted lips mouth the 'B' word – *Bunky*.

"That's not funny."

Zavonne's bucked eyes tell Bernadette no joke is being played.

The rapid rise in her body temperature gives Bernadette the sensation of incubating an internal flame. Her mouth becomes dry, preventing her from speaking to her sister.

Zavonne points to the window. Bernadette does not need to look to see that Will and Julia have arrived.

Being the consummate hosts of the property, the couple cross the threshold with two freshly baked blackberry pies. They acknowledge the guests before proceeding to the kitchen. Bernadette's attempt at joining her grandparents is aborted by one of Julia's patented *go away* looks.

Extreme heat intensifies inside Bernadette. A light spasm causes her left leg to twitch the way it did during lengthy speeches that came before her father's switch meted out her punishment for disobedience. She sits on the arm of a nearby chair. The second and third involuntary tremors are not noticed by anyone except Zavonne.

Conversation regarding the expansion of Nee Nee's salon into a full-service spa is a welcomed deterrent for Bernadette. As interested as she is, her subconscious is focused upon what she knows is transpiring in the kitchen. In that room her grandparents will expertly combine social graces with interrogation to select threads of information from Hayes. Those threads will be used to weave together their representation of who he appears to be. Their opinion of his worth will determine if he possesses the qualities deemed worthy of being seamed into a suitable covering for her.

Hayes rises from his seat to greet Will and Julia.

"Pleased to meet you, young man," Julia says accepting the seat Hayes offers her.

"Would you mind taking a walk with me?" Will says already headed to the door.

Hayes follows taking in Will's skin barely a shade lighter than Bernadette's. He is well put together in crisply pressed khaki pants, matching shirt and shiny, black Johnston & Murphy shoes. His erect posture and steady gait portray the self-assuredness of his slightly built frame.

Hayes accepts the seat he is offered near a bed of over-sized white calla lilies. Will remains standing. He makes eye contact with Hayes. With words, spoken with a thick southern accent sprinkled with down-home vernacular he says, "You just met Bernadette's grandmother. Since you have, you know we ain't what most people call typical. If you gonna be 'round Bernadette you gonna have to deal with us 'cause we're a people who do business unusual. That means we watch out to see what the other might not see."

Hayes nods, but does not offer a response.

"A few months ago I asked my granddaughter what dating meant. She gave me her definition. I want you to give me yours."

Hayes' left forefinger and thumb massage his chin before responding. "Dating to me encompasses spending time getting to know one another and exploring new territory."

"Are bed privileges with my granddaughter included on your exploration map?"

"Sir?"

Will's eyes sweep over Hayes. One step forward is as deliberate as his next words. "Let me make this plain. It's Twinkle's choice to keep company with you. It's my business to let you know I'ma old school man and I don't play 'bout my kinfolk. You *will* respect my grandbaby, and I'm not talkin' 'bout that new fangled stuff y'all call respect. I'm talking 'bout godly standards. If y'all part company that's between the two of you. If y'all have to part company 'cause you pressin' her to do wrong or you puttin' your hands on her, you and I will definitely meet."

Eleanor's so-called thrown together meal of smothered chicken, turnip greens, corn on the cob and hot water cornbread, is the setting for phase two of the seniors' interrogation.

As predicted, Hayes is asked to retrieve things from places considered off-limits to one in his position. Conversation laced with questions to the Hillises put Bernadette on edge.

After socializing for a period of time following dinner, the elders excuse themselves.

Zavonne and Bernadette walk them to the door. All are kissed and hugged by Zavonne before she returns to her guests.

Bernadette embraces, then kisses Will and Julia. A curt goodnight is extended to Eleanor.

Eleanor allows her hosts to depart before expressing her dissatisfaction for Bernadette's distant behavior.

Hostile words leap from Bernadette's mouth. "Why didn't you tell me you were here when you called this morning?"

"I come and go as I please, young lady. Unlike you, your grandparents understand the necessity of my presence at this time. I am a welcomed guest in their home."

"But not mine!" Bernadette spits out.

Not wanting to damage their relationship any further, Eleanor quells her desire to put the insolent Bernadette in her place.

Two women, more alike than either one of them realize, face off like opponents inside a boxing ring. Two steps forward by Eleanor minimizes the space between them. Eye contact rings the bell for the verbal bout. Eleanor strikes first. "I'm here at the invitation of my dear friends – your grandparents. We have much to discuss regarding you and this young man."

Sharp words stagger Bernadette causing her to flinch. The involuntary motion reminds Eleanor of how in the past her blunt remarks would bring the adolescent Bernadette close to tears.

Bernadette rolls her eyes. Eleanor – a seasoned boxer, blocks that with a fierce look of her own.

Bernadette slips in a jab when she tells Eleanor, "Guests are invited into my home. In the future you are to ask permission to enter my home rather than barge in unannounced."

Willingness to leave Bernadette without bruised feelings is set aside. Eleanor's next words push Bernadette against the ropes. "Your permission for what I do or where I go is not necessary, especially when it pertains to your well being."

"I'm a grown woman who can take care of my own affairs. I'm doing very well without your interference, Mrs. Burton."

The formality of Bernadette's reference coupled with the venom in her tone is the surprise left hook that staggers Eleanor.

Their brief stare down is broken when from between clenched teeth Bernadette sneers, "Stay out of my house and away from my place of business!"

Her follow-up packs a wallop, but not enough to take Eleanor, who counters with a combination of her own. "My responsibility to this family did not end with the marriage of my daughters. Like it or not you're included in the purpose I will fulfill."

"When did you say you were leaving?" Bernadette nastily inquires.

Eleanor's experience cuts the circumference of their ring. Bernadette's inexperience is circled with intimidating silence.

Bernadette's lowered head leaves her unprotected, allowing the delivery of a powerful uppercut. "If it takes until the day after eternity to find out all I need to know about this boy and his people, that's how long I will remain."

Eleanor's departure leaves her inept opponent at the end of a standing 10 count.

Shrouded in defeat, Bernadette and her bruised feelings return to her guests.

Zavonne and Nee Nee challenging Roosevelt to become more in tune with his feminine side, at any other time would be humorous. At the moment, nursing hurt feelings of her own prevents Bernadette from joining the harassment.

Hayes' intense stare from across the room reminds her that he is fresh from the Lewis/Burton interrogation camp.

"Hayes?"

He stands, adjusts his shirt, then moves to her side. "Take me somewhere we can talk in private," he whispers in her ear. Hayes is escorted to a limestone terrace filled with large flowering clay pots.

"Hayes?" She says to his back as he walks to the opposite side of the terrace. Rigidity in his posture chills her like a strong winter gust.

"You did not tell me Mrs. Burton is your grandmother. Nor did you tell me that she would be here. Most importantly," he says not allowing her to interrupt, "you refrained from telling me how lethal your family really is."

Bernadette sits in a nearby chair. Thoughts of how her no-holds-barred grandparents may have manhandled Hayes' ego is a fleeting thought. She is too emotionally spent to address the issues that he has just mentioned.

Two hundred plus pounds landing in front of her is startling. "You scared me leaping through the air like that," Bernadette says while straining her neck in order to focus on Hayes' face.

"Now you understand my position when Rambo's kinsmen sprang from the bush on me."

"They couldn't have been that bad, Hayes," Bernadette laughs knowing all too well they could.

"Allow me to give my synopsis of your grandparents, Ms. Lewis."

"What do you have to say about my people?" she laughs.

"I fear few people. I have a healthy fear of your grandparents."

"Why?"

"I believe their words may have placed my manhood into neutral. Time will tell me if I should shift into drive or reverse."

CHAPTER 9

People, who don't rob, steal, murder, so on and so forth, the ones we classify as nice people, are in just as much danger as the outwardly sinful. They may be going to hell in droves because they have not surrendered to God...Sometimes it isn't us. It's their refusal to accept an invitation to church.

Sleep has abandoned Treva.

Pastor Filmore's words running continuously through her mind have brought her to a state of in-depth self-examination. For years, attempts at becoming a church attendee have not worked for her. The few times she did grace a sanctuary, the experience left her wondering why she ever tried.

...Have you taken personal time to show someone the way to Jesus by exuding Christ-like characteristics?

There is no denying Bernadette's very nature is what led her to accept her invitation to visit Trinity. Despite her receptiveness of Pastor Filmore's messages, she fears the positive experience will diminish.

Treva's light brown eyes stare into darkness. Unconsciously, her right hand searches until it finds her bedside CD player. She presses the play button. "He's standing...surrender your all today."

The soothing words bring serenity into the room. Repeat mode keeps the song playing long after Treva falls into a peaceful sleep.

***

"Do people who are good-hearted, but don't go to church go to hell?"

"What you really want to know is, are you in jeopardy?"

Teeth with a slight overbite appear then disappear as Treva ponders the response. "Yeah, I guess that's what I'm asking."

Bernadette's bare feet make slapping noises upon the decorative soapstone floor as she makes her away across the kitchen.

"There are a lot of very kind people who don't go to church who are very kind. The issue isn't attendance at the building where we worship God. The issue is the lack of a relationship with God." Bernadette allows her words to marinate within her new friend as she moves about the sun-drenched kitchen preparing their lunch.

Treva allows her eyes to roam about the kitchen. A short wall separating the kitchen from the pantry is papered with papyrus. *As For Me And My House – We Shall Serve The Lord*, is repeatedly etched into it in bold script. Treva walks to it. Her right hand adorned with a sterling silver band on the index finger and a diamond and pearl ring on her pinky finger move over the words as if she were reading Braille.

Bernadette observes Treva without being too obvious.

"How do you serve God?" Treva abruptly asks.

Bernadette moves to the stove. "True service begins with choice. Christ chose to die for us. It's each individual's choice to decide if they will die to self in order to live for Him."

Treva continues to caress the wall as if it were a familiar lover.

Purple and gold hand-painted china weighted with melon, pineapple and kiwi is set upon the table. Treva returns to her seat. After grace, the two eat their fruit in silence. Several times they make eye contact, but remain silent.

Treva's glances at a bible lying on the nearby counter and then to Bernadette do not go unobserved.

As if cued, Bernadette and Treva reach for the bible at the same time. "Is it okay if I get more juice while you find the scripture you want to show me?" Treva laughs.

Bernadette nods her consent.

She removes the gold clamp holding her hair up as she walks away.

Treva returns to the table with a full glass of juice. Bernadette opens the bible to the desired scripture without having to search for it. "Let me show you something my pastor spoke about last week," she says pointing to a scripture with a glossy fingernail. *"But he shall say, I tell you, I know you not whence ye are; depart from me, all ye workers of iniquity.* In this chapter of Luke, Christ is calling people to repent and is teaching about the Kingdom of God. We need to repent because all of us have sin in our lives. He is teaching about the Kingdom because people who come to Christ don't always understand what is expected of them. Many think if they keep the laws and busy themselves with works they have earned eternal life. They haven't."

Bernadette pushes the bible across the table until it is directly in front of Treva. "Tell me if I'm out of line. You're searching for something to fill a void in you."

Treva flips forward and backward through the text before her, then looks Bernadette directly in her eyes. "How much time do you have to spend with somebody who took the words 'drop by anytime,' literally?"

"As long as you're willing to stay."

Treva taps her fingers on the table, then asks a straightforward question. "Are you just being polite, or are you really okay with me dropping by unannounced?"

Bernadette tilts her head to the side. Her nose wrinkles. "I'll be real honest with you. I hoped you would accept my invitation to drop by. I'm a pretty private person. I don't welcome people into my home that I don't like. Since you're staying for a while, let's move out to the terrace where we can get a little more sun."

"You're willing to help me out?"

"Why wouldn't I?" Bernadette offers, leading the way outside. "It's all about sharing what you have with others, so they can share it with someone else."

Treva follows her hostess while unconsciously humming the song she heard the first day she visited Trinity.

"I love that song," Bernadette comments.

"I do too. I heard it for the first time at church a few weeks ago. I bought Addie Lewis' CD and play it nonstop in my car and all night at my bedside. When I'm in the shower, I close my eyes and pretend that the lady at Trinity is singing it to me."

Treva's halted speech, wide eyes, and too much attention paid to her hands define the moment.

"It's okay, sis. I've seen you every Sunday you've been at Trinity."

"Why didn't you say anything?"

"If you wanted me to know you were there, you would have told me. I just kept praying that you'd keep coming." Bernadette's face brightens. "I tell you what. If you have dinner with me after church this Sunday, I guarantee you I can get my grandmother to sing the song for you."

***

"Black women have way too much booty to be wearin' low-rider pants. And they should have enough sense not to wear thong drawers if they do. Ain't that right, Hayes?"

An upraised hand is Hayes' response.

Like strings attached to a puppet, each pull of his hair manipulates the gripping then loosening of his hold upon the arms of the salon chair he is in. Nee Nee winks at her talkative manicurist who in turn seeks to goad Hayes into conversation.

"Man of my dreams, I know you have a lot to offer women seeking the affection of someone as fine as yourself. Talk to me, baby."

An ego so huge it is said to require luggage to be carried around, prevents Hayes from speaking. He refrains, fearing his voice will crack and ruin his suave reputation. Nee Nee pulls more hair into place, causing him to cross then uncross his long legs.

Three hours after planting himself in the chair, Hayes is released from what he calls the death grip. Pain shoots through his temples.

"Baby, your girl got your wig on lock down. You'll need a pardon from the warden to walk around with that style."

Hayes' cell phone ringing intensifies his pain. The number on the display irritates him. "I am not in the mood. I will not meet with you. I have taken the last call…once I hang up you are to expunge the memory of my existence from your mind…"

Hayes' venomous words, overheard by many in the shop, start a buzz of conversation. The topic – Who Is Mr. Hayes Davis?

Hayes' hair is braided so tight that the corners of his eyes seem to have turned upward. Having taken the legal dose of pain killers, he searches for anything else to relieve his agony.

He tries to concentrate on a scripture, but his vision is blurry. *Perhaps prayer will detour my thoughts*, he thinks as he grasps for something to distract his mind from the pain.

Morning devotion was never an option in the Davis household. Under the watchful eye of their mother, Hayes and his siblings praised, prayed and worshipped every morning.

It was a part of life that lessened in Hayes' adult years, but not even his courtship with waywardness could completely detour him from prayer. Now determined to devote his life to Christ, Hayes spends hours reading the scriptures and praying for clarity. Worship is now serious. Often he awakens filled with a need to praise.

Familiar lyrics from a praise song pop into Hayes' head. He hums the tune softly. Humming turns into a low-pitched song. Rhythmic tapping upon his chest initiates corresponding footwork. Louder and louder Hayes sings.

Praising carries him from his bedroom, through the house to the Florida room and onto his manicured lawn.

Light dew upon the grass feels cool between his toes. His uninhibited dancing joins soul-deep adoration being sent upward. He removes his blue linen shirt. His glasses join the hastily discarded shirt as the intensity of his praise increases.

Hayes praises until exhaustion renders his perspiration-drenched body upon its back. He relishes the coolness of the damp grass. Tears from his eyes and sweat from his pores act as cleansing agents, ridding Hayes of the toxins poisoning his body and soul as he begins to worship.

Rings from his cell phone interrupt his holy communication. He answers, "Yes, Brown Man."

"I see you can talk. Guess Nee Nee didn't weave your tongue into your hair."

"Tell your woman…"

"What happened to your headache?"

"I praised it away. Remember your lecture on getting out of self?"

Roosevelt grunts.

"I placed so much emphasis on Him, self was forgotten. When I came to myself, my pain had subsided."

"You can apply that to every aspect of your walk, man. This walk ain't all about you. It's about who God called you to be. Man up and answer the call."

Further words reveal the true nature of Roosevelt's call. "Heard your girl is still callin'. What's up with that?"

Hayes sighs.

"You just talked about the joy of praising."

Another sigh.

"Nee Nee told me how you blessed that girl out today. How you gonna praise God with the same mouth you used to berate one of His children?"

Hayes cannot respond.

"Read Romans 12 verse 2 and James 3 verses 9 and 10. We'll talk about it when I swing by the store for lunch tomorrow. Don't order me nothin' that has a goat in it 'cause I might go postal on you this time."

***

The advantage of being with your girl is the ability to be yourself.

Falimah's entrance into Treva's home without knocking and kicking off her shoes is all too familiar. Her fluted skirt is hiked beyond public acceptance before she leaps onto Treva's exceptionally comfortable sofa.

"What happened to the back of your leg, Falimah?" Treva asks with a bit of concern.

Springboard action brings Falimah to an upright position. She lowers her raised skirt, then firmly plants both feet on the floor. "I was a little too aggressive on the stair climber at the gym. I missed a step and bruised myself up pretty good."

Treva recognizes the avoidance tactic when Falimah asks to be fed, so they can go out to party.

The subject change concerns Treva. Her concern is how Falimah will act when she tells her that she has made other plans.

"Do you want salad or a baked potato with your steak?" Treva asks heading to the kitchen to buy herself some time.

Ten minutes later she reappears with a dinner tray. "I made dinner earlier so all I had to do was pop your plate into the microwave."

The two have known each other far too long. Falimah's stiff posture and stare convicts Treva.

She pretends not to notice.

"What's going on Treva?"

"Will you act like a human when I tell you?"

Falimah's crossed eyes guarantee nothing.

"I have to finish packing. I'm flying to L.A. for a little power shopping. I'll be back Sunday afternoon."

"You going with some new friends?"

"Yeah."

"Is it Bernadette?"

She shakes her head yes.

Falimah takes her plate and leaves.

***

Soft growling from behind a high-back chair cause the small group of juveniles to huddle together for protection. Scraping sounds made by the chair as it inches forward heightens their anxiety. The chair stops. Slowly, a twisted mane appears, but then quickly disappears. Without warning, the crouching predator leaps from behind its barrier toward the children. Stunned bodies fall like bowling pins, preventing their escape. Herculean strength lovingly scoops up their little bodies. They struggle from his grasp then pile on top of him with laughs and screams of joy.

Pandemonium rings throughout the house. Moving rapidly, Zavonne's feet barely touch the floor on her way toward unknown mayhem.

"What is going on in here?"

"Grrr…"

Her flying cup meets the hardwood floor, as her piercing scream fills the air. Screams continue as she is taken down. Her landing is cushioned by masculinity.

"You said you would get her Mr. Davis!" the children shout.

After startling the children with his impromptu ending of their afternoon story, Hayes coerced them into helping him play a joke on Zavonne.

Zavonne warns Hayes not to tell anyone in their friendship circle how he pulled a fast one on her as she rises to her feet.

She smiles inwardly as she watches Hayes and the children set about straightening the room. Over the past few months she has come to know him as a man of his word. In addition to the story hour, Hayes often does minor repairs or whatever else is needed at Saving Grace.

Blaine is Hayes' number one fan, but keeping up with the content of the stories is a struggle for him. Although he has been fitted with a hearing aid, doctors predict he will be totally deaf within six months. When he learned this, Hayes enrolled in American Sign Language courses along with Blaine and his mother, Dinah. He and Blaine formed a strong bond, becoming virtually inseparable.

Zavonne sends the children back to their parents, then invites Hayes to sit with her.

"You've been spending a lot of time with Blaine. Unfortunately, it's easy for children to become attached to that. It's not uncommon for the parent to become attached too. I see the way Dinah looks at you. I hear her tone when she talks about you."

Pulling at a lock of hair while rubbing his neck, he frowns. "What are you suggesting?"

"Blaine has already lost his father and suffered from living on the streets. He's allowed himself to trust again because of you. If you're not going to be in his life for the long haul, make sure he doesn't become dependent upon you."

***

A week in California tending to business and spoiling three energetic nieces has drained Bernadette's energy.

Hanging out with Treva for a few days gave them the opportunity to really get to know one another. Even Terry was impressed by her. Despite her charitable mood, once Treva flew back to Seattle, Terry cracked the whip across Bernadette's back.

Marathon sessions with staff and artists associated with Three Praises tested Bernadette's stamina. Just when she thought she had a moment to rest, Terry produced a list of executive tasks she saved specifically for her.

Throughout the day Bernadette received calls from the triplets on her cell phone demanding that she come home and bring them presents. Each evening they greeted her in the driveway, then shadow her like CIA agents throughout the house. Although she went to bed alone, Bernadette awakened each morning with the trio in her bed. By week's end she was happy to be fleeing Los Angeles.

Thirty minutes after landing, Bernadette and her four pieces of luggage wait at the airport for Hayes.

Twenty, thirty, sixty minutes later and Hayes has not arrived.

Bernadette's usual calm demeanor goes from concern, to irritation, to all-out anger. "The nerve of Hayes Davis leaving me stranded!" she mumbles under her breath after placing another unanswered call.

She kicks a suitcase which leaves a scar on the tip of her shoe. This only serves to raise her anger level. *He ain't so fine he can't be replaced.*

Her simmering anger makes the lengthy ride home uncomfortable for the friendly cabby, whom she instructs to just drive and to save his conversation for someone else.

She tries to apologize for her behavior with a generous tip. The gratuity is accepted, but Bernadette and her bags are left in the driveway.

Having to drag overstuffed bags up the stairs only intensifies her rage.

Terry's untimely call receives her wrath.

"Whoooa girl! You need to chill! I just called to see if you made it home safely. Sounds like you flew in with the flyin' monkey squadron. What happened?"

Bernadette's anger rises while telling Terry about being stood up.

"Twinkle, calm down. Before you assume anything, you need to find out what happened."

Bernadette is not listening to reason. "Hayes left me to fend for myself after he…"

The buzz from the front gate distracts Bernadette. The sight of Hayes' car on the security screen sets her off again. "You know that boy has the nerve to be ringing my bell? I'm not letting him in!"

"Let him in, Twinkle!"

"No!"

"I know you're a better woman than what you're portraying right now! You don't let a man or what he may do cause you to lower your standards. You let him in and handle your business like the woman Mama raised. You hear me, Twinkle?"

There is no way she cannot.

She takes the advice and opens the gate. She steps onto the porch wearing Hayes' favorite red dress. The grin of approval she had sought hours before is no longer desired.

"I am sorry I was unable to escort you home."

She cuts off his apology with loud angry words.

"Stop shouting at me, Bernadette."

"You left me stranded, Hayes! Why weren't you at your office? Why is your cell phone turned off?"

Storm clouds can literally be seen forming inside Hayes' onyx pupils, and thunderous words leap from his throat. "I came to apologize, but since you refuse to listen, I am finished here. Understand me well though, never again believe I live only for you."

"Get off my property!"

Clinking keys announce Zavonne's arrival.

Luggage strewn about says that Bernadette is in a foul mood.

Zavonne finds her disheveled sister in the kitchen sipping from a deep mug. Her apology is immediate. "I'm sorry I messed up, Twinkle. Hayes couldn't make it to the airport. I was supposed to pick you up. I got stuck behind that accident on 405...left my cell phone...couldn't call anyone."

Hayes takes time to collect himself before entering the pediatric intensive care unit. Blaine's well-being must be his only focus.

Bernadette felt lower than a penny looking for change when Zavonne explained the situation. A truck that ran a traffic light hit Blaine the morning of her return from Los Angeles. Hayes asked her to pick Bernadette up in order to remain at the hospital for moral support.

Hayes refused to accept Bernadette's calls. When she visited the hospital, he refrained from speaking to her.

Prayers for forgiveness and intercession for Blaine's recovery and Dinah's strength keeps Bernadette awake at night.

Despite favorable reports from the doctors, a blood clot claimed Blaine's life three days after the accident. Zavonne's call with the shocking news seemed to deplete Bernadette's lungs of air.

Although the chapel is sparsely populated, Bernadette chooses to sit in the last pew.

Apprehension toys with her mind. *What if he doesn't acknowledge me? I wouldn't blame him. The one time that he needed me I wasn't there for him. Even if he doesn't speak to me again, I must apologize.*

Bernadette forces herself to go through the reception line. The emptiness in Hayes' once sparkling eyes leaves her short of breath. His widely spread arms welcome her. She holds him tight as he openly sobs over the loss of his young friend.

CHAPTER 10

Delicious aromas from Treva's kitchen fill the air.

In an effort to appease Falimah, she has invited her and Bernadette over for an evening meal and conversation. When Brian finds out about the dinner he tells Treva he will swing by to pick up a plate to go.

Treva is lost in deep thought while preparing the meal. Concerns about whether she has done the right thing by inviting both Bernadette and Falimah tonight weigh heavily on her mind. She tries to push down the anticipation and anxiety.

At the stroke of seven, Brian arrives carrying his own plate, utensils and a wide grin. Boldly he strides past Treva, finds his way to the dining room and seats himself beside Bernadette as if he were an invited guest. He rises upon Treva's entrance to assist her into her seat.

Wit and unabashed conviction about the topics discussed over dinner keep the ladies entertained with a male perspective.

Treva catches herself sneaking more than casual peeks at Brian whenever he moves about the room. His zipper front knit sweater over crisply ironed jeans looks good on him. His shoulder length black hair has just enough body to keep it from being limp.

Falimah is in tune to all eye contact between the two. She expresses her disapproval with glances of irritation toward Treva.

Fried catfish, red beans, rice and cornbread satisfy the palates of all.

"Show me what you have in the garage," Brian urges.

Treva points to the garage. Falimah follows Brian while Bernadette helps Treva tidy up.

Brian finds the Fairlaine and Mustang parked side by side.

Falimah eyes him intently. Despite the snide remarks she often sends his way, her attraction to him has been building. She seizes what she believes is her moment. Boldly, she jumps onto the hood of the Mustang and lounges like a car show model. Exaggerated posing moves her short skirt upward. Her breasts often on display beneath snug sweaters and blouses move freely.

Realizing that her attempt at seduction is not getting an immediate response, Falimah removes herself from the vehicle. "I know about men like you Brian Chin," she says, her voice low and sexy. "You have high expectations." She steps toward Brian. Lust illuminates her body like a radioactive glow. He takes two steps backwards.

She steps toward him again. "You want a woman who's the fully equipped package."

Falimah allows her hand to sweep across the front of her skirt before moving upward to outline assets which most men find irresistible. "You like being in control. That's good because a real woman can appreciate that."

Treva's arrival brings a full grin to Brian's face. Leaning close to Falimah's ear Brian softly speaks words that fertilize Falimah's garden of hope. "You're right. My expectations are high and I don't settle for less than what I want."

His next words cause her garden of hope to wither and die.

"Treva's definitely a fully equipped package. That's why I wouldn't try to control her – but I'd definitely take good care of her."

Falimah works hard to hide her embarrassment as she returns to the house.

Brian walks toward Treva extending his hand. She takes it. "Show me the rest."

Treva sucks on her lower lip while staring into Brian's eyes. She lets go of her lip and then demands to know how he found her house. His answer, whispered into her ear brings tears of laughter. When she regains her composure she leads Brian to an adjoining structure that houses some of her most prized possessions.

In addition to the two Fords she alternately drives, Treva owns a canary yellow 1955 Thunderbird convertible. The black 1935 Pontiac, with suicide doors and a hemp trunk, is her father's preference. Her favorite, a 1965 Pink Cadillac Calais hard-top sedan completes her five-car fleet.

Treva's laughter gets Brian's attention. He summons her with his index finger. Treva runs back to her guests. He playfully takes off after her.

Their performance comes to an abrupt end when an acrobatic move lands Brian in front of Treva. His surprise move allows him to capture her. Attempts to break his hold are as false as showgirl eyelashes. "You guys are gonna have to keep this boy away from me now that he knows what I have."

"Not going to happen. I will wear you down."

Falimah looks as if she has bit into a lemon.

Before leaving, she takes Treva aside. "Looks like you have an admirer, girl."

"Brian's just after my cars."

"You may think that, but we both know he'd jump through a ring of fire if he thought you'd give him some play. You gonna give him some?"

Treva's push sends Falimah backwards.

"You need to save that strength for wrestling with Brian."

Treva's rolling eyes beg to differ.

"Let me give you the results of the office pool. Big money is on Brian ta get cha before Christmas. You heard him say he's going to wear you down."

"We work together. I can't date him."

"Let me explain the world to you. You can date him and while you're at it...," she whispers into Treva's ear.

"Girl what have you been doing behind closed doors? Do I need to check you for cooties?"

Falimah laughs at Treva's response to her offbeat suggestion. "I do what feels good. The question now, is what's good for you?"

"Nothing. This smack you're talking is pure speculation."

"No it's not," Bernadette says stepping from the shadows of the doorway. Falimah flushes.

"Tell me this, Treva. If you had a choice of dating Mr. Chin without fear of office turmoil, would you?"

Wide grinning and her fanning hand tell Bernadette what she already knew.

Bernadette places a very important call from her car.

"Yes, Ms. Lewis."

"Okay computer boy, I let you follow me here and I got your information for you. You just make sure you remember you owe me."

***

Deciding how to color coordinate toe and fingernail polish with this week's wardrobe is as serious as cornbread with greens for Bernadette and Zavonne. Their process is interrupted by Zavonne's cell phone call.

"Yes Bunky."

Bernadette rolls her eyes.

"No ma'am. I don't want doves released after the ceremony. No. No. Bunky! We said we didn't want the formal sit down dinner, or the caviar, or our full names carved in ice. We just want a simple candlelight buffet with the menu we selected. Will you do this for us please?"

Bernadette chuckles softly as she listens to Zavonne debate with their grandmother about her wishes.

"Twinkle, um..."

At the mention of her name, Bernadette sprints down the hall to the bathroom.

"Twinkle. She's, ah, in the bathroom. Thank you for calling to discuss this, Bunky. I know you want the best for me and I love you for it. Please just do what's on the list. I'll call you tomorrow. Love you."

Bernadette exits the bathroom. Shamelessly she returns to her sister's side.

"You almost made me tell a lie, Twinkle. Don't do that again. As a matter of fact, you need to grow up and deal with your issue with Bunky. She may have been kind of cold when we were growing up, but she's not that same person. She really does love you."

Bernadette's furrowed eyebrows disagree.

"She does. Someone who doesn't love you wouldn't have flown out here to see about you even though she knew you didn't want her here."

Bernadette's cell phone call detours her acid response.

"Hello."

"I miss my love. Will you reserve time for me tomorrow?"

"Depends on if you will make it worth my while."

"Determine that for yourself."

Hayes hangs up. He sends her a phone photo with his candy apple red clad body holding three pair of designer shoes with the message, "Are these worth your while?"

She calls him quickly, "Where are you?"

"On U Street, at a store that has your name written all over it – Wild Women Wear Red. Which of these shall I purchase for you?"

"How much will it cost for all three?"

"Five crisp Benjamin's should suffice."

"I can give you three hundred. Zavonne's good for the rest."

Zavonne's verbal protest is clearly heard by Hayes. "Make sure your sibling understands that as a businessman I leave no stone unturned to collect what I am owed. If forced, I will put her in a headlock until her debt is paid."

"Deal! If they carry sizes for a fully grown woman, get me a size twelve. If they run narrow, get a half size larger. "

Hayes' soft chuckle causes her pulse to quicken. Very sweetly she asks if he will need a ride from the airport.

"I will call you when I return. I like you, Twinkle."

"I like you too, Hayes."

"Hayes-and-Twinkle-sitting-in-a-tree-K.I.S.S.I.N.G!"

Bernadette laughs at her sister's juvenile antics.

In a split second, Zavonne's expression changes from amusement to seriousness.

"We need to finish what we started, Twinkle. You love Hayes. Bunky loves you. She's not in your business. She cares about who's in your life. She flew out here to meet Hayes and check out his people because she can see what you can't, or rather won't see. You need to pray about who he is, Twinkle. You need to know who he is by the spirit."

"You're a wise woman."

"I'm just passing on what Daddy taught me."

The two go back to painting their nails.

Bernadette does not speak again until Zavonne has placed a base coat on her fingernails.

"His relationship with Christ, the storytelling and his time with Blaine has done something to him. He's driven to figure out ways to lessen the stress for deaf children. For the last three days he's been in Washington D.C. at Gallaudet University doing research about educating deaf children."

"Can you handle his drive for what he's doing?"

"What do you mean?"

"If the two of you haven't discussed your purposes, you should. He can be fine as wine, and he definitely is, but if your purposes don't connect, you shouldn't consider being anything more than friends."

Bernadette thinks about the many times Hayes has shared his thoughts on how to help children like Blaine. His genuine desire to educate himself for the sake of helping others has intensified her attraction to him. Early in his ASL course, Hayes more than excelled with his hand communications. He made the choice to become Blaine's mentor and had begun to teach him some important things about manhood.

Zavonne's words interrupt her thoughts. "Would you cross the line to keep Hayes?"

Pointed words linger in the air like smoke from a Cuban cigar. Bernadette does not respond.

Zavonne fingers Bernadette's two-carat diamond ring. "When Daddy gave us these rings he said we might meet a man that's so appealing we might be tempted to offer ourselves to him. These rings are a reminder of our pledge. Nothing God requires of us or what Daddy and Mommy taught us has changed. Hayes is not your husband."

Bernadette frowns.

"Have you and Hayes…?"

"No."

"Have you been tempted?"

"I have to be honest and say that I've thought about what it would be like."

"Listen to me, Twinkle," Zavonne says with a little force. "I know you've been holding out on me about Hayes. I don't like it, but I have to respect your space. While you and Terry have been talking, I've been praying."

Bernadette tenses up.

"What I'm about to say to you I need you to hear with your spirit and not your flesh."

Bernadette's nod indicates she will.

"You just said you've thought about what it might be like to be intimate with Hayes. That says how much you really like him and how careful you really have to be. He says he's turned his life over and he's trying to be straight, but he's still a man. A really fine man, who's used to having his physical needs met. He's a man like the ones Gram T always warns us about."

Memories of bold words spoken by their great aunt come to the forefront of Bernadette's mind. At every family celebration Gram T takes it upon herself to sit all the single women down to give them a good *talkin' to* as she calls it. Bernadette chuckles inwardly at the words she has committed to memory. *Y'all been brought up in Jesus. That's what makes ya so pretty. It's my job to talk woman business to ya. Don't none of y'all be 'barrassed 'cause I'm a old woman. I'm old and livin' holy 'cause the women folk in this family talk plain 'bout life. That's why I knows what I knows and I'm tellin' y'all so you know and teach your younguns when the time comes. 'Cause of what the women folk in my day told me and I knows what I'm talkin' 'bout when I say pretty for a woman can mean trouble. Trouble, 'cause all kinds of mens gonna be tryin' ta get from you what ain't theirs to have. It's easy for 'em if you ain't got no woman trainin'. You gots to be careful 'bout what you let a man say to ya. Y'all know the ones I'm talkin' 'bout. Them slick mouth Johnnies. The ones that be touchin' ya with they eyes. Thems the men that's so smooth they got gals' legs spreadin' wide as eagles wings in flight 'fore they open they mouth. Y'all ain't on this earth to be nothin' but godly women. Y'all gots to be on the lookout. You do that by takin' every man 'round you to the Lord so's ya know they spirit. If'n somethin' ain't right, the Lord will tell ya. When He do, you listen.*

"Are you looking out the way you should, Twinkle? Are you praying about Hayes the way you should? Are you careful how you let him talk to you? Do you let him touch you?"

"I'm handling my business!" Bernadette snaps.

"Twinkle, I asked you a question and you didn't answer. Would you cross the line to keep Hayes?"

***

"I understand and I hate to push, but I really need you to get those shoes for me."

Bernadette's personal shopper, Angela, places her hand over the receiver to muffle her laughter. Of all the people who frequent Marabel's, it is only Bernadette or her sisters that she would go the extra three, four or five miles to secure a must have item.

"I'm doing my best to get the shoes for you, Bernadette."

***

A number of absences due to illness and vacations has Treva dividing time between her desk and the executive suite. With only she and Bernadette occupying the Penthouse, the week has been more like executive training camp. Serving as Bernadette's assistant has made her privy to inside information as well as opened doors to more possibilities.

Treva's presence in the executive suite has also fueled Falimah's jealousy. Envy has the green monster on edge and full of catty comments.

Treva picks up the ringing phone. "This is Ms. Lewis' office. How may I help you?"

"Ms. Scott, this is the security office. I have a Mr. Davis here to see Ms. Lewis."

Treva remembers that Bernadette has no appointments prior to two o'clock. She double checks the appointment calendar.

"Ms. Lewis, there's a Mr. Davis in the lobby to see you. He's not on your itinerary."

"Buzz him up, Treva. I'll be out in a minute."

The stainless steel elevator doors open like stage curtains. Hayes steps from it wrapped in a purple, green and metallic gold woven cloak projecting an aura of regality. The same colorful fabric is intricately wound about his head. His erect posture and casual surveillance of the surroundings give the impression that all about him is his possession.

He sets his wicker basket and a large shopping bag down. Treva smiles, intrigued with the man before her. He takes her hand in his, squeezes it gently, tilts his head in cordial greeting, then releases her hand.

"Hayes Davis. Ms. Lewis is not expecting me. If she is unavailable, please let her know that she is well worth the time I will spend waiting for her."

His eloquently spoken words keep the grin on Treva's face.

"May I sit?"

Treva stumbles over her own words. "Yeah. Yes. Yes. Please have a seat, Mr. Davis. Ms. Lewis will be out momentarily."

Treva turns to her keyboard. She quickly sends a message to Falimah. "I'm sitting here in the presence of one of the finest brothas I've seen in a long, long, time. His name is Hayes Davis. You heard of him?"

Falimah touches her mid-section then, allows her fingers to tap out a response. "Yeah, I've heard of him. He owns The Written Word."

"He's the one? I've been getting a monthly calendar of events in the mail from that store. Bernadette must have put me on their mailing list."

Falimah's fingers arch over her keyboard. Her pursed lips kiss the air then relax before sending her response. "He has a store in Tacoma too."

"Bernadette's a bookaholic, so I guess knowing him is a plus," Treva types back while keeping one eye on Hayes.

"Hold on." Treva ceases typing.

Bernadette enters the waiting area wearing a different dress than the one she'd arrived in. Their tender embrace indicates more than a casual relationship.

"Okay girl, Bernadette has him," Treva types.

Falimah responds, "Beam me up Scottie. I'm headed to the elevator."

"What brings you here, Mr. Davis?" Bernadette asks while trying to conceal a smile.

He waves the wicker basket full of treats in front of her face. She playfully grabs at it. "Have a seat until I return," Hayes softly commands giving her one of his patented smiles. He waits until she is seated before slipping out the door to retrieve the shopping bag left in the reception area.

Falimah, conveniently positioned at Treva's temporary desk, has a clear view of Hayes when he enters the hallway. She fools no one with her attempt to look busy with the papers in front of her. Hayes flashes a smile to acknowledge her presence before returning to Bernadette.

"That boy is sure 'nuff fine. I'm surprised he's dating Bernadette. From what I've heard, he's been around, if you know what I mean."

"What do you mean?"

Falimah leans back and then crosses her legs. Her lips twist into a half smirk. "*My* cousin worked part-time at his Tacoma store. "*My* aunt warned her not to date him because of his reputation. Girl talk around town says he gets what he wants from the ladies. I didn't take Bernadette to be *one of those kind of ladies.*"

Treva catches Falimah's intentional reference to blood relationship while questioning Bernadette's reputation.

"People change, Falimah. If what you say about him is true, then *my* girl is definitely a woman worth changing for."

CHAPTER 11

Patience, not one of Bernadette's strongest virtues, is a struggle to maintain as she watches Hayes fuss over his presentation.

Hayes' black cashmere sweater is just snug enough to showcase the broadness of his chest. She takes in his trim waist, strong backside and athletic thighs that are clearly defined each time he bends to place items around the rich purple and gold spread upon the floor. *Why did this boy have to show up wearing exactly what he knows will make me lose my concentration?*

Focus girl, focus! Scripture, think of a scripture. – Whatsoever things are honest, whatsoever things are just...pure...lovely'. This is not working. This sight is far too LOVELY.

Hayes extends his arms to invite Bernadette to eat.

She sits down to her favorites – mustard greens with a hint of pepper sauce, hot water cornbread and a medley of okra, corn and tomatoes.

"Are you pleased?" Hayes inquires.

Her long lashes flutter. "Almost," she smiles.

Following the blessing, Bernadette uses her hands to sign the words "My name is Bernadette. How was your trip?"

Hayes smiles while signing back, "My name is Hayes Davis. Who taught you ASL?"

Not knowing how to respond with her hands, Bernadette verbally tells that Dinah has been helping her.

They enjoy their lunch in silence.

Bernadette breaks the silence by asking what prompted the surprise meal.

"There is nothing that I would not do to put a smile on your face."

"*Nothing?*"

"Your question is rendered to measure the amount of control you have over me?"

"If I have to control you there would be no need in our being together."

Rather than respond Hayes begins to unwind the fabric on his head. His tresses fall downward and outward framing his face like a lion's mane.

Bernadette's eyes widen.

He responds with roaring laughter. "It has been a bad hair day. The wrap makes me presentable."

She presses her lips together to hold in laughter as she points at his unruly hair.

Hayes brushes his hair backwards then asks when her parents will arrive for the Thanksgiving holiday.

"What?"

Sign language and audible words ask a second time. "When do your parents arrive?"

"Why?"

"I have met your grandparents."

Bernadette wrinkles her nose.

Hayes changes the subject by asking about Zavonne's wedding. Her response is interrupted when he asks what type of wedding she prefers.

Bernadette is caught off guard.

"Will you tell me?"

Visions of an event planned since the age of twelve come forth. "My wedding will be my covenant pledge to God. I only want immediate family and those who pray for me on a daily basis at the ceremony. I wouldn't mind a larger reception though. What about you?"

"I have not given it much thought."

Bernadette is unable to conceal her disappointment with his answer.

"Do not pout my love. Marriage has only entered my thoughts of late. The majority of my time is consumed with maintaining a successful business while keeping you from surrendering yourself to me," he says jokingly.

His next words are aborted by a yawn.

"You need to get some rest Hayes."

"I concur. But would you mind if I spend a bit more time here?"

Bernadette checks her watch. "How did you get here?"

"Taxi."

"I have a consultation with a potential client, a briefing with one of my staff and then some paperwork to go over. If you don't mind waiting, you can take a nap in my private quarters. When I'm finished I'll drive you home."

He accepts her offer.

Hayes makes small talk about the upcoming holiday while they pack up. Bernadette skirts around his question about how she will spend the holiday by asking about her shoes.

The large shopping bag tied with a brilliant red ribbon is placed into her hands. She can barely contain her excitement.

Hayes' opposition to accepting the five hundred dollar check she offers for payment almost ruins their afternoon. They go back and forth until she stuffs the check into his shoulder bag he left leaning against the wall.

Rather than extending the debate, Hayes clears his throat, then asks, "Do you teach on Sunday?"

"Why?"

"Because I would like for you to join me for Sunday service and dinner with my family?"

"You…you want me to meet your parents?" Bernadette stammers.

Belly deep laughter shakes Hayes' body. "As long as you obey my every command my father will see you as the subservient woman I am meant to have." He winks.

Quick reflexes catch the flying napkin she throws.

Opportunity to develop and oversee a project rarely extended to a novice is exciting. Treva has been given this chance and is determined to do an excellent job.

Early morning rising and late nights include researching statistics and consumer marketing trends. Monday's deadline is three days away, and Treva is way ahead of schedule.

She is satisfied with what she considers a job well done and decides to relax for a moment. Leaning back she closes her eyes and dreams about her future success. The blissful moment is interrupted by a crackling sound. She jumps up and opens her eyes to sparks and smoke coming from the surge protector beneath her desk. There is no way to safely disconnect her computer from it.

She frantically dials the lab.

"Brian Chin." Brian answers.

"Cut all power to this floor now!"

"What?"

"Just do it!"

Within seconds the lights go out.

Falimah's shouts come through the door before she does. "What happened to the electricity?"

"I'm not sure how this happened, but I have to go down and thank Brian for saving me again."

Falimah's expression suggests she is about to say something off kilter.

"You know Treva, I can cover for you, so you can give him a proper thank you. In fact, while you're down there you could try a little…"

Treva's eyes widen "That sounds painful."

"What's a little pain between partners? It's all for the sake of fulfillment."

Treva knows that Falimah is trying to get a rise out of her. She walks away to find Bernadette to tell her the bad news about the company computer.

Bernadette's displeasure at learning a valuable piece of equipment has been damaged is obvious. As displeased as she is, her mood is not spoiled. Hearing Hayes say he has thought of marriage recently and also inviting her to meet his parents literally has her floating.

She walks to Falimah's office for their afternoon briefing.

Curiosity is written all over Falimah's face. Regardless of the look that is an invitation for girl talk, Bernadette declines.

Falimah pushes for what she wants, "So, is that your man or is he auditioning to be your man? If he isn't your man, are you setting him up to be your man? If the answer to both questions is no, then will you introduce me to him?"

Bernadette smiles, then seats herself in the chair nearest Falimah. "I knew you would ease your happy hips upstairs when you got wind of Hayes being here. For the record, let me answer all three of your questions. Hayes is all mine." She smiles impishly. "His visit was a pleasant surprise."

Falimah digs deeper, "And now that he's surprised you, what have you planned for his homecoming?"

She's a bold-behind sista.

"After I finish with my client I'll wake Hayes up and drive him home; then, I'll drive to my home."

Falimah literally falls forward pressing her palms flush on the desk for support. "Where is he right now?"

Amusement at what she knows Falimah is thinking causes the corners of Bernadette's mouth to turn upward. She casts the line into the waters of Falimah's curiosity. "Asleep in the Penthouse."

"Ooooh, you guys been bad."

Careful sista. This conversation is telling me more about who you really are than you think. "You think we been up there doin' the do, don't cha?"

Falimah's accusing eyes confirm that is exactly what she is thinking.

"Do I look like a woman who'd give it up for a pot of greens and some cornbread?"

Falimah laughs. "So you're saying a brotha has to put the rock on your finger before you give him some?"

Is this girl slow or what? "Even if Hayes proposes and puts the Hope Diamond on my finger, he still won't get *none* till the preacher pronounces us man and wife."

"Girl, you too tight for me," Falimah waves her hand.

A woman without a plan is a woman who will most certainly fail. These words have been the foundation for virtually all that Treva has set out to do. The destruction of her hard drive cost her two hours of precious work. But thankfully she had saved the rest of her work on two back up CD's.

She had not envisioned spending two hours past her quitting time in the computer lab. Determined not to fall behind schedule she forges ahead with her task, but is nowhere as enthusiastic about it as she originally was.

"Why don't you take it home?"

Brian's words startle her.

"You scared me Brian!" she says while clutching her chest.

"Put that file on CD before you lose it again."

She follows his instruction. She proofs her finished project several times, then emails a copy to Bernadette.

Her attention is more focused on Brian now.

"Why are you still here?"

"Manual system checks."

"I'm sorry. I know you could be doing other things on a Friday night."

"Actually, I was going to ask you out to dinner?" He quickly blurts out.

"You were? I mean why? I mean, um…"

Brian laughs at Treva's surprised reaction. "Look Treva I'll be straight with you. I've been interested in taking you out for some time."

"I don't think it's a good idea for us to get involved in anything more than friendship."

He pauses, "Then as your friend and constant rescuer, may I take you out for a quick bite?"

She studies him. His expression is so innocent.

"Yes," she says.

They head out to Casuelita's for a meal and conversation. Treva takes the opportunity to get personal information about Brian.

"Are you an only child?"

"Nope, I have a younger brother and sister."

She makes a checkmark in the air with her index finger.

"Are your parents still married?"

"Yes."

A second checkmark is made.

"Are you needy in terms of requiring constant care, or can you be self-sufficient in solitary time?"

Brian winks, then leans forward. His expression indicates a moment of seriousness. "We all have needs," he says without removing his gaze from her face. "In my solitary time I go to car shows, watch old movies and jog. Most of my time alone or in the company of others, I'm thinking about how to enhance or create a software program."

Treva eats a portion of her entrée, then sips from her water glass before continuing.

"You have any physical ailments?"

"What?"

"Do you have seizures, tumors, high blood pressure, psoriasis, toe fungus?"

Brian's loud laughter draws the attention of several diners.

Treva smiles, then presses for more.

"Any history of mental illness in your family?"

"Some may question the possibility. However, I beg to differ," Brian responds while rubbing his stomach and patting his head at the same time.

"Check, check and double check," she says as she marks the air.

The two joke back and forth not caring that others are staring at them. During dessert Brian tenders the same questions to Treva.

"Only child?"

"Yes I am."

"Parents together?"

Treva's smile momentarily disappears when she states her mother died when she was an infant.

The smile reappears with Brian's next statement. "The fact that you keep blowing up my phone with pleas for help tells me you're needy. Your choice in friends makes me question your sanity. So tell me, are you hygienically sound? Any fungus, rashes, extra toes, or chest hairs?"

Laughter from the next table gives away the fact that the diners have been eavesdropping.

Treva shakes her head no.

"Are you productive while you're alone?"

"I like tinkering with old things like cars and dolls. I grew up watching classic movies with my dad and I still love them. Most of all, I value my privacy."

"Is your need for privacy the reason why you wouldn't tell me about the cars?"

"No, I didn't tell you about the cars because you don't need to know all my business," she says with a mischievous smile.

The two continue their playfulness as they walk to their cars. Despite her protests, Brian insists on following her home. He remains at the curb until the garage door closes.

To her surprise, she hears him knocking rapidly on her door.

"What do you want Mr. Chin?" Treva sings through the door.

"Booty call!" is offered as cheerfully as 'Avon Calling'.

His zany pleas for entry make her laugh.

"My dad said that when I escort a woman home, I should make sure she's safe once she's inside. Are you safe in there?"

"Probably more so than if I let you in."

More hilarious barbs are exchanged before Treva asks if he would like to come in and see her dolls.

"Yes."

She opens the door and tells him to make himself comfortable while she disappears down a hallway. Within moments she returns with an arm load of her collection. She points out those that were once owned by her mother and grandmother.

Easy conversation flows between them until Treva notices the time.

"Your expression tells me that I need to go."

"Yeah it's pretty late."

"Your point?" he laughs.

"The point is that since I've been entertaining you. I haven't gotten the work I should be doing done. Falimah and I are painting my dining room in the morning. I was supposed to have all the molding taped by the time she gets here."

"You bake me a cake and I'll do your taping for you."

"Not tonight my friend."

"You're really putting me out?" he says through another laugh.

"Yes."

A loud banging on her front door awakens Treva. Keys turning in the door tell her Falimah has arrived.

"You better get your sleepin' behind up outta that bed, girl!" Falimah shouts from the doorway of the mistress suite.

"I'm not getting up. I had a late night."

"Doing what? Playing with your dolls? I saw them all over the place out there," she says pointing down the hallway.

"Do you mind if I cancel today? I'm too tired to paint."

"Fine with me. I'm not in the mood anyway," Falimah obliges.

Falimah retreats to the living room. She glances at the dolls lying about like children at naptime. The sight is uncommon in the home of her meticulous friend. Being a neat freak herself, Falimah is compelled to put the dolls away. She hears a thud after picking up an arm load. She looks down and spies a man's wallet. Treva's precious dolls are tossed aside like dirty dust cloths. She discovers that the wallet belongs to one, Mr. Brian Chin. Her imagination moves to the shady side of the street.

"Hmm...I need to find out what's transpired here," she says while tapping her chin suspiciously.

"Trevaaaaa! I knew it would only be a matter of time before you two got together. How was it?" She yells while walking back toward Treva's bedroom.

"Get your dirty mind out of the gutter!" Treva yells then pulls the covers over her head.

Falimah pulls the sheet away, then waves the wallet in front of Treva. "What is Brian's wallet doing here if things didn't get hot and heavy?"

Treva snatches the wallet, then retreats beneath the fresh linen. "Get out Falimah!"

Instead Falimah jumps in the bed with Treva.

"I ain't going nowhere till you tell it all."

"Okay, Falimah. Here are all the sordid details – I stayed late after work. We went to dinner. We came here. We talked some more. The end."

"I told you that boy is hot for you."

"No, he's not," she retorts as she sits up. "But he is someone that I can be friends with."

Falimah pulls her back down to the pillow. "Skip friendship! That boy is yours – the hook is in his nose. Girl you betta work that."

Falimah reaches over Treva to answer the ringing phone. "Treva's Palace.

What's your pleasure?"

"Falimah?"

"Brian Chin?"

"Yeah."

Falimah winks at Treva.

Treva snatches the phone. "Hello."

"Did you pick my pocket last night?"

"Falimah found your wallet."

"When is she leaving?"

"Soon."

"Call me then. I'll come by. When I do, those four one hundred dollar bills better still be in there."

"Only four?" she asks teasingly.

"Yeah. You ate up a hundred dollars worth of food last night…"

Treva hangs up on Brian in mid-sentence, then stops Falimah before she can say anything. "Don't even start with me. He's just coming to pick up his wallet."

"If you say so. But tell me this. How'd he get your telephone number so soon?"

Thick brows above smoky eyes peering from beneath a Smooth Jazz promotional cap are a delightful sight when Treva opens her door.

Brian's swagger is somewhat cocky as he moves past her to the dining room.

Treva stands with her hands on her hips and waits for him to speak.

"I came to make a deal. You paint two walls. I'll paint two walls and the ceiling. Then I'll order pizza while you bake me that cake you promised me."

"I did not promise you a cake and I'm not real big on pizza. I'll call my uncle. He goes to Willie's Taste of Soul every Saturday. I'll have him pick up something for us while he's there."

Humorous banter helps to pass the time. Brian works rapidly. Treva does not. "You need me to get you a double shot of something to get you in gear, Ms. Scott?" he says over his shoulder.

She does not respond.

"I said I'd help you, but I didn't say I'd stay the weekend to get the job done. I'm halfway through my second wall and you're over there finger painting like you're in kindergarten."

"If you can do better and do it faster, then have at it Chin," she barks extending her brush toward him.

Brian accepts the challenge. It actually takes more time to get Treva to admit he has done a good job, than it did to complete the painting.

Her uncle stops by a little later with the food. He introduces himself, makes a little small talk then leaves.

"Your uncle seems pretty cool," Brian comments.

"Don't let his manners fool you. Just because he was nice to you doesn't mean he, my dad and brothers won't beat you down if you don't treat me right."

"I thought you said you were an only child."

"I'm my father's only child. But Uncle Randall treats me like his own."

Brian rubs the stubble on his chin.

"You didn't make the connection, did you? His name is Randall Meyer as in the father of Falimah Meyer. Falimah and I are more than friends. We grew up as sisters."

A low grunt is Brian's only response as he takes paintbrushes and pans outside to clean while Treva sets the table.

After watching a Bette Davis movie, Brian tells Treva that a full coarse meal to be rendered upon request is the required payment for his handyman services.

"Is it always about food with you Brian?"

"Yes."

"Get out of my house!" she says jokingly as she pulls him toward the door.

"Earlier you said if I didn't treat you right your uncle, dad and brothers would come after me. Will you give me a chance to be good to you?" he asks as he resists her efforts to send him away.

Deciding to play it cool she says, "I could use a good friend."

The tip of his finger brushes her nose. "You should know I really value friendship."

Curiosity gets the best of her and she takes the bait, "Tell me what you mean."

"Accountability and honesty."

Treva's face shows she is a bit confused.

Brian explains. "When I give you my friendship I expect total honesty. I give you license to speak into my life even when it hurts. I'll do the same for you."

"Brian," Treva softly says.

"Let me finish, Treva. I'm not what most expect and I'm not afraid to make my feelings known. I have a lot of acquaintances, but few friends. You and I are different and alike in many ways. Because of that I feel that we can really relate and accept each other for who we are."

Brian's unexpected words fill Treva with warmth. On a whim she asks him to join her for one of her hobbies.

Brian sees yet another side of Treva Scott during their two hours at the shooting range. She tells him that after high school she went into the Air Force. Her goal as a Reservist is to serve her country and end her career with an excellent retirement package.

Their drive back to her home is filled with a string of jokes Brian has about Treva being a possible security risk. As he walks her to her door he asks, "Does your military service mean that you are skilled in hand-to-hand combat and you carry a gun?"

Two quick light jabs to Brian's mid-section before pinning him to the ground answers his first question. Patting her hip leaves him wondering about the second.

CHAPTER 12

The smell of steaks sizzling on an inside grill is enticing.

Hayes digs into Roosevelt's bowl of pasta, "Get outta my bowl, man."

Hayes eats several more servings before moving to the grill. He slices a bit of the meat, chews it then frowns. "Did not marinate, did you?"

No response comes from Roosevelt, who has taken over cooking the evening meals due to the extra time Nee Nee is spending working at her hair salon.

"Allow me to help you, my friend."

Roosevelt has no objections. He sits at the table. His hands tap out a rhythm then slide backwards to grip the edge of the table.

"What?" Hayes says without turning.

Roosevelt stares at Hayes' back.

"What do you have to say, Brown Man?"

"More than you want to hear."

"What?" Hayes barks.

"You need to check yourself man. You're getting in tight with Bernadette, but you still have Renata on your trail. She ain't ever been high on my list, but I know how she operates. You do too, that's why you doggin' her. End the madness so you and Bernadette can deal without the extra baggage."

Hayes is furious. He whirls around and stares at Roosevelt. The stare down lasts until Hayes shouts, "You are out of pocket. Renata will get over me in time. As for Bernadette, I take great care to guard her from my past."

Hayes' less than polite response does not detour Roosevelt from his point of view. However, his ugly remarks and progressively bad attitude, gets him an invitation out the door.

Propped upon king size pillows Hayes reaches for his bible. He begins reading where he left off the night before. And the LORD said unto Moses, Yet will I bring one plague more upon Pharaoh...

The phone rings interrupting his concentration. Caller ID announces who it is. Hayes does not pick up. The caller will not give up. He answers the sixth call.

"Why do you persist in pursuing me?" he shouts into the receiver.

Renata is determined to be heard, but Hayes drowns her words with callous ones of his own. "A woman of worth would recognize when her company is no longer desired or necessary. I do not want you as a lover or a friend." Her muffled sobs do little to soften his hardened heart. "Do not call me again."

Hayes is not able to calm down even with resuming the reading of his bible. His thoughts wander to Roosevelt. He dials his friend's number, but only gets a recorded message. "We bless you in the name of the Lord. Please leave a message."

He bends down on his knees and asks the Lord for forgiveness before placing another call to the Hillis home. "Do not let the sun go down on your anger. Forgive me for the way I spoke to you, Brown Man. What you said was spoken in love."

Although he has prayed and asked forgiveness of his friend, Hayes cannot rest.

In and out of sleep, he tosses and turns. At one point, he awakens sweating profusely.

He falls to the floor on his knees, "What is it Lord? What do you require of me? Help me to hear…"

Sleep soon overtakes him. Within his subconscious he hears, *And the LORD said unto Moses, Yet will I bring one plague more upon Pharaoh…*

***

Common sense dictates that when a desired result does not come from repetitive action, one's method of operation must change.

Change has been a challenge for the analytical Treva Scott. For her, if it cannot be seen or proven by scientific fact, it does not exist.

Despite initial skepticism, Pastor Filmore's series on 'Total Surrender' is having a profound impact upon her. Spirit-filled words have become the serum necessary to counteract poisonous voices that have inhabited Treva's dreams. For years, these voices have told her she is not worthy of love.

Wednesday night bible studies have intrigued Treva and drilled holes in the views she uses to make life decisions. Simple words from a complex man state that surrendering to God is a matter of choice.

Words encouraging and assuring her that God will take her surrendered pain, now gently and incessantly ring at the door of her carefully constructed fortress. So much so that despite past disappointments, Treva dares to surrender to what she never would have before – blind faith.

Until circumstances prove otherwise, Treva chooses to believe that God will do just what Pastor Filmore says. She prays asking that if God really loves her, that He help her comprehend why bad things happen to good people.

Peace beyond what she has ever imagined is becoming a welcomed companion. Often, she opens her bible to scriptures that answer her numerous questions. An insatiable drive to align herself with the word of God, so that her prayers continue to be answered, sends Treva to Bernadette. Her simple request is that she teach her how to pray properly.

Necessity to minister responsibly put Bernadette on her knees. A day later the two meet. Rather than presenting prayer as a ritual to be learned, Bernadette begins by introducing Treva to who God, Jesus and the Holy Spirit are. Subsequent conversations include the purposes of prayer, praise and worship.

What consistently remains with Treva is the word choice. It is *your choice* to believe. It is *your choice* to give your burdens to God. It is *your choice* to surrender all.

Whenever Treva asked Bernadette if she thought she should get saved, she was reminded that accepting Christ is a matter of *choice*.

Daily, Treva scours the scriptures. Anything that grabs her attention, is brought to the ever patient Bernadette, along with a barrage of questions. Regardless of what she has been receiving and feeling, Treva remains on the fringe of accepting what Bernadette and Pastor Filmore present as biblical truth. During this morning's prayer, Treva declares that if God is worth surrendering to, someone other than Bernadette will speak to her about her current search for truth.

Falimah is another issue for Treva. Often when they are together, Treva has very strong feelings that something is wrong.

***

Pacing about her bedroom suite yields no answer for Bernadette, and neither do the dresses and suits scattered across her bed.

What am I going to wear? I know what Hayes likes, but I need to make a good first impression in front of his parents. What can I wear that won't make me look too wild, just in case they're not as demonstrative as Hayes? Since it's the shoe that makes the outfit, maybe I should start there.

Entry into the ten by twelve space reserved for her steadily growing collection of accessories does not help. Eight wooden tiers, each with the breadth to hold twenty-two pairs of shoes, greet and overwhelm her at the same time. Standing before the menagerie causes Bernadette to address reality – she has far too many shoes from which to choose.

The buzz from the front gate sends Bernadette into a tizzy. *Of all days why is Hayes here two hours early?* She enters the code that allows entry onto the property, then commands Zavonne to entertain Hayes until she is ready.

Gold pinstripes on Hayes' black suit cause Zavonne's eyes to widen more than the door she answers.

"I brought sustenance."

"Somehow I thought you'd show up with something. That's why I spent the night. Come in, Hayes."

His courteous arm nobly escorts Zavonne toward the dining room as his exquisite diction pokes fun at her. "You doubt my sincerity, Ms. Lewis?"

"Should I?"

Speculation about Zavonne's suspicious nature is as strong as perfume in a ten by ten sanctuary on Sunday morning. Rather than respond, Hayes places focus upon the task at hand.

With great care he removes a heavy Baccarat crystal vase filled with Bird of Paradise from the center of the table. The table is covered with a delicate violet sari embroidered with gold. Upon it he places covered dishes filled with fresh fruit, spinach quiche and two large jars filled with fresh, squeezed orange juice.

Boldly, Zavonne examines the suit he designed and had made by a local tailor. To assist her perusal Hayes models for her. The presentation ends with a dramatic flourish.

Zavonne smiles, then asks about his shoes.

"Since you are driven to pry into my personal affairs, I will give you information that I know will reach the ears of my woman before the sun sets."

Zavonne laughs at the truth of his words.

"My father taught me to never allow my nine-to-five to be my only source of income. As a clothier, I design and wholesale to an elite group of customers, and a few upscale boutiques around the country," Hayes proudly informs her.

Zavonne takes a seat.

He continues, "The bookstores and the clothing are venues that, for now, satisfy my intellectual, business and personal needs. I have made it my business to grow and retain my resources by becoming skilled in the market place. Paying market value for any item I can obtain at cost or negotiate downward is abhorrent to me. My car, and other luxuries that most presume have placed me in deep debt, are paid for in cash or, at most, within a period of time that will minimize compounding interest. Currently, my only debt is my home and Tacoma store. Both will be paid for in half the time stated in my contracts."

What he perceives as a look of desire for more personal information is read on Zavonne's face. Rather than indulge her, he places the conversation in her court when he asks about her father.

Zavonne grins proudly. "Simply put, Daddy is the first man I fell in love with."

The unexpected description moves Hayes to a chair.

"Growing up, I always understood how much he loved me. It's his kind of love that taught me how special I am and tapped me up with a switch to make sure I understood he meant business."

Hayes' open hand disturbs the air as it moves back and forth.

"Yes, we got the switch when we got out of pocket. People look at the way our father treats us and the things we have and believe we're spoiled rich girls. We're not spoiled – we're blessed. We're blessed because of the people in our lives."

Hayes nods.

"My dad's parents moved in with us when Terry was born. We lived in Los Angeles with people from the Old Country – Alabama. Our summers were spent in Birmingham. We can work the land as well as we can write a business proposal because my parents were determined that we would be modern women with an old-fashioned upbringing."

Hayes nods again, then goes back to setting the table.

"You've met my California grandmother. Most people don't care too much for her because she's really straight-forward."

The crystal pitcher in Hayes' hand is filled to half its potential as his interest in Zavonne's words increases.

"She's very particular about who is allowed into our inner circle."

Zavonne stares deep into his eyes. "It doesn't matter that others don't like or even fear my grandmother. It matters that she loves us and will allow nothing to detour her from protecting us. I'm a lot like her in that area. There's nothing I won't do to protect my sisters."

Hayes' straight teeth partially appear. He takes several steps towards Zavonne. "You believe I need to be watched?"

Zavonne takes two steps in his direction. "The fact that you're being watched tells you that Twinkle comes from people who are connected to someone," she says lifting her hand upwards.

Both take another step, which brings them within inches of one another. Hayes' dark pupils look downward into Zavonne's unblinking gray pools. "You bad, Ms. Lewis?"

"I can be."

"Jump."

Zavonne leaps upwards bumping chests with Hayes as if he is her ball court buddy. His strong arms steady her landing.

"Tell me about your father, Hayes," Zavonne says returning to her seat.

His tongue examines the inside of his mouth before a response is given. "My father is unlike any other. He is a strong-willed man with an enormous sense of worth and family. All that I am is because of what he has poured into me."

Zavonne nods.

Hayes grins then purses his lips before sharing what few are privy to. "People believe me to be conceited. What they unknowingly observe is confidence that has been bred into me from the womb. I cannot remember a time I have not desired the best. I do not see that as egotistical. I view that quest as living to expectancy."

Vertical shaking of her head causes Zavonne's uncombed hair to float about. Valuable information is interrupted by Bernadette's entry.

"Twinkle?"

"I can't find anything to wear." Bernadette laments.

Hayes is emphatic that when he escorts her to church, Bernadette will be wearing something other than the T-shirt and jeans currently adorning her body. Eyes that have ignited the fires of women he does not know, scrutinize Bernadette.

"Do you possess apparel similar to this?" he asks making a full turn.

"You want us to match?" she asks.

A deep crevice appears in his left cheek.

Zavonne watches Bernadette struggle to keep from grinning as she leaves the room.

Hayes' disposition brightens when Bernadette returns. She has risen to the occasion by matching Hayes' vibrant ensemble. Her gold and black double-breasted mud cloth suit fits in all the right places. Bernadette's thick braids stand tall with the support of a gold scarf strategically tied around her head.

The matching amber and cowrie shell necklace and earrings she selected are the perfect complement.

"Show me your shoes, Twinkle."

She points a size-twelve shoe in Hayes' direction. The same jewels festooning the toe of the three-inch, black linen shoes match those of her jewelry as well as the black linen purse hanging from her shoulder.

Zavonne's choking laughter demands their attention. "Take a long look at you and your golden boy on the way out. With those shoes and your hair stacked up like Marge Simpson, you're taller than he is today."

"Does not matter – she is stunning. If distance was not an issue, I would walk her to church," Hayes pronounces.

"Swaddled in all that gold, you two will attract attention whether you're in or out of the car."

Hayes' eyes display a hint of mischief as his grin allows his teeth to appear then disappear several times.

Zavonne again watches her sister fight to keep her lips together. Bernadette is taken aside before she and Hayes reach the door.

"It's Hayes' smile and that look in his eyes that sets you on fire," she whispers. "We need to have a serious talk when you get back here tonight."

Zavonne must have telepathically transmitted her comments to Roosevelt. When he and Nee Nee greet Bernadette and Hayes at the church entrance he demands to know how many inches Bernadette had grown since their last encounter.

The resemblance between Hayes and his father is so strong that Bernadette correctly identifies him in the church foyer before they are introduced.

Hayes goes to his outstretched arms; they embrace and release. Hayes pulls him to Bernadette. "Bernadette Lewis, this is my father, Allen Davis."

Introductions are barely complete before haughtiness named Renata Taylor, dressed in an electric blue pantsuit, overtakes the elder Davis. Their warm embrace certifies a mutual like for one another. She turns, grasps Bernadette's hands and smiles widely before reaching out to Hayes. His abrasive words abort her attempt at contact.

Hayes' display of rudeness creates awkwardness for Bernadette. It is the elder Davis who soothes the moment by escorting the offended woman to the sanctuary. His promise to correct Hayes' abhorrent behavior is heard by the two couples left staring after them.

Bernadette is disturbed by the sullenness of the man she has fallen deeply in love with.

Hayes' brooding prevents him from entering into the praise and worship service. Civility marginally returns mid-way through the message. He touches her hand and gives her a nod. She returns the gesture, but her preoccupation is with repetitive words from her inner voice whispering, *out of the abundance of the heart the mouth speaketh.*

Dinner is a definite eye-opening event for Bernadette.

Thembelani (Tim-Ba-Lonnie) Davis, the quintessential hostess engages Bernadette in conversation of interest.

They find that they share similar interests and talents. Both are youth ministers and accomplished keyboardists. Passion for teaching has made its way into the daily workings of B.L. Lewis. Thembelani's thirty-year teaching career was elevated with her promotion to principal five years earlier.

As discretely as possible, Bernadette studies her exotic hostess. Emerald-green rayon, hand painted with touches of red and black, brings life to her floor-length caftan. Jewelry unlike what she has seen before effectively complements the outfit. Achromatic skin, the same as her own, gives no hint of what her true age may be. Thembelani's speech consists of a diverse vocabulary used with care and showcases intellect that inspires rather than condescends. When the opportunity presents itself, Bernadette asks about the land of her origin.

"I am a native of Zimbabwe."

That bit of information clarifies many things about Hayes to Bernadette.

Hayes' brother Sundai (Soon-dah-ee) and sister-in-law are quite pleasant. However, in stark contrast to his mother and brother are his father and sister Mudiwa (Moo-dee-wah).

Her disposition is one of a person having failed every charm school course in which she was ever enrolled. Bernadette is grateful that the same behavior is not displayed in her three-year-old daughter, sitting politely beside her.

Allen Davis' posture at the head of the table is as proud as a ruler sitting upon his throne. Disregarding Bernadette's presence, he and his daughter make constant references to Renata's personal and business accomplishments.

Blessedly, an afternoon comparable to having a tooth pulled without anesthesia comes to an end when Hayes announces a need to depart.

The normally talkative couple is silent for some time. Hayes breaks their silence. "I apologize for the behavior of my father and sister. I had no idea they would openly campaign to become models for a dysfunctional family poster."

Bernadette soothes him with sympathetic words. "There's not a family that doesn't have their special people. You haven't seen anything until you meet my great uncle. He'll be here for Zavonne's Christmas party and wedding. When you look up *extra special* in the dictionary, you'll find his picture there."

Silence is resumed, then interrupted when Bernadette asks a direct question. "They still like her, don't they, Hayes?"

His hands tighten around the stirring wheel. "Renata is my sister's best friend. Her presence in our midst spans more than fifteen years."

"Why do you hate her so much?"

The remainder of the ride is in uncomfortable silence.

Inside the Hillis home, Hayes warns his friends not to ask about the time spent with his family. Nee Nee disregards his request by painting a picture of what she believes took place.

As the evening progresses, the level of intimacy between Hayes, Nee Nee and Roosevelt is discussed.

"What we share with Hayes is something most don't understand. They don't because true friendship is a rarity. We love Hayes. And because we do, we look out for him," Roosevelt states.

Tentativeness rises in Bernadette.

"It's not what you think. We're vulnerable and we have license to speak into each other's lives. Hayes sleeps here, eats here and loves my wife like the sister she is to him."

Not one thing is relayed that Hayes has not candidly revealed to Bernadette. Choosing to be equally as honest Bernadette makes her position clear. "I know how close the three of you are. I just need you to understand that our business is our own, not yours."

"Fair enough," Nee Nee responds. "Now that you know how tight we are, tell us how honest he's been with you."

A somber expression takes possession of Bernadette's dusky face. Months ago, Hayes openly spoke of the trysts of his past and what he referred to as a lightweight affair with pharmaceuticals.

From his prone position on the couch Hayes mumbles. "Thank you for your public intrusion into my business Mr. and Mrs. Hillis. Have you any additional comments while I am down here on my back?"

"As a matter of fact I do," Roosevelt announces. "Your production has ended. This means your sabbatical is officially over. I expect you at choir rehearsal next week."

Bernadette's head turns to Hayes. "You can sing?"

"I can hold my own."

Roosevelt's large feet stomp the floor. "Brotha man has one of those voices that will make you throw your money at the preacher."

"You're saying he can out sing you Mr. Hillis? You were working that song so hard today I was waiting for angels and a chariot to come down to take you on to glory."

Nee Nee's entrance into the conversation propels Hayes across the room. His hands, that are as soft as most women's cover Bernadette's ears. "You have said more than is necessary, Mrs. Hillis. I believe we should depart before Twinkle decides I am not worth all the effort she is putting into pursuing me."

CHAPTER 13

A need to know grows like weeds inside Bernadette. Those weeds, fertilized with her impatience, rapidly move upward, then out her lips. "Have you told me everything about Renata?"

His lack of response is irritating. Stares at the side of his head are ignored.

"Tell me the truth, Hayes."

Hayes licks his lips, but remains mute.

"How long were you two intimate?"

Silence is maintained.

Bernadette turns sideways in her seat fixing an unblinking stare upon him. When the car stops at a traffic light, she unbuckles her seatbelt, then reaches for the door latch. His hand firmly grasps her arm. "Please do not go."

As he moves through traffic Hayes reveals that intimacy between him and Renata began during summer visits home from college. Two years earlier they became exclusive. The introduction to Bernadette severed their ties.

His honesty satisfies her query. But, his earlier behavior in the church and pitiful attempt to avoid discussing something very important for her to understand, raises a barrier of concern. The concern is so strong; it keeps Bernadette from inviting Hayes inside after escorting her to the door.

"Hello."

"It's me Treva. You have a minute to chit chat?"

Bernadette marks her place inside the novel she is reading with a gold-plated bookmark baring her initials. "What's up?"

"I wanted to tell you a couple of things and then ask you a question," Treva says lifting one of her fragile dolls upward. "I just met Faith."

"Who?"

"My doll. Her name is Faith. She's almost fifty years old and in real bad condition. I believe I can turn this one into the crown jewel of my collection, that's why I'm calling her Faith."

"I like that."

Treva repositions Faith. She fingers the matted hair as she ponders how to proceed in the conversation. Rather than extend the silence, she speaks. "Have you ever had to step into a friend's business knowing they wouldn't like it?"

"Yeah," Bernadette responds as she walks from her bedroom toward the kitchen."

"Did you know before you did it they might wild out on you?"

"No, but one of the biggest fights I had with a close friend stemmed from caring enough to let her be mad at me. We almost knuckled up in public because of what I told her. After we cooled off we were able to discuss the situation. We're closer now because of it."

"That's good," Treva replies.

"You said you had a couple of things to tell me. You only told me one thing."

A grin comes to Treva's face. "I met with my banker today. My bid for the building was accepted. I'm now the proud owner of 6,000 square feet of commercial property."

Readying for bed, Bernadette thinks about Hayes. Spending time in the home where he grew up and with the people he grew up with spoke volumes about the man.

It is obvious Hayes received his charm, style and insatiable drive to conquer intellectual boundaries from his mother. With personalities that can be bottled and used to minimize overcrowding in any room, Hayes' father and sister placed themselves on Bernadette's 'avoid as often as possible' list. What is most disturbing was seeing Hayes in the two of them.

She closes her eyes wondering just who Hayes really is.

Snatches of sleep bring a repetitive dream. Bernadette is standing before a house with three doors. The first door is open. She bypasses it and moves to the door on the far end. She knocks, then enters. When she is gently pushed out, she is in tears. She knocks on the center door, but no one answers. Determined to enter, she turns the knob. Each time she does, the foundation beneath her feet begins to quake.

Despite misgivings, Bernadette accepts Hayes' invitation for lunch at the bookstore.

He stands to acknowledge her presence, then immediately comments on how great she looks in her firebrick red, glove-leather outfit.

"How long can you stay?" he asks as he seats her on a nearby couch before sitting in a chair opposite her.

"I can stay as long as it takes," she responds setting her purse at her feet.

The two engage in casual talk over a fruit platter, deli sandwiches and tea. Hayes' revealing plans to housesit for Roosevelt, indicates he doesn't really have plans for Thanksgiving and is fishing for an invitation to her table. She avoids the obvious by asking a rather blunt question. "Tell me who you are, Hayes Davis."

Hayes leans back in his chair all the while keeping his eyes on Bernadette. Before he can respond, the door bursts open. Mudiwa strides in and sits beside Bernadette as if she is queen upon her throne. Her words spoken to Bernadette are harsh. "We have private business to discuss. You need to leave us alone – now!"

Not being born yesterday, Bernadette clearly deciphers her ulterior motive. Rather than speaking words that might lead to physical contact, Bernadette diffuses the intentional insult with laughter.

Hayes pulls Mudiwa to her feet. Their war of words is loud and angry.

Bernadette gathers her belongings and departs. Hayes catches up to her mid-way through the store. "You have no reason to depart. There is nothing so private…"

Sarcasm drifts from Bernadette's words. "Privacy isn't the issue here, setting boundaries with your sister is. You need to handle your business."

"When will we meet?"

Bernadette's less than warm stare does not speak to an invitation for his company any time soon. She refuses his offer to escort her to her car.

Simultaneously, they turn their attention to someone walking towards them. It is Renata.

Bernadette reads the fury upon Hayes' face before he steps in front of her.

"You dare to accost me in my place of business. I have warned you for the last time," he roars.

***

Falimah's approach brings Brian to his feet from behind Treva's desk.

Her seductive eyes feel like hands performing a body search.

"I see my girl has you in the right position. I tell you what. When you tire of the same ole same ole, I have a position or two I'm sure you'll like."

His response is halted by Treva's return.

Falimah laughs her way down the stairs.

"Where would you like to have lunch?" Brian asks irritated by Falimah's lingering laugh.

"I have enough food to share. We can eat in the lounge." Treva suggests.

Garlic wafting through the air as the food warms heightens Brian's anticipation of a home-cooked meal. He voices his aversion to the meatless sauce when Treva places a plate before him. She offers him the option to take it or leave it. He leaves it. To ward off comments he does not care to hear, he blesses the meal.

He watches Treva eat for a few moments before moving ahead with what is on his mind. "Since you've sabotaged my meal, let's talk about why you invited me to lunch."

"You perceive that I have an agenda, Mr. Chin."

His steepled fingers rhythmically tap one another. "My perceptiveness is one of the reasons you like me."

Her look is inquisitive.

Brian gently caresses Treva's hand. Adoration for her is evident in his expression. "You like me, Treva. I like you. One reason you're hedging about getting more involved with me is because we work together. The other reason is that you're concerned about my ability to really handle who you are. I'll tell you like I told someone else. I wouldn't try to handle you. I'd take care of you."

Attempts to remove her hand from his are unsuccessful.

"You're a determined woman. You know what you want and don't mind doing what it takes to get it. I like the fact that you're not helpless. Because you aren't, most people haven't figured out how to love you the way you need. That's why you're still searching."

He lets go of her hand. She pushes her half empty plate away, then begins to suck on her bottom lip.

Brian runs a hand through his hair. "You wanted to have lunch today, so you could tell me you want us to go slow while you're trying to understand why you're searching for God."

"How'd you know?"

"I wouldn't waste my time on a woman I wouldn't pray about." Brian pushes his chair back, then stands and stretches. Leaning down he brings his lips to her ear. "Much as I care for you – God cares more. Me pressing you right now would interfere with the best relationship you will ever have. I'm a patient man. You do what you need to do. Just understand this, when other men start buzzing around, you let them know you've already been found. I'll be ready when you are."

Treva stares after Brian. When he disappears, she bows her head. "Thank you God for answering my prayer."

***

"I appreciate you keeping me informed. I'll give you a call next week to check on the status of my shoes."

Bernadette hangs up cloaked in an aura of hopefulness. The waiting list for the shoes she seeks has dwindled to ten buyers, but there are only four pair remaining.

On a whim, she logs on to the site of the designer to take another look at the coveted footwear. The glimmering shoes are as hypnotic on the screen as they were in person. *I'm gonna have these shoes even if I have to marry somebody to get them.*

Business sense snaps her out of her trance. She picks up several files, then heads out the door. As she approaches Mrs. Bell's desk she is told that a Mr. Hillis has just arrived.

Bernadette sets the files on Mrs. Bell's desk, then heads down to greet her surprise guest.

Roosevelt is welcomed with a big hug. The two engage in a little small talk as Bernadette gives him an impromptu tour of the building.

When they reach the upper landing, she speaks of the function of those occupying the junior executive wing. Falimah and Treva's entrance put a halt to their conversation.

"Good afternoon, Ms. Lewis," Falimah says. Her lustful look sweeps over Roosevelt.

"Falimah Meyer, Treva Scott, this is a friend of mine, Roosevelt Hillis."

"Hillis? Nee Nee is my sister's beautician. Is she related to you?" Falimah asks.

"She's my wife."

The three of them read disappointment on Falimah's face before she disappears behind her office door.

Bernadette escorts Roosevelt to the Penthouse. Her hands roam over the lapels of the chocolate wool overcoat he drapes over the back of the chair he seats himself in.

"It's a gift from Hayes," Roosevelt offers.

"Was it your birthday?"

"Naw. Me and Hayes are so tight we pick up stuff for one another that catches our eye. He brought this back from D.C."

"What did Nee Nee get?"

Overhead lighting causes the diamonds on Roosevelt's wedding ring to sparkle when he rubs his chin. "You're good, girl. But, just for the record, know that as close as we are, Hayes ain't fool enough to ever buy a piece of clothing for my wife."

"So now that we have that straight, tell me what brings you here."

"Hayes. I already know about what went down at the store today."

Bernadette wrinkles her nose. In her opinion, leaving Hayes to deal with his sister and past love was wise, but is still annoying.

"Let me tell you what I know. Because Mudiwa and Renata are in cahoots to make your life with Hayes miserable, the two of you are now at an impasse."

Bernadette squares her shoulders. Her posture relaxes under Roosevelt's gaze. "I'm not fool enough to think that women stopped pursuing Hayes since we became exclusive. But it's up to him to honor what we have."

Roosevelt invites her to sit beside him. Taking her hand he gently touches the large diamond ring on her left hand.

"It's a gift from my father."

Roosevelt nods, then relays what is on his mind. "I need to be up front with you, Twinkle. We both know Hayes is going through a process. That process is being challenged from every side. Being a true friend means looking out for one another."

Words of truth pull up Bernadette's wall of defense. Roosevelt speaks through it. "Are you his friend?"

She nods positively.

"Friends pray for friends and won't interfere with purpose." Roosevelt says reaching for his coat.

"Hello."

"Instruct your husband to open the garage door."

"He's not home, Hayes."

"Where will I rest my weary head?"

"You bought a home for what purpose?"

"If I did not have an incoming call I would have time to express my current thoughts to you Mrs. Hillis. Goodbye."

Hayes clicks over to his second line. "Yes, Brown Man."

"Where you at, man?" Roosevelt asks.

"My original destination was your house. Your wife denied my entry."

"That's what she's supposed to do, boy," Roosevelt laughs. "I'll be home in about ten minutes. Meet me out front."

"Thank you. Now call your wife and command her to allow my entry, should I arrive before you."

"Why are you here, Hayes?" Nee Nee demands when Hayes enters the kitchen behind Roosevelt.

"I have a resting place on these premises I intend to occupy this evening, Mrs. Hillis. Now that I have satisfied your curiosity, please go to the kitchen and prepare our meal the way a good woman is trained to do."

"Don't mess around and get whupped," she says taking a step in his direction.

Hayes' upraised hands move backwards with him.

"Hey. Did you forget your man is home, or is Hayes priority tonight?"

She kisses Roosevelt passionately, then directs his attention to a covered dinner plate.

Hayes rushes to the refrigerator. His search yields no prepared meal for him.

"Brown Man, must I enlighten you on how to rule your woman? Food prepared in this home must be sufficient for two healthy men and the cook."

Roosevelt roars a response. "If you want food you'll have to cook it yourself. When you do, make sure you leave some money on the table."

"I want Nee Nee food!" Hayes shouts as he simulates a child's tantrum. Nee Nee laughs her way out the room.

Hayes points to Roosevelt's plate. Roosevelt laughs. "What Nee Nee cooks is for me and me alone."

Carrying his plate, Roosevelt continues his repartee as they walk to the family room, just off the kitchen.

Hayes takes a cushion from a chair, goes to the floor. He props the cushion under his head, then closes his eyes. After a few minutes his eyes open and focus on the intense stare Roosevelt is sending his way.

Hayes lightly tugs his ear. The gesture is reciprocated when Roosevelt places two fingers upon his lips, then his chest.

"I had an interesting afternoon with Bernadette," Roosevelt says rather nonchalantly.

Hayes springs upward like a Jack-In-The-Box. "Why were you in the presence of my woman?"

"Because I have your back."

"Talk to me."

"No, no, no my friend. A second ago you were sweatin' me 'bout bein' with her, now you want what I got. What's it worth to ya?"

"Your privacy. You tell all, I will not become your nightly guest."

Seating himself on the floor, Roosevelt takes the scenic route by telling every mundane detail Hayes could care less about. Hayes takes off his shoe and waves it in a threatening manner. Roosevelt's laughter irritates him.

When his amusement subsides, he relays what transpired.

"Ya wanna know something? It wasn't so much the words she said as it was the way she said them." He studies Hayes for a moment, then asks, "Can she trust you?"

The reasonable question annoys Hayes, but compels him to respond to Roosevelt's underlying reason for asking.

"My change of life is short-lived. Memories of who I was are a concern for you, understandably so, since I have been tempted on many fronts. However, I assure you, my heart is with Twinkle. She can trust me."

Agile movements bring Hayes to his feet. He stretches through a yawn. "Since you were so astute at fulfilling friendship duties, I will retire to allow you to rock your baby to sleep. Be sure she understands that in return for your early release, I expect my breakfast to be ready when I come to the table in the morning."

CHAPTER 14

Hayes' outstretched hand fumbles about until it finds the ringing telephone. "Hello."

"Hayes Kokayi (Koh-Kah-Yee) Barak (Ba-Rock) Davis. Your sister informed me of your scandalous behavior. Don't let the scent of this other girl jeopardize what you've vested in Renata."

Hayes is offended by insulting words referenced to Bernadette. He works hard to stifle his volcano-intense anger. In order to head off an eruption capable of eradicating every positive step made in his newfound life, he hangs up the phone.

Keys in the door announce Hayes' arrival. His long strides take him into the kitchen where he knows his father is waiting. Without a word, Hayes accepts a cup of what his mother calls instant surge.

Men known for their extreme intellect, ambition and arrogance sit opposite one another.

Excessively strong coffee slides down Hayes' throat. That sip is followed by a second and third. Upon finishing his coffee, Hayes sets his personalized mug next to his father's.

The touching of his chin with his index finger is the father's signal for the son to speak.

Hayes loves his father unconditionally. But as strong as his affection for him is, the time has come for Hayes to assert his individuality. He prays to be given words to speak in love.

"I must apologize for being so abrupt with you last night."

Allen nods but does not reciprocate with a verbal acceptance.

"I know how much you like Renata, but our paths have taken different directions. Now that I've given my life to God my goal is to submit all I am to Him."

Perplexity covers Allen's face. His left index finger rubs his chin. "You have been raised in the church Hayes. I don't understand what you're talking about."

Painfully, Hayes must acknowledge his father's lack of understanding. Over the months he has been seeking clarity, Hayes realizes that teachings from, and the actions of his father are clearly identified as the root of the views he has embraced.

"I have never had a personal relationship with God. Now that I do, I no longer seek the superficial."

Allen traces the rim of his mug with his index finger. He inhales deeply, then speaks. "I do believe I understand what you're saying son. Now, understand me. Do what you want with this girl; just be discreet. Renata's a rare breed. You won't find too many women who can deal with the type of men we are."

Hayes' emphatic words proclaiming love for Bernadette are followed by permission to speak candidly.

Permission is granted.

Hayes relays truth with a modicum of reserve. "What you suggest I do to Bernadette and Renata is a prime example of lack of godly relationship. You and Mama insisted the family be in church without failure our entire lives. We learned the scriptures and accepted communion, but we were out of order. No disrespect Dad, but mixed signals from you and Mama taught me how to be a double agent. I acted one way around Mama and while at church. But, when away from church, I have broken most of the Commandments and I've done it with your approval!" Hayes emphasizes forcefully.

He halts Allen's attempt to interrupt by speaking over him.

"Dad, please hear me. The way I treated Renata and others was wrong." Hayes pauses, looks his father directly in the eyes, then takes a deep breath. "We were both wrong in our treatment of women."

Allen's displeasure for Hayes' words becomes obvious when his eyes narrow to the size of slits. His fist making contact with the table causes the remainder of his coffee to slosh about.

Hayes finishes his discourse with a simple statement. "Dad, I love and I accept you for who you are. I am asking you do the same for me by respecting my choice."

Exchange of non-compatible viewpoints takes father and son to new heights of candor and revelation. The discussion ends with each of them acquainted with someone they had not previously known.

Determined to handle all family business, Hayes makes his way upstairs to his sister's suite. He finds her lounging on a fuchsia patterned chaise. Without raising her head from the paper she is reading she snarls, "What do you want to say to me, Hayes?"

"Dee, I will not mince words. You and your girl are to remove your dastardly tentacles from my business immediately. Your dislike for Bernadette is foolish. It will also cause problems between you and I should you dare to perform as reprehensibly as you did in my office."

"You can't do anything to me. Daddy will…"

Hayes' muscular hands remove the Wall Street Journal™ from hers. Gently, yet firmly, his index finger raises her head until eye contact is made. "You are looking at a man who controls his own life."

His assertive language ignites venomous words wrapped in a thick layer of accusation. "She whipping it on you so good you'll turn on family?"

Flames shoot from Hayes' eyes. Rather than speaking words that would char the skin on her face, he remains silent.

The time displayed on the bedside clock tells Hayes he must depart. He let's out a soft sigh. "My feelings for Renata are no more. Do not waste time seeking to manipulate me into a choice I will not make."

His sister's onyx-colored hands tingle from Hayes' soft pinch. She reciprocates with one to his cheek. The exchange acknowledges all is well between them.

***

The image of Hayes' car on the security camera brings a smile to Julia's face. "Hayes is here, Addie," she announces inputting the code to allow him onto the grounds of her home.

One of two bouquets in Hayes' arms is offered to Julia when she opens the door. Her experienced nose savors their fragrance. She acknowledges the gift with sophisticated words seasoned with a southern accent.

His white teeth appear, showing acceptance of her kind words.

"Are Mr. and Mrs. Lewis in?" he asks.

"My son is out with Twinkle. My daughter-in-law will be pleased to meet you," Julia states already walking away.

Hayes follows Julia down a hallway. He pauses just inside the kitchen door to study the wall on his right. It is a magnificent hand-painted mural depicting a slave woman holding a fruit bowl. The index fingers on each hand are missing. Silhouettes of two children flank her.

"She is our reminder to be thankful for what the hands of this house prepares," Addie says to Hayes' turned back.

He spins in her direction. "Forgive me, ma'am. I was taken aback by the depth and symmetry of the artwork. I did not mean to forget my manners." He bows deeply before presenting Addie with the bouquet in his arms.

Her head tilts and her nose wrinkles. "How did you know yellow roses are my favorite?"

"Twinkle sent a bouquet for your birthday."

"I see you're an attentive young man," Addie observes.

Pointing to the chair beside her, Addie invites Hayes to sit. A bit of uneasiness is detected in him. "Relax young man. I won't bite unless you give me just cause."

Alarm expresses itself across Hayes' face.

"Are you okay?"

"Your words are the same spoken by Mrs. Burton at our first encounter."

"I heard she bit you hard. May I offer you breakfast to help heal your wound?"

"Yes ma'am."

Hayes consumes generous portions of delicious food. During light conversation, Addie takes visual inventory of the man holding her daughter's emotional and intellectual attention.

"Tell me about your livelihood Hayes," Addie says before taking a sip from her second cup of green tea.

Hayes does not hide his pride in realizing his dream of owning bookstores.

Pertinent information is stored in the minds of two of the family's gatekeepers while their hospitable demeanor disguise their interrogation. Neither woman is surprised when Hayes insists upon cleaning the kitchen before his departure.

With his chore complete, Hayes bids the women farewell. At the door, he expresses the desire to meet Bernadette's father before he leaves town.

"You're not joining us for Thanksgiving dinner?" Julia inquires.

He looks slightly embarrassed. "No ma'am."

Julia eases his discomfort by stating that they are a late night group. He is invited to stop by to sample her custard pie and bread pudding after he fulfills his family obligations.

Hayes thanks Julia for the invitation and departs.

Drumming her fingers on the table Addie says, "Twinkle's got a lot of nerve. She didn't invite that boy to dinner because she's not ready for him to meet her daddy. Don't tell little Miss Smarty Pants you invited him."

***

That if thou shalt confess with thy mouth the Lord Jesus, and shalt believe in thine heart that God hath raised him from the dead, thou shalt be saved. For with the heart man believeth unto righteousness; and with the mouth confession is made unto salvation.

Slightly trembling fingers move from Treva's heart to her mid-section. Each time she reads these scriptures she gets a rush.

***

Concentrating on scheduling authors who have tentatively agreed to participate in the first annual Written Word Fest has Hayes on fast-forward.

At six in the morning he is teleconferencing with the Atlanta, Philadelphia and North Carolina authors. All have schedules that will allow them to fly to Seattle for the dates Hayes prefers. An hour later he places a call to Ohio. Favor is bestowed upon him when that author's schedule accommodates his need. The same transpires after conversing with the Los Angeles writer.

Two calls to Delaware prove futile in reaching Hayes' desired party. He sets irritation aside in order to forge ahead. At noon speed dial connects him to his boy in Chicago. The two college friends rehash school days, then get down to business. In an effort to assist a friend, the novelist rearranges his busy schedule. Additionally, Hayes is provided with the cell number of the Delaware author who had flown to New York to participate in a literary panel. He is reached and all is set in place. Hayes hangs up, then goes to his knees to give thanks for being granted everything for which he had prayed.

The impetus keeping Hayes moving forward is his afternoon appointment.

James Wilder has been a member of Zion Faith Temple longer than Hayes has been alive. Four months ago he became a daily fixture at the bookstore. For hours he would sit caressing books and eyeing Hayes without speaking. To give honor to one in need Hayes transformed a storage room into the classroom where he is teaching James Wilder to read.

By four o'clock, Hayes is traveling south on I-5 toward an evening shift at his second store in Tacoma. Soft jazz from the CD player blends with the sense of peace enveloping him. Thoughts of his meeting with Addie Lewis are pleasing. Although an invitation to join the family for Thanksgiving has been extended, it would have meant more coming from Bernadette.

Customers standing in line with items to be purchased are a pleasant greeting when he enters the store. His courteous smile pleases and charms patrons as he opens a second register.

When the lines thin, he moves throughout the two-story bookstore straightening displays and offering assistance to customers. Light conversation between patrons reading in the loft while sipping flavored beverages, blends with the voice of the featured storyteller entertaining children and parents.

Inside the first level reading room Hayes finds two of his favorite customers, Tamara and Craven Sterling. This duo spends two days a week in the store completing homework while their mother works the late shift at the legal aid firm next door.

Hayes' outstretched hand is filled with school papers.

Looking over Tamara's paper, he is pleased with the quality of her work. From his wallet he draws four tickets for the opening of the Black Nativity, her reward for work done well.

Turning his attention to Craven's math paper, Hayes finds a few errors. Instead of telling him so, he sits down to help him work them out. A bright smile lights Craven's face when Hayes places a big star over the correct answers.

"Go pick out a new book for yourself and one for your parents."

"Thanks, Mr. Davis," they squeal then run off to find new treasures.

Walking into his office, Hayes reaches for the mail. He stretches, then sits before going through the stack of eight or so envelopes.

Electronic messaging reveals six messages. The four from Renata are immediately deleted. The one from Bernadette is promptly returned. She cannot be reached at her office, home or on her cell phone.

Hayes calls his mother. He is greeted by her voice message. "Thank you for calling. If this is Hayes, meet me and your father at Kallaloo for dinner. Leave me a message to confirm our date."

The call jogs Hayes' memory. He asked his parents to meet with him to discuss details for his move to D.C. Now that he has received his acceptance letter from Gallaudet University, he must quickly prepare for his January departure.

Leaning down, Hayes removes his shoes, then places his feet upon his desk. Solitude behind drooping lids allows him to analyze the root cause for his change in career goals.

There is no doubting his friendship with Blaine, and the one he maintains with Dinah is the instrument used to show him his true purpose. Coming to understand the challenges faced by the deaf has become a source of frustration for Hayes.

Acceptance into Gallaudet University did not come without cost. Preparation included many nights turning into days with little to no sleep for the goal driven, Hayes Davis. It has been worth the effort. Once the education degree is received, he will move on to step two – opening a school that meets the needs of deaf children.

***

"Twinkle, listen to this."

Bernadette slowly opens one eye.

"You listening to me?"

"Yeah," her drowsy voice says with irritation. She stretches her legs upward then brings them to rest on the arm of the sofa before drifting into slumber.

"Wake up!"

Bernadette's long feet at the end of her flailing legs almost kick Zavonne in the throat. She looks up into Zavonne's angry eyes.

"Don't start trippin'. I'm tired and you've been going on and on and on about the wedding. I love you. I love that you're getting married and getting out of my house. Right now I'd love to roll over and sleep for the next ten hours. Can we talk in the morning?" she asks leaving the room.

Zavonne and her whiny attitude accompany Bernadette to her room. "I'm only getting married once. I want to share everything with you and Terry."

Bernadette lies across her bed. She pats the space beside her. Despite her drowsiness she allows Zavonne to ramble on about the wedding. In the midst of a sentence, Zavonne holds up her left hand. On her ring finger is the three-carat diamond placed there by her fiancé. Beside it is the two-carat diamond promise ring Joseph placed on her finger on her sixteenth birthday. She fans her hand in front of Bernadette.

"You wanna stop that before one of them rocks slash my face?"

"Remember how proud Daddy was when Terry gave her ring back to him at her wedding? It's going to be the same when he gets mine. You'll close the circle when you give yours back on your wedding day, Twinkle. Terry kept her pledge and I have too. You can't break the circle. You have to come to the altar pure – not for Daddy, but for God."

Wedding plans dominate conversation between mother and daughters. Strong opinions regarding likes and dislikes ruffle some feathers, but do not distract from everyone's desire to make this a cherished event.

When Zavonne goes in search of her father, Addie seizes the opportunity for a private conversation with Bernadette.

Her words cruise down Casual Boulevard and pause at the corners of an upcoming speaking engagement, and Joseph's philanthropic awards. A sharp left at the intersection of Hayes Davis and Bernadette Lewis brings the conversation to a slow roll.

Bernadette decides that Candor Avenue is the best route to take and answers an obvious question before it is tendered. "I didn't invite Hayes to dinner tonight because I don't want him to have to deal with Daddy's madness."

"There's something else, Bernadette. What is it?"

The use of her birth name often indicates displeasure or concern harbored by her parents.

Bernadette moves close to her mother.

"Tell me how he really makes you feel," Addie whispers into her ear.

"Mama," she sighs, "he's more to me than you think. "Do you remember I used to say I didn't want to be kissed by anyone except my husband? I was serious. I believe if a woman is supposed to save her virginity for her husband, she should save her kisses for him too. Other than friendly pecks on the cheek from family members and male friends, I had never been kissed before."

"Had never?"

"For the first time in my life I'm dealing with the man Daddy warned me about. The one I might want to give every ounce of myself to. Hayes is so good to me."

"How good?"

"Good beyond what I ever believed a man could be." Bernadette fingers the fringed edge of her royal purple cashmere sweater. Its softness, rich color and fit are why she purchased it. She runs the edge over Addie's hands.

Addie is pulled close. "He's the one, Mama. The one who makes me feel like purple. Hayes and I have kissed."

Without a word, Addie repositions herself and waits. Bernadette stretches to full length, allowing her long legs to cross her mother's lap. Instinctively, Addie massages them.

"I love him so much."

Addie's tone emphasizes her concern. "Then we should talk."

Bernadette sits up and prepares for the combination of maternal wisdom and ministry to come forth.

"What if you decide you love him so much you disregard all you know to be right?"

"I wouldn't do that."

Addie chuckles. "That sounds good while you're sitting in front of me, but go down this road with me. Say you decide your need for Hayes outweighs common sense."

Discomfort in Bernadette is as detectable as lipstick on a cheating man's shirt collar.

Addie presses. "Say the affection you give him shifts total focus to you and away from purpose. Where do you go from there?"

Her attempt to reply is futile.

"Don't be fool enough to believe the taste he receives from the honey jar will come without expectancy. He will expect you to sleep with him again and again."

Bernadette blurts out that Hayes loves her.

Her defensive words do not faze her mother. Addie's head tilts and her nose wrinkles as she inspects her maturing daughter. "From what I've been told, Hayes does love you, but that isn't the issue. What you would become is the issue."

Words of truth shake the foundation of Bernadette's weak defense of herself and Hayes.

"You love this boy Bernadette?"

Vertical nodding gives Bernadette's answer.

Generational eyes of gray connect. Duty to motherhood breaks through their moment of silence with more truth.

Addie leans in, grasps Bernadette's hands and squeezes. "You're a grown woman so I won't cut my words. Loving a man is serious business; a business that no woman can afford to fail at. I didn't always know I would marry your daddy. But, because of what my parents taught me, I did know about my Kingdom business."

Bernadette smiles knowing that what her mother received from her parents has been passed down and often reiterated to her and her sisters.

"Your daddy awoke a sensuality in me that scared me. I can see in your eyes that Hayes has awakened the same in you."

Bernadette tries to hide from the reality of her mother's words. Her facial expression betrays her.

"You cannot allow your love for Hayes to cause your business to fail. Until you become a wife, a portion of that business is to remain steadfast to your vow of purity. We've talked often about what that includes. Do we need to revisit anything baby?"

The love poured into Addie's words puts Bernadette at ease.

"Loving Hayes is a natural emotion. What would be unnatural is if you forget to *love* and *respect* yourself; that's another thing that will cause your business to fail."

"Mama," Bernadette says with a bit of force.

Addie halts her words with a hard look. "Listen closely because whether you like it or not you need to hear this. "You don't need to be in a rush, Bernadette. Take your time to pray about who he really is. Your young man has made quite an impression on you in this season of introduction, but men have many seasons. If you're truly serious about Hayes, you need to find out how he'll act when winter storms come. See if the rains of spring shrink his point of view when something doesn't go his way. It's okay if it does, but when that hot iron of summer's reality hits him in the face, you should be able to see him straighten out. Most importantly, you need to know beyond a shadow of a doubt that the man you desire won't scatter like leaves in the fall when the winds of pressure begin to blow."

Bernadette folds her arms across her chest and throws herself into the cushions of the sofa.

"Life isn't a fairy tale, Ms. Lewis. Reality bites and it bites harder when you enter a relationship blindly."

Bernadette unfolds her arms and removes the frown from her face.

"You weren't placed on this earth to be yoked to a superficial man. Hayes has just recently come into his walk with Christ. He needs time to get good and saved and develop into a disciple."

Silence.

"Take this boy to the Lord to find out who he is and if he really is the one God has for you. When you do this and obey, you will do what is right, even if it hurts."

Addie's outstretched arms are offered. Bernadette accepts her invitation to come near by placing her nearly six feet and one hundred fifty-five pounds into the lap of love.

"He's a good man, Mama."

Warm breath caresses Bernadette's ears. "He may be, but keep this in mind. A good man pursuing you does not erase your option of choice or obedience."

Mother and daughter continue conversation until they fall asleep locked in an embrace.

Joseph stands watching his wife and daughter in slumber for some time before entering the room. Going to his knees at the foot of the couch he prays. "Father, I thank You for covering this child with Your shield of protection...I have prayed and You have shown me..."

CHAPTER 15

Restlessness prevents Hayes from finding comfort in his bed. Reflecting on the thoughtful words from his protective mother keeps him turning.

Mama is impressed with Twinkle, he reflects as he turns yet another time. *She says the standard of her family was revealed through the presence of her grandmother.* Hayes moves from beneath expensive linens. Unconsciously, he rubs his chin with his left index finger as he ponders his mother's sentiments. *I must agree with Mama's advice. I owe Twinkle more respect than waiting until a day or two before I depart to tell her about school. I must tell her now.*

Bernadette tosses and turns from one side of her bed to the other.

For the third time this evening her recurring dream is vivid and disturbing. She finds herself before three doors. The first door slowly opens. Hands invite her inside. The invitation is refused. She runs to the third door. She is inside for a brief moment, then is escorted outside. She stands before the locked door, brokenhearted.

Determined to have what she wants, she seeks entry through the middle door. Each attempt to enter causes the foundation beneath her to shake. The spirit of rejection becomes overwhelming. Tears of anguish flow downward increasing her feelings of inadequacy.

Through the density of her bitterness a voice from the first door is heard. She goes to it. Arms reach out to pull her in. Instead of receiving the love being offered, she runs away.

***

Epson salt added to a steamy tub of water helps to relieve the pain in Falimah's left thigh. The digital display embedded in the marble vanity shouts her lateness. The expected ringing of the phone tells her she must hurry. She allows voice mail to answer in order to not have to argue with Treva for being late. "Thank you for calling. After the tone please leave a message."

"Hey baby it's me. Cancel whatever plans you have. I'm on my way."

Identification of the caller further constricts knotted muscles.

The next call is from Treva. "Hey sis, I got cash. I got a credit card with a large, unused balance. When that runs out, I got checks attached to an account with money, money, money, money. What I don't got is you. Where you at, girl? Hit my digits quick. I'm ready to shop."

***

"Hello."

"Zavonne, this is Hayes. I need you to put me in touch with your father."

"Why?"

"It is a matter that does not concern you."

"Okay cool. I have to go. Peace."

"Do not hang up on me."

Her laughter irritates Hayes as he pushes for what he wants. Their momentary silence is replaced by a few clinks, then a strong southern voice. "This is Joseph Lewis."

"Daddy, I have Twinkle's friend Hayes on the line. He wants to talk to you." Her prolonged drivel about nothing ends when Joseph dismisses her.

"What can I do for you, young man?" Joseph asks.

Hayes does not hedge. "Mr. Lewis, my name is Hayes Davis. I have been seeing your daughter socially for several months. I would like a little of your time."

"I'm pretty free tomorrow. Can we meet then?"

"I have an early appointment, but I can be in the city by noon."

"We can meet for lunch here, or if you'd be a bit more comfortable…"

Hayes squares his shoulders as if Joseph can see him. "I will be there no later than noon. Goodbye Mr. Lewis."

***

Six unsuccessful attempts to reach Falimah for their planned shop till you drop date tests Treva's resolve to remain civil. Her lead foot brings her to the home of her hot and cold friend in record time.

Using her own keys, Treva lets herself inside Falimah's lavish home. Male clothing strewn from the door to the bottom of the stairs tells all. Treva retraces her steps to her car.

Rather than sulk about yet another of Falimah's shows of inconsideration, Treva decides to make this a banner day. She finds Bernadette's number in her cell phone directory.

"Hello."

"I'm on my way to buy accessories, then to find something to eat. What are you doing?"

Bernadette hastily returns cleaning products to their place. A beeline to her room to gather purse and keys is made. "Tell me where to meet you. I'll help you with the shoes."

Shoe shopping with Bernadette is likened to performing in a triathlon. Her relationship with literally every sales associate they encounter at Nordstrom amazes Treva.

At another shoe salon, inside information on when a rather expensive pair of shoes will be on sale is pleasing. It is more pleasing when the associate tucks them away assuring Treva they will be waiting for her when the discount becomes applicable.

As if life long friends, the duo laugh and tease one another on their way to lunch. Treva has become aware of Bernadette's fetish for shoes and books. Bernadette is now acquainted with Treva's penchant for purses and carry-bags.

Bernadette spots one of her church members through the large window of the Cheesecake Factory as she and Treva wait for a table. Without inhibition she raps on the window until she gets her attention. "Are you hungry?" Bernadette shouts.

"Hi Sister Bernadette," the teen giggles coming through the door. "I'm hungry but I have to save my money for a pair of shoes I need for the Scholarship Banquet," she whispers.

Bernadette pats her purse. "I think I have enough to feed you."

"Thanks," she giggles again.

"So tell me about the dress that will go with your new shoes," Bernadette says honestly interested in the young lady's response.

Her head hangs down. Peripherally, she looks at Treva then back to Bernadette and whispers, "Don't tell anybody, but I can't afford a dress. When your feet are as big as mine, you have to spend a lot of money to get something nice. I don't have a job yet, so my aunts got together and gave me money for my birthday, so I could get some shoes."

Tears threaten to spill from Bernadette's eyes. During one of their teen overnighters this young lady shared her pain of knowing her family could not afford to send her to college. The group of twenty or so teens and chaperones prayed and encouraged her to stretch her faith. By faith, she applied for and received a four-year scholarship to Javis Christian College where she will pursue an English degree. In two weeks, she will be honored for her accomplishment, but cannot afford a dress for the occasion.

For I was an hungered, and ye gave me meat; I was thirsty...Naked, and ye clothed me... These words whirl around and around inside Bernadette's head.

"You okay?" the young lady asks Bernadette.

"I'm fine, honey," she says patting the girl's hand. "As a matter of fact, I believe I may have a lead on a job for you if you can handle working in a high-tech environment for some rather interesting people."

Treva chuckles.

"I was just thinking," Bernadette says with a smile in her eyes and on her lips, "you've done so much to help me on Sundays I'd like to do something nice for you to show my appreciation. How 'bout we do a little belated birthday shopping after we finish lunch?"

"You'd do that for me, Sister Bernadette?"

"Yes I would."

The excited teen accepts the offer.

Bernadette introduces the young lady to Treva. She smiles broadly at Treva before commenting. "I see you at church. You're the one who always cries when you praise. You really love God don't you?"

Treva nods positively.

***

Wearily, Zavonne turns from her stomach to her side. The motion is made cumbersome due to entanglement within sheets and blankets. When she is able to focus, the early hour displayed on the clock stares at her.

Thump, scrape, thump, scrape. Barely focusing eyes peer about the dark room. Thump, scrape, thump, scrape. Zavonne strains to identify the sounds that brought her out of her much needed sleep.

More sounds identified as coming from outside her front door causes anxiety to push past the usually calm demeanor under which she is notoriously known to function. What sounds like someone jumping about on what her mother calls her Sunday brunch porch, is now clearly audible.

Hysterical laughter leaps into the air as the image of Hayes dancing across her porch is viewed on the security screen.

"Get off my property, ya savage beast," she shouts through the speaker.

His dancing becomes more animated as the volume of the Caribbean song he is singing increases. "Open, open de doooor. It's cold out here and me wanna come in."

Zavonne's long feet with toenails sporting a French pedicure hit the floor, then slide around until her slippers are located. She throws on a cashmere robe over her satin pajamas, then heads down to engage in a verbal battle with Hayes.

"What do you want, Hayes?" Zavonne shouts when she throws open the door.

Hayes' pupils bulge outward. He picks up his garment bag, rubs his eyes, then shields them as he moves from the cold into the warmth of her abode. His soft chuckle is irritating.

"What do you have to say Hayes?"

His head moves from side to side then up and down. "Being that you are the sibling of my woman, I am compelled to be honest. You are not attractive at five in the morning."

Perusal of Hayes in worn jeans, a faded sweatshirt and a head full of hair trying to escape from the colorful knit cap on his head brings forth laughter. "I wouldn't be so quick to criticize, Island Joe. Due to the fact that you seek refuge from the elements inside my home, I'm the finest thing you've seen this morning," Zavonne replies running a hand through hair that looks like the crown of Medusa. Moving closer to Hayes, she sniffs the air, then wipes her lightly crusted eyes. "You're a bit on the funky side. You forget to pay your water bill?"

Hayes flaps his arms and spins causing Zavonne to cover her nose with her hands.

Through laughter he tells her he has raked the yards, swept the porches and stacked the wood for the three houses.

"You saved me a lot of time and labor today. I almost feel grateful enough to cook you breakfast."

Hayes leans against the wall with a huge grin on his face. "Enlighten me, woman. I have Twinkle, you and Nee Nee. Why do I stand solo by the stove?"

"We don't carry your name, boy. You comprehending what I'm saying?"

"Clearly."

Pointing to his armpits, Hayes makes his way to the basement bedroom he now calls his own before Zavonne can respond. When he returns freshly showered and dressed for the day he is given a package Dinah left for him. He tucks it under his arm.

"What's on your agenda for the remainder of the day?"

"Joseph Lewis."

Zavonne stares at Hayes strolling out the door as if he is on his way to pick up a million dollar check.

Will studies Joseph as he moves about the kitchen making preparations for the Thanksgiving meal. Pride in the man his son has become, rises in him like cream to the top of milk.

Chuckling, Will pulls out a chair. "Sit down, son. We need to talk 'bout why you need to keep crazy in your back pocket when Twinkle's boy comes out here today."

Joseph submerges another bunch of greens into a nearly full sink of water before joining his father at the family table. A pocketknife that is always with him is taken from his front pocket. He sits then begins cleaning his cuticles. "Why do you feel you need to warn me about how to act?"

"I know you inside and out Joseph Lewis. You ain't been 'round these two, but you been prayin'. We both know this boy's got it bad for Twinkle. More than that, she's got it bad for him too."

"It's not like they're getting married."

Loud laughter permeates the air. "Been with you and your younguns a long time. Twinkle ain't never brought nobody 'round here for us to getta look see at. The woman you and Addie raised up is the reason that boy is runnin' up on you today. When he comes up in here, you see to it you in tune with the Holy Ghost and this boy is dealin' with the man I raised."

"Daddy I know you mean well but I'm her father."

Will laughs in his face. "I'm your daddy and I know what I'm talkin' 'bout. Hayes ain't like most of them jarhead boys 'round here. He's comin' ta show you he's a man in love with your daughter."

Shortly after these words are spoken, Addie enters the kitchen followed by Hayes. Without reservation he walks to Joseph and extends his hand. "Sir, I'm Hayes Davis." Joseph accepts the extended greeting.

Reaching out, Will shakes Hayes' hand. "Good to see you again, Hayes."

Will winks at Joseph on his way out of the room.

Pointing to the table, Joseph tells Hayes to have a seat. Instead of sitting, Hayes walks to the sink. Pointing at the greens he asks, "Are these in need of preparation?"

Joseph encourages Hayes to indulge in the monotonous chore. Hayes' kiwi green mock neck sweater is removed. A nearby towel is tucked into his waistband and the process of cleaning greens begins. Joseph moves to the second sink in order to rinse them.

No time is wasted getting to the root of his visit. "Mr. Lewis. Twinkle does not want us to meet just yet. I took it upon myself to come here today because I feel that we should."

Joseph says nothing.

"I am not an apprehensive man, Mr. Lewis. I desired to meet you and your wife in order to remove any measure of concern about who I am from your mind."

A soft grunt is Joseph's only response.

The two work in silence until the first batch of greens have been picked, washed and rinsed. Joseph doesn't miss the fact that Hayes lets out the dirty water, then cleans the sink before starting on a second batch of greens.

Hayes occupies Joseph by asking about his business, likes, dislikes and points of view on a variety of subjects. Joseph answers without much outward emotion.

Eyeing the end result of their labor, Hayes asks what meat is being used for seasoning.

Joseph points to simmering pots on one of the two six burner stoves in this state of the art kitchen. "We'll use ham hocks in some, smoked turkey for the rest."

"I will prepare the onions."

A smile of impression comes to within inches of being displayed on Joseph's face when Hayes rubs down the butcher's block with a lemon.

Nonchalantly, Joseph asks Hayes how he feels about Bernadette's need for his approval.

Hayes pushes the mound of onions he has chopped aside with the cleaver in his hand. He leans against the preparation island.

Joseph waits for an answer.

Hayes' words are blunt. "In all honesty Mr. Lewis, I would like us to become friends. Your opinion of me will not change how I feel about Twinkle."

Joseph shifts the conversation to Hayes' walk with Christ. Honestly, he speaks of recent changes and a few more on the horizon. He refrains from divulging what those changes are by citing the first discussion must be with Bernadette.

Hands on the clock convict Joseph. Hayes has been working nonstop preparing greens that smell so good he could eat them out of the pot, yet he has not offered him refreshment.

"You hungry?"

"Yes sir."

Further conversation is interrupted by Zavonne's entrance.

"You need me?" she mouths to Hayes. Horizontal movement of Hayes' head indicates he does not.

"The boy said no. Go away." Joseph laughs at his interfering daughter.

"Okay, I'll go, but it'll cost you, Daddy." Reaching into Joseph's back pocket Zavonne takes his wallet. From it she removes several bills and one of his credit cards.

"Why do you need the plastic?"

"Terry's plane is delayed in L.A. I'm getting the keys to the Caddy from Papa and taking Mommy and Nana out for a little power shopping. They'll appreciate how generous you are."

"You got enough, Puddin'?"

"Yes."

If Zavonne's voice were any sweeter, Joseph would need an injection of insulin. His adoring eyes and smile follow her out of the room.

Joseph speaks as if answering a question when his attention returns to Hayes. "It doesn't matter what Zavonne took out my pocket. My girls want for nothing. That includes prayer, emotional support and finances."

Hayes extends his hand to thank Joseph for his time. Walking Hayes to the door, Joseph poses a final question. "What if I told Twinkle I didn't think you're the man for her?"

Hayes confidently responds. "Should Bernadette suggest separation due to your disapproval, I would set about praying you out of the way."

Ten telephone messages await Hayes' return to his office. Four from Renata are immediately deleted. The business calls are promptly returned.

Moving on to pleasure, Hayes removes his shoes, places his feet upon his desk, then dials Bernadette.

Sweet melodies coming from Bernadette's cell phone announces Hayes.

"Yes, my love?"

"Are you near the end of your day?"

Determination to complete a proposal she has been working on dissipates. "What's on your agenda?"

"Sustenance. In order to keep her touch upon me, Mrs. Hillis froze all food matter she believed I might consume in her absence. I have removed the most expensive cut of meat from her freezer that I will prepare tomorrow. Tonight, I will sleep in my home where food is bountiful."

Before they disconnect, Hayes' mischievous manner persuades Bernadette into bringing him food.

Her dedication to good business sense insists that she complete her task before heading out for the long weekend. Two hours later her indigo swathed body walks into The Written Word with several bags from Jones Barbeque.

Hayes barely acknowledges her before he goes for the bags in her hand.

"You're welcome." Bernadette says laughingly.

A drive by blessing is pronounced before a large rib is stuffed into Hayes' mouth. A second rib is consumed before he pauses for air. "Thank you."

Bernadette studies Hayes as he literally inhales a large piece of cake. "You know what? I've never cooked for you."

Twinkling eyes, revealed dimple, and an index finger rubbing his chin set the stage for his response. "Is presentation of palatable food a skill you possess, Ms. Lewis?"

Her hands find their way to her rounded hips. A sideways turn and slight tilt showcases African heritage.

Hayes' eyes sweep over her. "There is no denying your body is divine. However, that could be the result of food entering your system non-stop and exercise. I need to determine if you prepared those meals."

A razor sharp response is halted when Bernadette notices the time. "Mama's gonna have a fit. I told her I'd be home by six."

"Do not leave me."

"I have to go."

"Your debt to me is mounting, Twinkle."

"I owe you nothing, Mr. Davis," she says heading toward the door.

Hayes grabs her arm. "Allow me to escort you to your car."

***

Upon bended knees, Joseph offers sincere praise and worship.

In the quiet that follows, glimpses of the future flash before him. Revelation evokes an earnest response. "Father, thank You for showing me what I need to see. You have entrusted these children to me and I thank You for the honor. I know You give us free will. At this time I pray You would block every path that would lead to Twinkle's departure from her pledge of virtue and purpose. Keep her safe in Your presence."

***

Hayes' nightly exercise routine is rigorous. Tonight, it seems effortless; as he is distracted with thoughts about his meeting with Joseph Lewis.

Memories of the time spent with him accompany Hayes to the bathroom. Inside a glass-encased stall, residual of the strenuous workout are removed. He secures a red Turkish towel about his waist before stepping onto a floor warmed by heating coils.

Dimmed lights allow flames from candles about the room to create shadow imagery upon terra cotta walls. Sandalwood bath salts added to waiting waters send spicy aromas into the air when the Jacuzzi jets are activated. Pulsating waters caress Hayes' taunt body like an experienced masseuse, as he lies motionless in the liquid tranquility.

For the nth time he revisits his afternoon with Joseph. He surmises that Bernadette's directness comes from him.

Elapsed time and soothing waters allow his active mind to shift into neutral. Thirty minutes later, thoughts of an unopened package upon his bed removes Hayes from the cooling water. His wet feet leave size thirteen impressions in the carpet.

Droplets of water from his dripping body create a large puddle upon the blood red duvet. With care the lid from the two by two foot square box is removed. Inside, a variety of memorabilia from many of the places he and Blaine visited are found. He removes a bundle of numerically marked audiotapes from the bottom of the box. He taps the collection with his forefinger.

Remembering his redheaded chum as a big prankster, the need to know what is on the tapes propels him toward his expensive sound system. His hands trembling with anticipation, insert the first tape.

Hayes' heart leaps when Blaine's voice fills the room. "Mr. Davis, I got this idea from you. You kept trying to tell me stuff before I lost all my hearing. Thanks. Guess what? I have questions to ask that I don't want to sign to you. I found this old recorder and tapes..."

Unable to listen to another syllable, Hayes turns off the machine. Throughout the night, he cries tears for his lost friend.

CHAPTER 16

"If I come by later with my own containers, will you put whatever you cooked in them for me?"

One after another Brian strings hilarious one-liners into the receiver. Treva's sides hurt so badly she begs him to stop. When she catches her breath, she grants his demand for enough food to tide him over for several days. He accepts without knowing the food he will receive will come from the table of Falimah's mother.

Bernadette's number on her display lifts Treva's spirit even higher.

"Yes, oh great one who holds my paycheck in her hands," Treva laughs into the receiver.

"What's on your agenda today?"

Treva informs Bernadette she will be heading out to the Meyers' later. Bernadette does not immediately respond.

"Say what you need to say." Treva allows.

"I just wanted to say you're welcome to join us if you want to."

Grinning prevents Treva from immediately responding. "That's so sweet, but I'm set. Falimah's the only one who flakes on me from time to time, but thanks for the offer."

"Not a problem. Friends look out for friends."

Treva hangs up wishing she could bypass a long day with the Meyer family. Expectation of sitting at the family table, today, is not as appealing as it once was.

Zavonne's fiancée's brother flew to Seattle for Thanksgiving. He and Bernadette hit it off from the moment they met. Seated at the piano, they work out melodies as if they have been life long partners.

Bernadette is daring with certain chords and takes liberties with his offered lyrics. She laughs when he suggests that they collaborate on a musical project. The dinner bell belays another request for her to reconsider.

Zavonne and Terry seize opportunity to pull Bernadette aside before she reaches the dining room. "Watch out little sister. You have that boy looking like he'd eat out of your shoes," they warn.

"That's my plan. He's coming back to town for Zavonne's Christmas party. We're going to have a sing off." Bernadette winks. "He'll fly home thinking I gave him all I got tonight."

Bernadette shifts into diva mode. Swaggering toward the dining room she declares, "When I step away from the microphone that boy will bow down and kiss my big 'Bama feet."

Following the blessing by the long-winded triplets, Kentucky goes for his favorite side dish – the greens. He literally inhales the first serving, then reaches for more ignoring Terry's disapproval of his table manners.

Both her first and second sampling of greens is perplexing to Bernadette. Her taste buds embrace the unfamiliar, yet exceptionally tasteful delicacy. The process of elimination begins. Unfortunately, that process eliminates everyone at the table.

"Who made these greens?"

"Whoever it was put their foot all the way up to their shin bone in these babies," Kentucky whispers to Terry while trying to take some from her plate.

"Why?" Joseph asks without looking up from his plate.

"Because they're real good," one of the triplets offers with a mouth full.

Bernadette makes eye contact with each adult. Who made these greens?" she demands a second time.

"Hayes Davis," Joseph volunteers.

"My Hayes Davis?"

"Yes baby," Joseph repeats. While Joseph explains the events of the previous day, Kentucky fills a bowl he has lowered to his lap with greens.

"What are you doing?" Terry whispers.

"Be nice to me, Terry. You'll want some of these later."

Will goes to check the security camera when the buzzer rings. He returns shortly followed by Hayes carrying a picnic basket.

Terry assesses Hayes wearing a Kente woven scarf twisted about his head and knotted in the back. When he removes his coat, she admires his deep red turtleneck sweater over a pair of loose fitting, Kente print pants. Leaning toward Zavonne she asks how much hair is under Hayes' scarf.

"Almost as much as Twinkle has on her head."

Terry gives Hayes a second glance, then returns her attention to Zavonne. "You said the boy had a definite style, but you neglected to tell me how fine he was."

Terry raises her glass giving Bernadette her salute of approval. Her husband kicks her under the table. "Daddy, Kentucky kicked me," she laughs.

"I thought you weren't coming till later," Joseph says receiving Hayes' offered basket.

"Mama dismissed me."

"Did you bring more greens?" Kentucky asks slowly placing his stash beneath Terry's chair.

"No, but my mother sent a few pies as my admission to your table." Hayes quips pointing to the basket in Joseph's hand.

Following dinner, Bernadette and her brother-in-law return to the piano. The two are in sync while improvising on an array of tunes. When their shoulders touch to emphasize certain words, Hayes' relaxed posture tenses. His displeasure displayed for the brief encounter does not go unnoticed by Terry, Zavonne or Joseph.

"It's just a song, Hayes," Zavonne whispers.

"She is my desire. No one touches her except me."

Darkening eyes and pressed lips indicate Joseph, sitting to Hayes' left has overheard and is not pleased. In a tone so cordial it could have been mistaken for such, Joseph succinctly relays to Hayes who Bernadette is and to whom she belongs. Added to his commentary is the fact that he, Hayes, is not authorized to touch her.

Addie smiles from across the room. Joseph returns her smile as his words assert his position to Hayes. "I don't play about…you keep your hands off …I find out you…or you don't…if she lose her mind and…I'll…from…to…"

Instead of responding, Hayes returns his full attention to the singing duo.

To those who do not know Hayes the way Bernadette does, his wit and charm is as bold and engaging as ever throughout the evening. Because she does know him in a way others do not, Bernadette senses something amiss.

Their gazes connect and pull them close enough for Hayes to whisper, "We need to speak in private."

The two extend their goodnights. In silence, they make their way to the Slave Quarters.

Seated in the privacy of her home Bernadette asks, "Why didn't you tell me you came to see my father yesterday?"

Hayes rubs his chin, then grasps her hands. "You feared my meeting your father because you believed he may not approve of me. It should be you who decides whether I remain in your presence, not your father. Who I am is who I am. Who I am is why we must talk seriously now."

Rehearsed words cling to Hayes' vocal chords like a frightened child to the skirt of his mother. His need to express what lies ahead as gently as possible is threatened by his need to protect her heart. Valiantly, and with a mixture of adventure and pain, he speaks of his plans to obtain his education degree from Gallaudet University.

"Are you breaking up with me, Hayes?"

"Would it be presumptuous for me to believe you would wait for me?"

"What would I be waiting for?"

He does not respond.

Almost whispering she asks, "If you knew you were leaving, why did you go through all those changes to meet my father?"

"It was imperative that we meet now."

Hayes' head tells him what he is doing is correct. His heart yearns to erase the words that have brought pain to Bernadette.

Unexpectedly she says, "I appreciate you being honest with me now instead of waiting a day or two before you get on a plane."

Hayes stands. It is sheer will that carries him to the door. Knowing Bernadette is only a few feet behind, he pauses, apologies and then walks out.

The tears in his eyes make driving difficult for Hayes. When he arrives at his temporary home, prayers for help spill from his mouth. "Father, please help Twinkle. I know she's hurt. Please close every door she might try to go through that is not of You. I need You too Lord. Help me to be physically strong. Help me to resist temptation. Kill my flesh..."

Eleanor watches through the window as Hayes drives away. Intuition tells her all is not well. She slips from the house and makes her way to the Slave Quarters.

A quick prayer is offered before she enters. Bernadette's soft sobs make Eleanor's heart swell to the point of explosion. Softly she moves forward. Knees in the early stages of arthritis meet the carpet. Her hand touches Bernadette's tousled tresses.

Bernadette recoils from her grandmother's touch as if it were a hot poker. "Don't touch me!" Bernadette jumps to her feet. "Don't you ever touch me! I hate you!"

"Twinkle!" Joseph shouts from the doorway.

"I hate her. She never loved me and she still doesn't. She's just an old lady trying to get into heaven."

"Girl..." Joseph yells advancing toward Bernadette. Eleanor becomes the barrier between father and daughter.

"What's wrong with you?" Joseph yells.

"Ask her," Bernadette screams as she moves from behind Eleanor. "Ask her what she told Granddaddy on my sixteenth birthday." Bernadette's eyes flash with unmistakable hatred. Her stature towers menacingly over Eleanor. "You pretended to care so much about me. I know what you did. You sent me to Marabel's for a new dress, so I wouldn't be at the house when the photographers came. When Granddaddy yelled at you about it you told him I didn't need to be in the pictures. You said it was Mama's fault. You said you begged Mama not to have any more children after Zavonne because it might come out black like my daddy. You called my daddy names. You hate us because we're black."

Joseph catches Addie about the waist. "Mother, we need to be alone," he says rather brusquely.

"I'm sorry," Eleanor says as she leaves. "I do love you all. I hope you can forgive me."

"I hate you!" Bernadette screams as she runs toward the exit. She slows long enough to snatch her purse and keys.

Regardless of tears clouding her vision, Bernadette safely makes her way to Roosevelt and Nee Nee's house. She rings the doorbell incessantly until Hayes answers and without invitation, she steps inside.

"Twinkle?"

A condensed version of what transpired is given. He holds her close and allows her to shed her tears.

When her tears subside she finds her voice. "Let me stay with you tonight, Hayes. No one will ever know."

Hayes is temporarily immobilized by the request. He searches for a scripture. *A double-minded man...think on these things...the Lord is my...I need some help.*

"Stop, Twinkle," he warns as she moves close enough to be considered an appendage to his body.

"Make me," she whispers huskily.

Hayes groans. *Help me Holy Ghost.* Her nearness and vulnerability challenges his resolve to remain celibate until marriage. Physical longing is quickly overridden by spirit when words Joseph Lewis spoke to him earlier, roar within. *I don't play about the honor of my children. You keep your hands off my daughter. If I find out you're sleeping with her or you don't run if she loses her mind and offers herself to you, I'll cut you from here to now on!*

Bernadette's strength rivals his own as he seeks to remove her arms from about his neck. Her determination to remain attached sends them tumbling to the floor. Her arms and legs seem to be everywhere at once. When Hayes frees himself from the octopus named Bernadette he pulls her to her feet and towards the door.

Embarrassment for her rash actions causes her to lash out at Hayes as she readjusts her rumpled clothing. The loathsome look she gives him hurts as much as her words. "You don't have to push. I won't bother with you again. You ain't the man for me. My man will have the guts to make the decision he wants."

Hayes watches Bernadette drive away. His hurt feelings give way to irrational thinking when the taillights of her car fade in the darkness. Grabbing his keys, he runs to the garage. There is no response from the engine that should have immediately turned over. Ten failed attempts tell Hayes this car is going nowhere.

He wipes his face with his hand. *I have to focus.* He makes his way down to his room, then pulls several of Blaine's recorded tapes from their resting place. He pops one into the cassette player, then reclines on his bed. The pubescent tone in Blaine's voice reverberating from the speakers causes Hayes' heart rate to increase. "Mr. Davis, you said that when we ask God things in faith, He gives us what we need. You said that we couldn't just ask for God's blessings, we have to live right, so He can bless us. Last night when I prayed, I asked Him to help you live right, so He can bless you. I did that so kids like me can have a great big brother like you."

"We need to talk, Julia," Eleanor tells Julia when she returns to the house.

Drawing upon the need to believe all is not lost, Eleanor reveals the contents of the long ago conversation between her and her late husband. "My Eugene's dying request was that I seek God for a change of heart. I did that Julia, but Twinkle can't see it through all the pain I've caused her."

Faith in God puts the two women on their knees to pray for a granddaughter in pain.

Zavonne rises from her prayer position when she hears Bernadette entering the house.

"Are you alright, Twinkle?"

"I'm the same as I've always been – someone nobody really wants."

"Tell me what happened."

Bernadette refuses.

Zavonne urges Bernadette to let go of what is torturing her.

In spite of her vow to carry her pain to her grave, Bernadette rips off the bandage covering her past. Rancid odors from her decade old festering wound rush outward.

The stench assaults Zavonne's sense of fairness. Instead of responding negatively, she allows objectivity to filter the stench. It is that tool that allows her to inhale and exhale without expressing disdain for the source of polluted air. When she speaks she gives the best advice she can, but it is not well received. However, she does not give up. Gently, yet firmly, she speaks of the changes that have transpired in Eleanor.

Bernadette has no ears to hear. "Just leave me alone!" she shouts walking away.

The spirit of warfare rises in Zavonne. She prays as she walks to her own room. Lying prone on the floor, her prayer intensifies. Within the realm of heavenly communication, what she has to do becomes clear.

Zavonne removes a vile of oil from a small leather chest resting on a table next to a well-read bible. She pours a small amount into her hand and rubs it into her palms as she walks rapidly toward Bernadette's room. "Okay devil you wanna mess with folk – I got something for you."

She prays as she moves down the hallway. Stopping at Bernadette's bedroom door she anoints the doorposts and doorknob. Zavonne enters the room praying as she walks about anointing everything she is led to. Taking the vile from her pocket, she pours more oil into her hand. She pulls back Bernadette's bed linens and anoints every layer. Turning, she spies something wedged between the bed and the night table. It is Bernadette's 'Purpose Journal'. Without hesitation she anoints each page, then sets the journal on the night table.

Adrenaline will not allow Addie to sit still. She paces about the room speaking aloud to herself and occasionally to Joseph. In the midst of one of her ramblings, she whirls then leaps onto the bed where Joseph is silently praying. "How can someone be so hateful, Joe? Twinkle is her granddaughter, her own flesh and blood."

Joseph pats the empty space between them. "I have something to share with you."

"What is it?"

"I told you I prayed about asking you to be my wife."

"Yes."

"I didn't tell you my answer came in the form of a dream. In that dream I saw a portion of the future. You were there with me. I also saw the destiny of one of the girls. I don't know which one. I know the reason is so I wouldn't favor one over the other." Joseph clasps his hands together. "I pray for them all the time. I pray that they will always walk with God. I pray that they understand how blessed they are to have a family who doesn't neglect their responsibility to them just because they're grown."

Addie shakes her head in agreement.

"Most folk think being a virgin until they marry isn't important anymore. It is Addie. It is to God." Joseph stares into space for a moment before continuing. "The womb holds generational purpose. When God looks at us He doesn't see just one person; He sees generations. The womb has to be valued and protected. That's why the devil's after it. If he can't contaminate it through multiple use he'll try to destroy it through forced entry or disease. If that doesn't work, he'll try to get you to kill the fruit through abortion."

Joseph places his strong arms around Addie. "I pray about us too. I've seen portions of the ministry He has for us for marriages and parenting." Addie's attempt to free herself from his arms is negated when Joseph tightens his embrace. "I was told to marry you despite knowing the cantankery of your mama. I won't lie to you baby; it's been hard. She was so evil some days I didn't think I'd make it. But I couldn't turn my back on her. My love for her had to be like what God caused Hosea to have for Gomer. Mother didn't prostitute herself, but she's caused this family great pain because of her pledge to her idol – her skin color."

He presses his lips to her ear. "Your time for change has come."

Squinting her eyes minimizes how much of Joseph, Addie can see. The derisive stare she gives him is one he has experienced only one other time during their marriage. The strength of his arms around her does not allow her to move. "It's time to break the stronghold that has this family by the throat. That can't happen until you tell Mother how much she's hurt you too," Joseph gently explains to his wife.

Tears flow down her golden cheeks. Joseph gently brushes them away. "It's time, Addie."

Although his wife is in pain, Joseph continues to minister to her. "No one ever said that because we've been anointed for the ministry we wouldn't have trials. As hard and unfair as it seems, you'll have to decide if protecting Mother's feelings is more important than obeying God."

Taking Addie's hand, Joseph helps her to the bedside where they kneel in prayer.

Despite her prayer, Addie feels driven by her maternal instinct to avenge the wrong done to her child. Negative emotions and pride dare Addie to sever family ties. In her mind, doing so would exact retribution for the pain she can only imagine Bernadette has endured and what she has struggled to overcome for years.

Back and forth, spirit wars against flesh. The scrimmage rides Addie like a saddle as she makes her way to the door of Eleanor's suite. Addie pauses only for a moment before entering without knocking. Her anger-motivated steps take her through the sitting area to the sleeping chamber where she pauses, offended at the sight of Eleanor praying at her bedside.

"Mother, we need to talk."

Eleanor rises, smoothes her dressing gown and then sits on her freshly made bed.

Eternity seems to pass with the two locked in an intense glare. Eleanor breaks the link by patting the bed, her invitation for Addie to come near. Addie chooses the end of the bed instead.

Addie's words certify her anger. "I won't live the lie another day and at this point I'm not concerned with your feelings, Mother."

On and on Addie spews words of contempt for how badly her husband and daughter have been treated.

Eleanor draws a handkerchief from the bedside table. She dabs at the corners of her eyes, then begins to unnecessarily polish the wedding ring that has not been removed in fifty-eight years.

Addie holds up her own hand. The diamond upon it shines as brightly as it did the day Joseph placed it there. Fidgeting with her ring brings bitter memories of her wedding day. Addie speaks words she has written on journal pages safely tucked away in a trunk at home. "You made no bones about the fact you didn't approve of my marriage to Joe. Your not coming to my wedding has tortured me for years. You can't imagine how I felt coming down the aisle on Daddy's arm seeing everyone I love except you. What should have been the most treasured night of my life was spent crying in my husband's arms."

Eleanor remains silent allowing Addie to say everything that is on her mind. Addie falls silent in mid-sentence. For the first time in years she sees inside her mother. She perceives urgency in Eleanor's eyes. It is an urgency that comes with the desire for forgiveness. It is the desire for forgiveness and a yearning to give something that, until recently, has not been a natural act for her.

The urge to walk away and never speak to Eleanor again is considered. Joseph's words of wisdom help her regain composure. Addie takes a deep breath, then continues. "Throughout my entire married life I have refused to acknowledge what your meanness did to me. But it didn't matter because I was always aware that you knew what you did to us!"

The force of Addie's words startles Eleanor.

"Your determination to punish me and Joe for going against your wishes has gone too far. You hurt my baby with your mean mouth. Last night she ran away from us with pure hatred in her heart. If something had happened to her it would have been your fault."

Agitation moves Addie about the room. One sudden motion spins her one-hundred-eighty degrees causing her hand painted robe to spread like a cape in the wind. Her accusing finger stabs the air. "You have to make things right. As long as Twinkle hates you, she'll be separated from God. My daughter was not born to go to hell."

Thoughts of Hayes fill Bernadette's head as she lies in the fetal position on the couch. She berates herself for becoming susceptible to his charms. *How did I allow myself to be so vulnerable to someone who could do so much harm? He talked a good game and I played without counting the costs.*

She shifts her position to relieve the numbness building in her right leg. *How can he just up and leave me after opening me up to trust again?*

The image of Hayes' somber face appears as if he were in front of her. The noble plan he so proudly presented to her replays through her mind. Noble as it is, it only serves to block the flow of love to a heart that dared to be transparent to a man – a man with whom she had been warned to be careful. Her heart swells with so much pain that she believes she can literally feel it breaking. How could he take her fragile heart and then walk away, sentencing her to struggle with treading water yet again in the sea of rejection?

Prayer is the tool that assists Eleanor's every step toward the Slave Quarters. Her heartfelt desire to heal the breach born out of past ignorance turns prayer to praise. Wholeheartedly, she gives thanks for what she believes is the beginning of healing for her family.

Entering without knocking, Eleanor finds Bernadette again curled in the fetal position on her designer couch. Eleanor's presence is not acknowledged.

"All I ask is that you listen to me, Twinkle. How I treated you was wrong and I hope someday you'll find it in your heart to forgive me. Last night the man you love told you that he has to leave town, and now you're mad at him and God because you think they have rejected you the way I did, the way you believe most people will. Crazy has you believing you're not worth being loved."

Bernadette's eyes widen at the truth Eleanor speaks.

Love for her estranged and hurting grandchild releases all of Eleanor's inhibitions. She kneels before Bernadette. "Whether you want to hear this from me or not, you need to listen. The major portion of your purpose for God is in your womb. That's why you can't be intimately known by anyone other than your husband. Marrying the wrong man or the right man at the wrong time could kill your purpose. You will have what you long for when you obey and honor God with the fruit of your life. The one thing that will block your blessing is a cold and unforgiving heart. I don't say this because I want you to forgive me. Forgiveness is a matter of choice. I say this because it's what you need to know. Don't hate someone more than you love God, Twinkle."

Bernadette brushes pass Eleanor.

Inside her room she tosses her rumpled clothes to the floor like rags headed for the garbage heap. Layers of linen become the buffer of protection between her wounded soul and the seemingly cruel world from which she seeks refuge.

Loathing for the grandmother she has ritually despised prevents her from accepting sound advice. Bernadette beats her pillow with her fists. "How dare she come into my house demanding that I forgive her?"

Bernadette's agitation moves her from one side of the bed to the other. Constant motion and heat demand that she remove blankets from her flushed face. Her precariously thrown hand hits the journal on the night table. Her quick reflexes allow her to catch it before it falls.

Bernadette sits up, jolted by her promise to read it. She runs her fingers over the front cover. Despite her mood, she smiles. On the front cover is a picture of her with legs extending from pink shorts. The long extremities glisten from a layer of Vaseline she hastily applied prior to the picture being snapped.

On the first page is a drawing of an office building that appears to rise from deep blue waters. Above it, white clouds have parted and a dove, illuminated by sunrays, descends downward. In bold letters at the bottom of the page are the words, COVENANT PLACE. Written on the next page is: 'GOD MADE ME ON PURPOSE FOR HIS PURPOSE'.

Her journal entry is read aloud. "God wants me to be a businesswoman. He wants my business to be the example of what Kingdom principles and a godly person is. My business has to be blessed, so I can be a blessing to other people, so they can be a blessing to other people. If my workers do wrong I'll ask God how to be forgiving like Jesus, so they will see Him in me and want to know Him too. The name of my building will be Covenant Place because everything that happens inside it will be attached to my covenant with God. I want God to be pleased with me the way He was with Jesus at His baptism. I pledge to be an example of a Christian and to disciple the people God sends to me through my business. I will do what He says no matter what."

The reality of the message in this passage leaves her nowhere to run. In order to fulfill God's purpose for her life, she must submit to His will.

CHAPTER 17

Somberness, avoidance of eye contact and disheveled clothing indicates to Roosevelt that Hayes has suffered some type of emotional trauma. Determination to get to the heart of the matter keeps him on Hayes' trail.

When Hayes stretches out on the floor, late in the evening, Roosevelt lies close enough to inhale his expelled breath. "Talk to me, Hayes."

"I do not know where to begin."

"Just throw something in the air. I'll catch it."

Roosevelt listens intently as details of time spent with Joseph Lewis are given.

"What does he think about you?"

"His opinion of me will not change how I feel about Twinkle."

Roosevelt is familiar with virtually every mood possessed by Hayes. Without the tact he normally reserves for those he does not know well, Roosevelt voices his opinion. "Don't be too smug, brotha man. From what I've heard, he is the father to whom much respect is to be given. You been walkin' 'round here lookin' like a quiet storm all day. That tells me you may have tripped yourself up with him or someone close to your girl. Who was it?"

Roosevelt's blunt words purse Hayes' lips. Hayes sits up staring into space.

"Did not overstep my boundaries, Brown Man." The words are repeated like a mantra as Hayes slowly reclines to the floor. "However, the concern for what I may have done would be of consideration if Twinkle and I still had the possibility of a future together."

Roosevelt bolts upright. "What do you mean 'still had' the possibility of a future together?"

Hayes does not respond.

"Tell me what happened, man."

Hayes relays what transpired between him and Bernadette on Thanksgiving evening.

Roosevelt leans forward. He touches his own lips with his fingertips. Hayes repeats the motion, then slides his hand slowly toward his waistline. Roosevelt's stare demands an answer. Hayes points towards the exit. Roosevelt exhales.

"When you two gonna talk this out?"

"I have been dismissed. There is no further communication to be had."

Roosevelt pats his bare chest with both hands. The slow cadence evolves into a rapid drum roll. The irritating sound continues until Hayes speaks.

"It would be foolish to pursue her further only to leave her."

"Only for a foolish man. Don't think that once she cools off, she ain't gonna appreciate the man you are. I'ma be straight with you. Strong as my conviction to be a virgin on my wedding night was, if Nee Nee had presented herself to me I don't know if I would have made it."

Despite Hayes' look of annoyance, Roosevelt again gives his opinion. "When you turned to God, you gave up who you used to be. The battle of the flesh ain't over."

"You are correct. My flesh had me close to the edge all night."

Roosevelt's look becomes distant. Hayes waits for his next words.

Roosevelt pulls on his earlobe. "Listen to me. Last night showed you that your path ain't gonna be without challenges. If the enemy can knock you and Twinkle out, the Kingdom suffers a double loss. We need to pray."

***

Bernadette's crinkled hair, which gives the illusion of it trying to escape from her skull, is a hilarious morning greeting to Zavonne and Terry. Red, puffy eyes, the result of tears cried, halt their laughter. Terry makes room for her on the couch when she nears.

Without being prompted, Bernadette pours her heart out to her sisters.

"I'm so embarrassed…"

Bernadette does not realize how angry Terry is until she speaks. "He who has ears, let him hear," she barks.

"What?"

Terry stands and glares down at Bernadette. "Addie Lewis, Julia Lewis, Gram T, Terry Boyd, and Zavonne Lewis, all of us are bona fide women of standard. We've been constantly speaking life into you. You know your value and you know your pledge, but the first time you can't get what you want you decide to drop your drawers!"

Abrasive words bring Bernadette to her feet. "You must be crazy!" she shouts.

"I ain't crazy and you understood every word I said," Terry shouts back. Taking Bernadette's arm, she pulls her to a nearby mirror. "Look at yourself,

Twinkle. By virtue of your size and age, legally, you are a woman." Placing her hand over her heart she says, "In here, you have a lot of growing to do. Men have needs. If you want this man, you better find out what he really needs, and I'm not talking about lying in his bed."

Bernadette is abnormally speechless.

Terry leaves the room then returns with a comb, brush and oil. She sits and pats the floor before her. "Come sit, so I can fix your hair."

Bernadette does not move.

Zavonne nudges her forward. "Go on, Twinkle."

Bernadette sits silently before Terry.

Gently she sections Bernadette's hair. "You repent, Twinkle?"

"Yes."

"Hayes refusing your offer speaks to his growth. Whether you know it or not the two of you have made it to the next level. What you need to do now is open your spiritual ears and listen to what God is saying about him and you."

While Terry works on Bernadette's hair, Zavonne cranks up the music. The beat is good and the words are right. Zavonne dances into the room. Bernadette drums on the table. Terry tosses the comb aside. "Come on sis, let's get our praise on!"

The purring engine of Hayes' car is synonymous with that of a well-maintained vehicle.

Roosevelt laughs. "You said you asked for doors to be closed," he points to the engine, "here's a closed door."

Hayes walks from the garage to his room with Roosevelt on his trail. He reclines across his bed.

Roosevelt goes to Hayes' desk. He rummages through books neatly stacked upon it. *Understanding the Power and Purpose of Prayer* by Dr. Myles Munroe and *A Passion For Your Purpose* by Gloria Thomas Anderson, top the stack.

Perusal of Hayes' vast music collection finds artists such as Donald Lawrence, Dietrick Hadden, Donnie McClurken, Yolanda Adams, Vanessa Love-Davis, Val Taylor, Michelle Lang and Still Water, Walter Finch, and Israel Houghton. He turns to face Hayes.

"What?" Hayes asks.

Roosevelt advances toward him. Hayes sits up making room for him upon the bed. The two hulking men sit cross-legged, eye-to-eye.

Roosevelt begins. "God is like a pair of twenty-twenty glasses for you. Because you let down your guard and let Him in, you see the world the way

He intended. With that wide open vision, you found a woman with a full package."

"But?"

Roosevelt touches his lips before proceeding. "But is she for you?"

The set of Hayes' stare tells Roosevelt his words have angered him. It makes no difference.

"In order to see clearly, you have to keep your glasses clean. Just 'cause Bernadette's a full package don't mean she's the one you're supposed to have. You have a purpose and a vision and she does too. How do they connect? Do they connect?"

Hayes' look indicates to Roosevelt that somewhere between his words and Hayes' ears, rationale has been lost. Roosevelt's gift of perception kicks into overdrive. "I ain't said you wasted your time, boy! But I am saying you need to look at the whole picture. We keep hearin' 'bout what a woman is supposed to look for in a man, but we forget. We forget that as men we better look for the right qualities in the woman we're trying to get. Much as I wanted Nee Nee, if God told me she wasn't the one to be my wife I'd have let her go. It's not about the emotion man, it's about how you guys gonna work together for the Kingdom. You can be a fool and yoke up with pretty if you want. I'm telling you now, that yokes gonna bring you to your knees if it wasn't supposed to be on you in the first place."

"Clarify."

"Pretty works for a while, but y'all can't stay in the bed forever. Trust me, I tried. Put yourself before the Father and find out whatcha need to know. Y'all had that fight the other night but make sure when you leave here you got your business straight whether it's what you want or not."

***

That if thou shalt confess with thy mouth the Lord Jesus, and shalt believe in thine heart that God hath raised him from the dead, thou shalt be saved. For with the heart man believeth unto righteousness; and with the mouth confession is made unto salvation. For the scripture saith, Whosoever believeth on him shall not be ashamed. For there is no difference between the Jew and the Greek: for the same Lord over all is rich unto all that call upon him. For whosoever shall call upon the name of the Lord shall be saved.

Every reasonable avenue Treva traveled to prove God does not love her has only led to the assurance that He always has.

Lying prone in the midst of her bedroom floor, she pours out her soul. "Father, I did not want to come to You because someone said I had to. I did not want to just repeat words someone told me I had to in a place they say is proper. All that I have experienced tells me You are the only true and living God and that you do love me. It is my choice to choose eternal life with You. Tonight Father I choose to surrender all that I am to You. I confess with my mouth the Lord Jesus. In my heart I know You raised Him from the dead. I call upon the Lord as my salvation."

***

To every thing there is a season, and a time to every purpose under the heaven.

Change. Life is a continuum called change.

Although as constant as the rising sun, most are unprepared to meet the challenge change brings. They are unprepared due to their inability to properly exercise the freedom of choice. One must choose an avenue to travel or risk becoming the road traveled upon.

Choice – a simple yet powerful decision for every individual. You can choose to remain complacent, not realizing your full potential; or choose to step into the unknown and be the answer to why you were placed on this earth.

Throughout Hayes' life, choices have been presented time after time. Lack of truth attached to the opportunity of choice led him down a path of waywardness.

Choice, over a short period of time, has brought him into the full realization that his life is not his own. April's reflection is that of a self-consumed, womanizing businessman. All that he did was orchestrated to satisfy his over-sized ego and physical yearnings. December's image displays that of one transforming into a caring, community-minded seeker of God. Pursuance of a true love relationship with God has again presented him with choice. His thoughts no longer linger only on what is best for him. He has chosen to give up all he ever wanted to step into the unknown territory of change.

Unbraiding the last of what seems to be a hundred braids on his head, Hayes moves from the window he is sitting before, to the bathroom. The reflection in the mirror of crinkled hair jutting outward like exclamation marks brings spontaneous laughter.

His thoughts drift to Bernadette. Her willingness to surrender herself to him spoke to the depth of her internal pain. Submerging his head beneath warm water does nothing to wash her parting words from his mind.

While he allows his hair to air-dry Hayes sets about selecting ensembles for the upcoming week.

He answers his cell phone without checking caller ID, hoping it is Bernadette.

"Hayes, don't hang up. I, we, we really need to talk."

Irritated that it is Renata, Hayes responds with insane ire. Speaking at a volume capable of gaining the attention of the deaf, Hayes berates and humiliates Renata before hanging up on her.

Reality convicts Hayes soon afterwards. He has known for some time that he is to make amends with Renata. Rather than returning the call to apologize for his detestable behavior, he uses busy work to erase the memory of his far from gracious behavior.

Long into the night Hayes' clothes are washed, dried, ironed, steamed and hung with care. Every drawer is straightened. Shoes inside velvet lined boxes are polished and returned to their place of honor.

Fatigue eventually overcomes him. Silence in the room is broken by very clear words, "...*Hath the LORD as great delight in burnt offerings and sacrifices, as in obeying the voice of the LORD?*"

He looks around the room even though he knows he is alone. Focus goes to the telephone. He knows what he should do, but does not.

Sleep overtakes Hayes almost as soon as his head touches the pillow. As suddenly as he fell into slumber, he awakens.

The exercise of falling asleep and abruptly waking continues until Hayes decides to read. He turns on the light then puts on his glasses. It takes a moment for him to focus. When he does, he goes to the place he marked the night before – And the LORD said unto Moses, Yet will I bring one plague more upon Pharaoh...

***

A high priority message alert at the bottom of her computer screen prompts Bernadette to log into her personal Email account. The transmission, also sent to Terry and Zavonne, is from her father. *Zion Faith Temple presents their first Annual Family Conference. Featured guests – Elder Joseph and Evangelist Addie Lewis.*

Bernadette chuckles as she reads the date of the engagement. It just happens to take place when the majority of her family will be in town for the holidays and Zavonne's wedding. Joseph's postscript at the bottom of the page tells the sisters they are expected to minister in song.

Bernadette's reply to her father is humorous.

The send button is depressed just as Mrs. Bell announces Hayes' arrival. "Have him come up please."

Hayes enters before Bernadette has time to freshen up. His vulnerability literally reaches out to attach itself to her.

"How long can you stay?" she asks.

"As long as it takes."

As if taking subliminal cues, they silently move to Bernadette's private quarters.

When they are seated he takes her slightly shaking hands into his. "I depart in one month. I will not go until we are the friends we once were."

Yearning for Hayes, a man most women would give their sight for, shows in the grin she unsuccessfully tries to hide. Reciprocal affection is detected in Hayes' responsive smile.

"What will you do with your free time while I am away?" Hayes asks.

Bernadette removes her hands from his. "Contrary to what your ego would prefer, I will not be idly whiling away my time. My brother-in-law and I will collaborate on a project."

Hayes' countenance visibly changes.

Bernadette remembers Hayes' jealousy brought on by the amorous singer's flirtations on Thanksgiving. Delivered with authority, her words clearly and succinctly communicate the fact that she knows herself. "Take a look at me Hayes. I'm a woman who did not get to where I am without knowing how to handle myself. You need to quit tripping. Business is his only interest in me."

Hayes disputes her words by shaking his head.

She insists he is wrong.

His desire to chew on that opinion is tucked away like a stained napkin from the sight of a hostess.

Hayes takes her hands, "How do you see yourself, Twinkle?"

"I feel real good about myself.

"Now give me the truth. I have been closer to you than any man, yet something remains between us. Your pain is so immense you were willing to give me your body."

Shame lowers her head. He tenderly raises it. From his shoulder bag he draws a monogrammed pen and pad. INTIMACY – INTO-ME-SEE, is written upon the pad, then placed into her hand.

"I need you like I need air to breathe. I have chosen to be transparent by opening the door of who I am to you. Sex at this point, is not what I need from you. Without pretense, I aspire to see into you in order to know how to protect your heart and mind. What blocks my path?"

"I don't want to talk about it."

"Let me see into you, Twinkle."

Trust in this man, who is like no other, tears the veil. Defying inner voices imploring her not to testify, she tells Hayes everything about her relationship with Eleanor.

"From what you say and what I see now, your grandmother is not the same person you knew as a child. The only way you will step out of this is by forgiving her."

Bernadette frowns.

Hayes pulls her to the floor. "Pray with me, Twinkle."

***

Pain radiating from her shoulder to her elbow has not subsided two hours after Falimah ingested over the counter medication.

The ordinarily brilliant woman speaks to her reflection in the mirror. She unsuccessfully tries to convince herself that the bruise on her arm is not as bad as it looks.

At her bedside, the blinking red light of her phone silently shouts that there are messages waiting for her response. She depresses the play button. Message number one is from Treva reminding Falimah of their dinner date. The next two are political solicitations. Message number four causes tension.

Treva's military trained eyes scrutinize every step and motion Falimah makes. In an effort to find out all she can, she begins to snoop. "So sis, tell me about the one who is so good I had to pencil myself onto your calendar to spend some time with you tonight."

Falimah's decision to avoid eye contact is a red flag to Treva.

Rather than verbally responding, the bracelet on her arm is waved in the air. Treva merely glances at it. She is more interested in why Falimah winced as if in pain as she shows off her new trinket.

"You like?" Falimah inquires.

"I see you found someone who knows you're a collector," Treva says off-handedly.

Falimah moves towards Treva. "Watch how you talk about me, Treva."

"Back away, girl," she warns.

Falimah moves backwards sending an ugly glare before unleashing a catty remark and accusation. "You're getting a little high and mighty since you've been hanging out with Bernadette. You think you're better than me because somebody with position acts like they have an interest in you?"

Treva is so confident in who she has become that the snare Falimah hoped to set with her words does not work. She responds with words that takes Falimah off guard. "I'm still your girl. I'm just wondering if that's how you want things to remain."

Falimah touches Treva's arm. "It's on you. Since you've been brown-nosing the boss you've changed."

Treva recoils as if something vile has touched her. Rather than respond with words that would reduce Falimah to a puddle of liquid cynicism, she picks up the remote control as a diversion. Channel after channel is surfed. The ringing of her cell phone becomes the distraction Treva hopes will take her away from Falimah.

"This is Treva."

"Hey little girl, do you want some candy?"

Laughter lays Treva across the couch. "What do you want, Brian?"

"Just checking on you. Are you alone?"

Walking to the kitchen Treva can feel the daggers Falimah's eyes are plunging into her back. "I wish I were. Why couldn't you be the emergency I need to run to?"

"Careful. I said I'd give you room. I didn't say I wouldn't come running if you open the door."

What should have been a short conversation expands to an hour of pleasant exchange. It concludes with a promise to meet for lunch the next day.

Falimah flings words of rage regarding what she feels is a lack of consideration, at Treva the minute she returns.

"You're right Falimah that was rude, but talking to Brian was more enjoyable than sparring with you."

Their less than cordial words escalate with each exchange. Falimah insists Treva is wasting her time on a man who could never be any Black woman's soul mate. Treva counters with Falimah not recognizing quality in any man because of her concentration on his anatomy. Their prolonged verbal scrimmage hits lower and lower below the belt. In order to head off reaching the point of no return, Treva leaves.

Rather than allowing the situation to rule her, Treva decides to treat herself. A big smile crosses her face as she thinks of the items she will need to purchase for the triple scoop banana split she plans to devour.

As she walks the aisle of the supermarket her mind drifts to Falimah. She is certain her arm is injured.

Determination to think on something pleasurable places her thoughts on Brian. Memories of their earlier conversation places a wide grin on her face. Regardless of what Falimah thinks, Brian is the friend she needs.

The shrill ringing of Treva's cell phone interrupts her pleasant thoughts. Mentally she makes a note to reprogram the tone. "Hello."

"Are you ready for that candy little girl?"

"You are a quick witted boy, aren't you Brian?"

"I don't believe you're interested in little boys. If you are, you won't be able to keep pace with the man I am."

"I stand corrected. Now tell me what you really want."

"I was checking to see if you have any battle scars."

"What?"

"I clocked our conversation tonight. I know you paid for it."

"So you're saying I should have hung up?"

"You couldn't do that to me."

The line goes dead.

Drenched sheets cling to Treva. Being entangled with the bed linens is what keeps her from falling to the floor. She vows that she will never again eat two banana splits without exercising immediately afterwards.

Within two hours she has awakened three times from crazy dreams featuring Falimah as the headliner. Inside her dream, she is confused as to what she should do. Falimah seems to be pleading for help, but no audible sound comes from her mouth.

CHAPTER 18

"This is Brian Chin."

"This is Bernadette. Do you remember you owe me a favor?"

"Yeah, well no, well, maybe."

"Shut up and listen," Bernadette laughs. "I know this is short notice and I slipped up, but I need you. Are you willing to help me out with the sound system for my sister's Christmas party being held here tomorrow night? You'd be on the clock. It's a semi-formal affair and you can bring a date."

Brian agrees after his demand for triple time is denied.

Turning to his computer he types hilarious words. *Since you're keeping your phones off the hook I'll give you a chance to redeem yourself. I have a last minute invitation from Bernadette to attend a semi-formal event tomorrow night. There's a rumor going around that you clean up well. If this is true I'll swing by. Accessorize with a shawl of humility and I might let you hold my hand. Make sure you leave your firearms at home.*

Treva's response is equally as humorous. *Since you painted my dining room to get on my good side, I'll let you cut my grass for the privilege of being seen in public with me. You better wear something nice because I'll be gorgeous. Since I don't want the word getting out that we're getting close, just slow the car down in front of the house and I'll jump in. Because I'll look so good I'll need to be strapped to keep you off me.*

Every aspect of Zavonne's Christmas soirée exudes splendor.

What does not blend with the ambiance of the evening is the behavior of her visiting great uncle. Dressed in a custom made, blood red Brooks Brothers suit, he moves about the room speaking in a voice several decibels above normal. His red Stetson becomes the holder of legal tender as wagers are placed on who will be the winner of the singing competition.

Satisfied he has received all he can, he goes to the microphone. He disregards social etiquette when he roars, "Twankly! Where you at, baby? You ready to show out for Uncle?"

Bernadette stands on the seat of her chair. "I'm ready, Uncle!" she shouts equally as loud.

"When it's time you make sure you show 'em what Uncle taught you, baby!"

Terry reads the surprised look on Hayes' face. "Get ready," she says. "This boy thinks he can out sing Twinkle. It will not happen."

Hayes extends his hand to help Bernadette to the floor. She gives him a quick hug before being pulled away by Zavonne. He grins like a baby with gas watching Bernadette make her way across the room. As far as he is concerned, she should win on appearance alone.

Even though he was kept waiting fifteen minutes after he arrived, he had no complaints. Her entrance into the library where she found him caused Hayes mouth to fall open. What did not come from his mouth were spoken with eyes admiring her gold scoop-neck dress with its fitted waist and flare skirt that rested at mid-calf.

Bernadette twirled to give the full effect of her dress, then extended her foot to show off the latest addition to her footwear collection. Their hue is the same brushed gold as her dress. What makes them extraordinary are the three and a half inch gold and rhinestone heels. Hayes went so far as to admit that the sparkling footwear is so gorgeous he would consider being a woman for one hour just for the opportunity to wear them.

Show time!

Winning the coin toss, Bernadette opts to perform last.

Every eye is trained upon the chocolate man dressed in an Everett Hall suit strutting across the makeshift stage. Unblemished skin glows beneath the heat of overhead lights. With deliberate motion, he unbuttons the jacket of his suit. The premeditated move brings uniformed inhalation of breaths from many women. From an inner pocket, a handkerchief is removed. In what appears to be a single motion he pats his brow, tosses the kerchief into the air, then spins on one foot. By the time his spiral is complete he has caught the cloth behind his back, then launches into his performance. The exhaling of the many women nearly drowns out his first words. Showmanship works the song so hard literally everyone present are on their feet.

At the appointed time, Bernadette takes center stage. Instead of using the microphone provided for her performance, she takes the one in her competitor's hand.

"What is she doing?" Hayes asks.

"What she does best," Terry whispers. "Professional training from my mother and uncle has enhanced all of her natural ability. His song is about to become a fading memory. Twinkle's defeat of what he thought was a stellar performance will be so sweet we may have to check his blood sugar."

Bernadette does exactly what Terry said she would. 'Mesmerized', a tune she penned is beyond extraordinary. Bernadette's soul is poured into the song as her voice runs effortlessly up and down the vocal scale.

All are brought to their feet with the strong delivery of the last verse.

Every male in the room kneel before their seat to pay homage to the queen. Humbled by the mastery of her presentation her competitor bows at Bernadette's feet to concede his loss. In the meantime, her uncle takes pride in rubbing defeat in the face of those who wagered against Bernadette.

Hayes' eyes fondly follow Bernadette working her way around the room greeting guests and accepting praise for her outstanding performance.

"Man you just whupped," Roosevelt laughs. "Look atcha. You can hardly hear me 'cause your nose so wide open your nostrils coverin' up your ears."

Hayes' laughter comes to an abrupt halt when Bernadette receives a lingering hug from her not so covertly smitten singing competitor. Smugness covers his face when she expertly turns to avoid lip contact.

Roosevelt leans over. "Melody Man tryin' ta move in. You need to handle your business."

Joseph intercepts Hayes before he makes it across the room. Reluctantly, Hayes accepts the offer to chat in private.

They walk to the foyer. Joseph moves to the window. "You can't stand for any man to be close to Twinkle, can you?"

Hayes studies Joseph's turned back but does not speak.

"My wife is a beautiful woman. Because of the office she's been called to, she's very visible. There was a time when I went crazy if any guy got to what I considered too close to her."

"So you understand my position."

Joseph's response slices the air like a saber. "I understand that if you don't grow with her, Twinkle will soon lose interest in you."

Hayes does not respond.

"My daughter is a fine, fine wine. For the rest of her life she will attract the attention of men of all persuasions, ages and walks of life. You see how she took over that stage tonight?"

Hayes' nod indicates that he had.

"That's the confidence she wears with ease. Twinkle has to be confident with who she is in order to do what she has to do. If you want to be in her life you better find out if you can handle a full-time woman. If you can't, you need to take your half-stepping act away from my daughter." Intensity displayed in Joseph's expression matches that of his next words. "Her purpose can't work with a jealous or a slow-to-grow man hanging on her."

"I have no need to be jealous of any man." Hayes says standing a little taller.

Joseph walks to within inches of this massive man who desires his daughter. With no detectible emotion he drives home his point. "Every time you bristle up when any man comes near Twinkle, you're waving your jealousy like a white flag. What she and this boy are developing is a business relationship. He's picked up her scent, but she can handle him."

He chuckles in spite of himself. "There's no doubting that you and Twinkle have a heart relationship. I can feel your passion for her. It's the same I had when I was courting her mother. You watch yourself with my daughter. I don't know what you all worked out for when you leave for school. Whatever it is, you handle it right. I don't play when it comes to my wife and my daughters. You mess over or with Twinkle, you will see me."

Returning to the atrium Hayes searches the crowd for Bernadette. Front row center, on the dance floor he finds her beside her uncle doing the Electric Slide. He maneuvers his way between the two.

"Look out now young blood. Don't mess 'round and step on my gators while you tryin' ta hit a beat." Loud words are followed by an unusual version of the dance. Hayes responds with a fancy step and spin that tells onlookers he is no stranger to rhythm and finesse. When Bernadette shows off some fancy moves of her own, Hayes unbuttons his jacket then works it out. The three are a sight as they put their special twist on the choreographed routine.

When the music fades, Hayes dances Bernadette out to the foyer. Laughing she says, "Remember when I told you we all have 'special people' in our families?"

"You are referring to your uncle?"

"Isn't he great? Most people cringe when he's around because he's so loud. I love the way he sets the mood for a party good time. You see how he got you ta struttin' your stuff, Mr. Bo Jangles."

Hayes seats himself in a chair near the stairs. Bernadette accepts his offered lap. His sturdy arms feel good as he rocks her to the beat of the music coming from overhead speakers. Inside Bernadette's head, a rainbow of color lifts them upward. Warmth increases as Hayes' arms tighten about her.

"Come with me, Bernadette," he whispers.

Consideration of departing to a cozier atmosphere is entertained. What shatters the moment are remembered words spoken by her great aunt. *You gots to be real careful how you let mens talks to ya....beware of them slick mouth Johnnies. Thems the mens so smooth they got gals legs spreadin' wide as eagles wings in flight 'fore they open they mouth.*

Bernadette moves from Hayes' embrace. Realization of considering leaving with him convicts her like a twelve-person jury.

Desire's fire coursing through Hayes requires a few moments to get under control. He stands and then straightens his jacket before going to Bernadette's side. She stiffens under his touch. He leans close to her ear. "You need never to be uncomfortable in my presence. I am human. When you sang that song, your fire intoxicated my senses. I became consumed with a need to possess all of you. You have refused me. I respect your decision."

Bernadette returns to the empty chair. Hayes follows and kneels at her feet. "Didn't I tell you I could hold my own, Mr. Davis?" she teases in an effort to lighten the mood.

Hayes rubs his chin with his left index finger, but does not respond. Her second query also goes unanswered. "What about my new brother-in-law? Do you think the two of us can make a dime or two as singing partners?" Bernadette prods with a mischievous smile.

"Your voice is a goldmine more than capable of carrying a solo project. You have no need of a singing partner."

Bernadette seems to retreat into a world of her own, then returns. Lightly she caresses his hand. "The first man I ever loved is my father. I never believed I could love anyone more than him. That man, the one I loved first, knew one day he would have to release me to the one who will love me more than he ever could."

Hayes moves closer. His delightful scent fills Bernadette's nostrils, but does not detour her from her destination. "I didn't think I could love anyone more than Daddy until I came into the full realization of who Jesus is to me. I have a total passion for God and the purpose He's entrusted to me. You came into my life at a time when I needed no man."

Bernadette lets go of Hayes' hand. Tentativeness replaces his relaxed expression.

"You have to make a decision about who you are, Hayes." The tip of her index finger taps his right temple. "Are you secure enough and willing to grow with the full-time woman I am? If you aren't, we don't need to keep romantic hope alive because I won't allow a jealous or a slow-to-grow man to hinder me. I won't because my purpose, my gift from God, has no room for him."

Treva gets her chance to converse with Bernadette when she returns to the atrium. "So you and your people do this on a regular basis or is this party banging because I'm here?"

"We party hearty when the occasion arises."

Bernadette drapes her arm around Treva's shoulders. Speaking of hearty, where is Mr. Chin?"

"I had to put the hose on that boy and send him back to the sound booth."

Hayes' sensual looks sent Bernadette's way tells Treva his and Brian's minds are occupying the same space. "I see your man's heat is rising. I drove myself because I got off duty late. It's a good thing I did because I believe I need to take you home tonight."

"What?"

"You're the one who said friends look out for one another. I'm looking at Hayes, looking at you. The two of you do not need to be alone tonight. And neither do Brian and I."

***

Throughout the night, Bernadette's words speak to Hayes. Regardless of what he wants to believe, Hayes must admit he is a jealous man.

Unable to sleep he moves to his collection of biblical textbooks. From it, he selects multiple volumes. From an engraved holder he takes several pens.

Upon the floor of his room Hayes sits. He removes his glasses, rubs his eyes, then replaces the silver rimmed spectacles.

Titles of texts he has yet to study appear ominous before this learned man. Pages are fingered, then set aside. Ruby, burgundy and scarlet pens, gifts from family and amorous women, are fondly stroked, then placed upon closed texts when nothing worth writing requires their use.

"Where do I begin?" he wonders aloud.

Necessity for release drives Hayes like an animal in heat. He selects a pen. With fervor his penmanship proclaims the subject of his research – Jealousy.

Hours are spent pouring through pages of apologetics written by men and women revered in the theological field. He jots down a few thoughts, but nothing that quenches his thirst.

He battles to keep his eyes open in order to study the title of his paper. The word jealously silently screams as loud as a professional town crier. Again he questions where the road to his answer is.

"*Worship Me.*"

Hayes looks around for the source of the words he clearly hears.

"*Worship Me.*"

Hayes pushes books and papers aside. "Father, I worship You…"

Time passes without notice as Hayes surrenders his all to worshipping. When he finishes, he feels renewed. Gathering his books and papers he sets about placing them in order. Words written hours ago stare up at him from the page in his hand. Hayes bows his head. "Lord, give me Your instructions."

A thought instantly comes to Hayes. He grasps his pen. Beneath the word jealousy he writes – who has the right? As if on autopilot he opens his study bible to James 1:20 – *For the wrath of man worketh not the righteousness of God.*

Realization of his immature actions, unsettles Hayes. He begins writing several spaces below his first entry. One, fast to seek God's answers. Two, pray for humility, a broken spirit and contrite heart. Three, submit to the will of God.

More entries are written before Hayes tucks them into the back of his bible and then carries them to his bed. Fatigue washes over his body. Sleep overtakes him before he digests the first three verses of the fifth chapter of Mathew.

Roosevelt's entry into the room awakens Hayes. "What, Brown Man?" he inquires without opening his eyes.

Roosevelt seats himself in a chair near the dresser. As usual, he is silent. He is silent for so long that his eventual words startle Hayes.

"You been prayin', been prayed over and now you think you're ready for the big time. You're not ready yet, man. It's comin', but you're gonna have to wait on God's timin' for what He has for you."

Hayes turns to his side to face his friend.

"You have a responsibility to God to live right. You pray that prayer 'bout Twinkle?"

"Yes."

"You get a answer?"

"Yes."

"You doing whatcha 'sposed ta do?"

"Yes."

"You got faith to know it's all gonna work out in His time?"

"Yes."

"You got faith to obey?"

"Yes."

"Then I don't need ta say nothin' else."

Roosevelt moves to the door.

Hayes calls out. "Why have you remained close to me?"

Roosevelt turns. Two fingers touch his heart, then extend towards Hayes.

"Why did you choose me instead of someone on your spiritual and moral level?"

The so-called brethren who show open disdain for Hayes and his previously decadent lifestyle have consistently asked themselves the same question. Roosevelt leans against the doorjamb. He examines his disheveled friend who has moved completely into his home and will remain until he departs for school.

Large, strong, gentle hands touch lips that praise without inhibition, speak truth without regret and fulfill the passion of a woman who would choose to live alone rather than settle for second best.

"Let me tell you something, man. You think there wasn't times I was ready to cut you loose?"

Hayes sits up.

"You think 'cause you hadn't taken hold of your salvation you weren't on my level. God is no respecter of persons. God doesn't love me any more than He loves you. I know some serious scripture quoting Holy Ghost-filled brothas I won't spend ten minutes past service with. I love you 'cause of who you are not 'cause of what people say you should be. You've always been on my level. You just didn't know it."

Roosevelt walks out the door only to return to stand over his friend. He picks up the bible at Hayes' side and waves it in the air. "It ain't just 'bout what to do to get the woman you want. It's about that, and what you need to do to be in right standing with God, so He can bring the right woman to you."

***

Why is it that I seem to have more to do for Zavonne's wedding than she does? Instead of sitting in this restaurant waiting for Hayes, I should be home. Heat makes its way into Bernadette's face at the thought of Hayes. *How am I going to handle his being so far away?*

Hayes' diction that caresses the English language as if it were a bride upon the wedding bed, greets Bernadette before she sees him. Without reserve, he sings terms of endearment as if they are mandatory for his approach.

A slight turn of her head brings him into view.

From her vantage point, the full-length, leather coat and matching headpiece Hayes is wearing make him appear larger than he is. Bernadette's heartbeat quickens with each step bringing him closer.

Males sitting nearby shrug under the gaze of their dinner dates when Hayes strokes Bernadette's cheek, then gallantly asks permission to sit.

Conversation regarding the holidays and errands they have and have not tended to float between the two. Their conversation is interrupted by a call from Hayes' mother reminding him she is waiting for him to fulfill a promise with a deadline less than two hours away.

Bernadette accepts the invitation to accompany him to his parents' home.

A fast paced drive has Bernadette feeling like she's playing cat and mouse to keep up with Hayes. At one point he is driving so fast she has to call him on the cell phone to tell him to slow down. In less than fifteen minutes Hayes has led Bernadette from Capital Hill through the Rainier Valley to the entrance of Lakeridge where his parents reside.

Hayes pulls Bernadette through the kitchen door of his parent's newly remodeled tri-level brick home. Thembelani's greeting directs them to the living area. Mother and son's departure leaves Bernadette alone with a man she has no reason to be fond of. Allen's vague greeting does little to change her opinion.

Lack of social graces leaves Bernadette on her feet to deflect an immediate intrusion into her personal affairs. "My son and I have conversed regarding his feelings for you. He made it very clear that he's in love with you. Do you love my son?"

Bernadette takes the seat that has not been offered, then admits her love for Hayes.

Allen rubs his chin with his left index finger and thumb. His thick furled brows over his dark brooding eyes give Bernadette a glimpse of what Hayes will look like in thirty years or so.

"Now that we know the two of you have a mutual love for one another, what happens next?" Allen growls.

Bernadette does not respond.

"Let me put the question to you in a way you can comprehend. Hayes is a man in control of virtually everything around him. You don't appear to be a person who can be controlled. As a matter of fact I have no doubt you could get pretty much whatever you want out of any man, including my son."

Allen arrogantly continues. "My son is a good catch who is definitely going to be somebody someday. I'm sure that aside from his good looks and charm you're aware of his financial assets. There is no end to what he can offer. My question to you should be obvious. What do you have to offer my son?"

Now if I smack this ignorant man I'll have to fight with his wife and probably Hayes. Bernadette smiles. "Mr. Davis," she says with an unmistakable air of confidence, "I have to be honest when I say your words are rather offensive. However, with Hayes being your son, it is your right to look out for his best interests." She takes the time to remove her coat before continuing. "One thing you said is absolutely correct. I'm not a person to be controlled. Fortunately our mutual respect for one another negates the need for such juvenile behavior. Who Hayes is, not what he possesses, is my major attraction to him. As far as his assets are concerned it seems that he's doing pretty well for himself. I've heard he has a beautiful home. Personally I don't own one of my own."

Condescension in Allen's voice accessorizes his next words. "I didn't take you to be a *renter*."

Bernadette struggles to keep an unkind remark from escaping into the air.

"You don't make much money?" Allen prods when she does not respond.

Bernadette rises with the grace of the trained ballet dancer she is. Without speaking, she fingers what she knows are expensive items as she walks about the exquisitely decorated room. Before an expansive wall of windows that gives the inhabitants a great view of Lake Washington as well as giving their home a high six-figure value on the market, she pauses.

"Mr. Davis, from the looks of your home, it's obvious you and Mrs. Davis are closely acquainted with quality. I want you to look around this room, then take a very good look at me."

Allen's scrutinizing eyes move from Bernadette to a Jacob Lawrence original strategically hung over the marble fireplace. Not far from it hangs a Horace Pippin. His eyes travel to one of several bookcases. A majority of the leather bound books lining the shelves are rare first editions. Moving from there his gaze falls upon tapestry rugs and masterfully carved items upon shelves, walls and tabletops. The curio protecting his wife's extraordinary crystal collection was hand-carved by one of her African relatives.

When his attention returns to Bernadette she softly asks, "Do I look out of place here?"

Rather than answer her question, he gruffly asks if she has any tangible assets.

"Yes I do, but I don't make a habit of divulging my personal business to strangers."

"That is very wise," Hayes remarks as he and his mother enter the room.

"Tell me about your family," Allen briskly says from the edge of his seat.

"Via your pastors, you have met my maternal grandmother. I have no doubt her ambassador mission represented the core of who we are; a very protective and close-knit family not so unlike your own."

Thembelani's look halts Hayes' attempt to interrupt.

"What about your parents?" Allen barks.

Thembelani becomes the recipient of Bernadette's response. "Actually, you'll meet my parents soon. Elder Joseph and Evangelist Addie Lewis are speaking at your conference next week."

Allen shifts in his chair.

Bernadette picks up the latest copy of Paragon Magazine resting on the seat of a nearby chaise. The feature article makes repeated references to her parents self-made millions and philanthropic fellowships.

"This commentary speaks about the public life of my parents. I hope before they leave town you'll have opportunity to dine with us to get to know who they really are."

Turning to Allen she says, "As Hayes' father you're doing no less than my grandmother has already done in her quest to know who you are and how Hayes cares for me."

"How does he *care* for you now?" Allen asks.

In Bernadette's head the word *care* translates to *what does he buy you?*

Allen's corrosive words are handled with kid gloves. "The words you spoke earlier and the fact that you now insinuate that I may be prostituting myself for tangibles is very insulting. It is insulting to my parents and me. Most of all, it is insulting to Hayes. I know what you meant for me to hear. What I hear you saying is that you believe your son to possess a myriad of deficiencies. I hear you saying he may be so devoid of moral standards he needs to buy his women because he lacks what it takes to hold the interest and affection of a reputable woman such as myself. You're wrong in your assumptions."

Allen stands to his feet. His wife moves to his side. Flared nostrils and eyes that have narrowed to give only a glimpse of his dark pupils express his anger.

Bernadette stares back. "Mr. Davis, I have something else I need to say to you."

Allen's facial expression remains unchanged.

"You're wrong about Hayes. He's not going to be somebody. He already is."

Hayes moves to Bernadette's side. "Now that you understand the greatness I possess I offer you the opportunity to prove your culinary skills."

"Smooth move brotha," she whispers understanding Hayes effort to diffuse what could become an explosive situation.

Bernadette turns her attention to Thembelani. "I admired your collection of books on my first visit, Mrs. Davis..."

Hayes touches her arm. "Ms. Lewis, I will show you to the kitchen now."

Bernadette maneuvers her arm away from Hayes.

Drama over being hungry would have caused a previous girlfriend to beg for the honor of preparing a meal to placate Hayes' bruised feelings. His performance and demand for a meal have no effect on Bernadette.

"Mama, please help me," Hayes pleads at Thembelani's feet.

"Begging is so beneath you. Get up."

Turning to Bernadette, Thembelani says, "I have a private library I believe you will appreciate."

"You will leave me famished, Twinkle?" Hayes calls out to her departing back. Her loud laughter is his answer.

Allen beckons for Hayes to take a seat. "You found someone almost as pretty and as together as your mama, didn't you boy?"

Hayes' grin is wide and proud. "I cannot express how she makes me feel. I know you did not care for the way she spoke to you. Straight forward is how she is at all times. Either you like her or you do not."

Allen inquires about Renata.

The mention of her name slumps Hayes' shoulders. "We are no more. Please do not vex me with plots for reconciliation."

CHAPTER 19

Expensive stationery inside a linen envelope is the invitation only a select few will receive.

Months ago the invitation to Falimah's exclusive holiday gathering would have made Treva giddy with anticipation. Today it serves to remind her of the changes she has made concerning social affiliations.

Much has changed in the life of a woman few understand, or seek to.

Change has opened blinded eyes, enabling them to appreciate the simplistic beauty of true friendship. Within change, inhibitions about self-worth that encumbered like a lead lined frock, have been discarded. Removal of detrimental thoughts has allowed the over-comer to reweave a once suffocating garment into breathable fabric recognized as strength.

More than donning the new garment, Treva understands that ignorance about how to wear such a valuable article is dangerous. Past experiences have shown that without expert tailoring, strength is as ill fitting as an off the rack suit on a three hundred pound person.

Keen intellect concludes that far too many do not understand that strength has nothing to do with mind control that leads to oppression. It is an ability, a gift, to be carefully nurtured beyond the superficial in order to serve those about you.

For the third time in twenty minutes, Treva picks up the invitation to a party that will undoubtedly be the talk of the town for months to come. One she will bypass.

Rather than attending Falimah's conventional man seeking woman, woman seeking man celebration, her new found strength has opted to accept an invitation she will enjoy. She and Brian will deliver toys to Children's Hospital, dine, and then cap the evening by trimming his tree.

Predictably, Falimah did not receive the news well. What was unpredictable was an invitation for Treva and Brian to come to dinner a week before the party.

Brian made no bones about the fact that he did not want to go, but would do so for Treva. In return she must bake him a pie and a cake.

Looking down at the pad before her, Treva is aware that in the midst of her doodling she has written 'stand through the pain' in bold block letters.

Rather than occupying her mind with this subject Treva goes to her workshop to begin a task that has been put off far too long.

From a twenty-year old trunk she removes an armload of childhood friends. Friends who became the sisters, cousins and confidants she could share every painful thought with. With care she selects those to be restored then donated to the Children's ministry.

She examines Gabriella. Her torn arm came courtesy of Falimah the day Treva won the third grade spelling bee. Walking Talking Wendy was the doll every girl in the fourth grade wanted for Christmas. Only Treva received her. Wendy lost mobility and partial speech after being accidentally dropped from a second story window by Falimah.

If anyone ever asked, Treva would have to admit that a majority of the dolls nestled together like forgotten orphans suffered injuries at the hands of Falimah Meyer.

The bond between her father and Randall Meyer is the tie that has bound them for years. Respect for herself necessitates that change must take place. The crux of the matter is how to go about distancing herself from Falimah.

Words from one of Pastor Filmore's messages come to mind. *You do not have precious time to waste playing nursemaid to the offense others take regarding what God has called you to do. Just make sure it is God's will and it is done His way.*

Twice Treva picks up the telephone only to return it to its stand without dialing. She stares at it as if expecting it to ring. Two minutes stretch to ten. Twenty minutes later she dials Bernadette.

"Hello."

"Have you wrapped my present yet?"

"Present? I thought closing the office for a week was present enough for you people. Now you're begging for more."

"Do you have time for some serious talk?"

Bernadette does not, but makes the time for her friend. "What's on your mind?"

"I need to step away from someone I used to be real tight with. The problem is we're bound to each other in a lot of ways."

"You know you can be tight with someone for a long time, then boom, they're on your last nerve. You've grown immensely in the last six months and so you're probably seeing your friend with different eyes. Pray to make sure that what you're doing is predicated upon His will and not your hurt feelings, if that applies in this case."

Minutes of silence are deafening.

"You know it's Falimah, don't you?"

Bernadette lets out a low whistle.

"What you say is good advice. I hope it works because after I talk to her about some other things, the decision to separate may be hers."

Brain and Treva are at the height of their holiday bantering when they arrive at Falimah's. Big hugs and a tray of beverages welcome them inside the lavishly decorated house. Falimah introduces them to her date before returning to the kitchen.

Nasty is the only word that comes to Treva's mind as she gives him a quick once over. He moves towards her with a lustful look.

"Slow your roll," Brian warns.

The warning is ignored.

"Come talk to me," Treva says leading Brian to the dining room. Irritation at being eyed like the last chicken dinner at a church social, fuel her words. "Is he tripping or what? I don't like him, and I'm gonna let Falimah know she needs to drop that puppy off at the pound."

"I know what he's up to. If he steps over my line, I'll handle my business."

Treva frowns.

"Is there any type of artillery concealed anywhere on you?"

Both hips are patted as a mirthful smile crosses Treva's face before she goes to the living room where she finds Falimah's questionable partner.

New furnishings are a surprise. Treva fingers the textured pattern of the enormous sofa.

"You guys were gone for a while. I hope I didn't upset anything."

Simultaneous laughter comes from the duo. "Things couldn't be better between me and my man," Treva taunts.

"So it's like that?" he responds virtually licking his lips after each word.

"Yeah it's like that," Brian adds.

The scent of testosterone hangs heavily in the air.

"Treva, will you help me please?" Falimah calls from the kitchen.

Reluctantly she leaves Brian.

Reaching into the cabinet for plates, Falimah casually asks if Treva likes her furniture – her Christmas gift from her boyfriend.

"We priced that furniture two months ago, Falimah. It was around seven grand then. What are you doing to get him to let loose of that kinda of dough? How long have you been hiding him? And how come nobody in the family knows about him?"

"One question at a time girl," Falimah laughs while mixing dressing for the spinach salad. "Answer number one, you've been around long enough to know how things work. Answer number two, I haven't been hiding him. He's very private, plus he travels a lot. Answer number two also answers number three. And to set things straight he's been around long enough to get up off something. I know the way Brian's been following you around like a puppy isn't because of a lack of personal attention."

The urge to slap the salad bowl to the floor is hard to resist. Instead Treva places plates and utensils upon the serving cart. "You know you need to shut your mouth. Me and Brian don't sleep together and you make way too much money to be sleeping with anyone for tangibles."

"It's your thang, girl. You work it your way and let me handle my business my way."

Arrogantly thrown words are not surprising. Many of their conversations are held in this manner. In an effort to gauge how serious Falimah may be, Treva asks, "How do you feel about him?"

"This boy is digging me deep. Says he can't live without me."

Feelings alert Treva to something awry. "This may make you mad, but I have to ask. Can you live with him?"

Overpaid attention to the preparation of the dessert cart tells Treva, Falimah does not care to discuss the matter any further.

For the moment Treva drops the subject. She steals away to the first floor lavatory to collect her thoughts before joining the others at the dinner table.

During dinner Falimah's date dominates table conversation. His glowing resume of himself and other insignificant prattle, bores Treva and Brian. Pinches to Falimah's leg or arm offered as signs of affection as he calls her honey and sweetheart are disturbing to the couple.

Consumption of all the food on the table brings opportunity for an abrupt departure. Treva's offer to help with the dishes belays the exit.

Tiptoeing to place a platter on an upper shelf, Falimah loses her footing. Treva catches her before she falls. Falimah rubbing her upper left arm concerns Treva. "How long has your arm been hurting?"

Falimah ceases rubbing her arm. "I bruised myself when I fell off the treadmill the other day."

Red covers Treva's eyes. Within the haze, she sees Falimah struggling with the man sitting at her dining table nursing a brandy. Horizontal shaking of her head returns Treva to the present. "Let me see your arm."

Treva's request is denied.

In one quick motion Treva yanks Falimah's cranberry cardigan off her shoulder. Purple and blue flesh as large as the palm of her hand is exposed.

"Did he do this to you?" Treva demands.

Falimah pulls her sweater into place. "I told you before, what two adults do is between the two of them."

Treva glares over her shoulder at Falimah before taking the serving cart out to the pantry.

Brian enters the kitchen with more dishes. Falimah avoids eye contact.

Inaudible conversation from the living room begins to rise. Out of the mumble of words they hear, "Why are you hitting my sister?"

Brian and Falimah run from the kitchen like sprinters out of the blocks. Falimah moves past him to her suitor's side.

Treva again commands him to divulge why he is hitting her sister.

Squeezing Falimah tightly is his reply.

Hands on hips with feet slightly apart reflect Treva's mood. "Why are you hitting my sister?" she demands again.

Falimah commands Treva to cease her interrogation. When she does not, Falimah's boyfriend grips her shoulders. Falimah is thrust towards Brian and Treva, then roughly pulled back like a rag doll being offered, then snatched from expectant hands.

"*This – this* is mine to do what I please! Whenever I please!" he roars.

Tears of humiliation distort Falimah's face.

"My sister is not a this!" Treva shrieks.

Brian moves to her side. As delicately as possible he pats her down to see if a concealed weapon is hidden beneath her loose sweater.

"You need to cool down," Brian whispers into her ear. "I'll handle this."

Fingers that should be tender dig into Falimah's shoulders as her turncoat lover commands Brian and Treva to leave.

The order is not heeded.

Insults from a foul mouth are hurled at Brian. "You become a real man like me and you'll have that one begging for more like her girl here." He throws Falimah to the floor like an offensive inanimate object.

Treva catches Brian's cue. She covers Falimah with her body. The force of Brian's right jab stuns his foe. His left cross renders him unconscious.

Hysterical wailing greets Randall Meyer and his two sons as they enter the room. Falimah is snatched to her feet. "Is this the man Treva called me about?" Randall hisses while pointing to the crumpled body on the floor.

Falimah does not answer.

Randall goes to Treva. He whispers, "You need me to get rid of the evidence?"

"I didn't shoot him Uncle Randall, he's just knocked out," she whispers back.

Falimah finds her voice and unmercifully berates Treva.

Treva's temper is a match for Falimah's. "How nuts are you? That man beats on you at will and you turn on your sister who's trying to help you!"

"Who you talkin' 'bout, Treva? You don't have no sisters! You don't even have a mama!"

Randall catches Treva's fist in mid-air. "I got this baby," he says as he pulls her close then kisses her cheek.

Brian gently pulls Treva backwards.

Falimah's vile words assault the couple.

Brian struggles to restrain Treva as she screams her response.

"Let's go, Treva," Brian says pulling her toward the door.

Pain as immense as a black hole fills the inside of Brian's late model Acura.

Treva smiles weakly when he glances over.

Silence accompanies the couple from the car into Treva's home. Nothing but the need to soothe her is on Brian's mind. "Come sit with me so we can talk."

She curls up close to him on the sofa. "I've always admired the fire you have, but my level of respect for you went off the Richter scale after what I saw in you tonight."

"Falimah and I have been through a lot. I never thought she would sink so low," Treva barely whispers.

"She's taking her embarrassment out on you."

Brian rubs her hand. "Your need for family is your weakness. Falimah knows it and uses it against you when it's convenient for her."

A single tear makes its way down Treva's face. Brian gently wipes it away.

"You did what you believed was right. True friendship means being willing to stand through the pain that comes with your stance."

Her eyes widen. Softly she tells Brian that the words he just spoke are the ones she had written several days earlier. Vulnerability allows her to tell of the reoccurring dream where Falimah seems to be crying out for help, but nothing audible comes from her open mouth. A voice within her dream instructed her to do what was right and then stand through the pain.

"And so you will," Brian says. "But I have to say what's on my mind. I know your anger over what you knew was happening to Falimah caused you to confront that man tonight. That was not cool. You needed to let me handle things."

Pursed lips are her response.

"I can take care of you," Brian says cupping her chin.

He lets go, then takes hold of Treva's hands. "I told you being a friend means accountability and speaking into one another's life. I need to say all that's on my mind."

Treva nods.

"Your relationship with God has allowed you to outgrow your endurance of Falimah's madness. You're demanding that the people around you give you respect."

Tears moisten Treva's eyes. "Yeah, but it's costing me."

"Here's more truth for you. Anything worth having is worth the cost. You just have to decide if you'll pay or if you'll be cheap and hold on to dime a dozen misery."

Tears mixed with eyeliner and mascara become black streaks. Brian pulls her close allowing every sob to be released within his secure embrace. Time passes in silence. Their first kiss changes the course of their friendship forever.

Brian pulls away.

"I thought you said you go after what you want, Mr. Chin. What is it you want?"

His look is thoughtful.

"Brian?"

"I want you."

Treva sucks her bottom lip. Letting go of her lip, her mouth forms into a slight smile. It is not sultry, but mesmerizing enough to keep Brian focused upon it.

"I've been real with you tonight, Treva. I need for you to do the same. Tell me how you really feel about me."

"Here's honesty for you, Mr. Chin. You've always been my friend; a friend I respect and can share everything with. I enjoy being with you and I appreciate the fact that you don't try to make me be what you want. The day you told me you'd take care of me instead of trying to handle me was the day I knew I wanted to be closer to you. Your words then and now tell me you will care for me the way I intend to be cared for." She lightly slaps her own face, "Despite the move I just tried to put on you."

Brian's mood becomes mischievous. "I know it's been hard for you to keep your mind off of me." A quick, light jab halts his next words.

"Where do we go from here, Brian?"

"Forward."

Treva jumps to her feet. One forward step is taken.

"Development of our friendship."

Another step.

"Not absorbing your every moment."

Step three.

"Praying to see if our purposes line up."

Step four.

"Taking care of you."

She turns on Brian. "I can take care of myself. I don't need or want a man buying me clothes, giving me money, paying my bills or expecting me to do what he says because he's seeking to be my man. I come and go as I please. And I won't be cleaning your house, cooking your meals, buying you clothes, giving you money, or paying your bills. Can you handle that?"

"Yes ma'am."

Artificial harshness softens as she puts big soft eyes on him. "Then what I'll say is we can work on developing this."

Brian's expression indicates there is more to be said. Treva draws near. "Speak truth to me."

"Truth is, my type of caring has to do with your heart, not your upkeep. Can you handle that?"

"Yes sir," she says saluting him.

"Now that we have that settled, you need to tell me what time you get up in the morning."

"Why?'

"I'm coming by with my laundry. It wasn't on your list of what you wouldn't do for me."

***

Christmas spent with family in Seattle combined with putting final touches on Zavonne's New Year's Eve wedding has been hectic. It has also kept the three sisters virtually inseparable.

This evening Terry helps Bernadette select her outfit for the next day. Their conversation goes from humor to business to personal.

"You have some issues to deal with, Twinkle," Terry says after selecting boots to go with her cashmere jeans still in need of a top. "Remember when we were younger and we prayed that Bunky would show you that she loved you?"

Bernadette tenses.

"She's always loved you. She just didn't know how to show it. We kept praying and now you have what you prayed for. Problem is you think you're too good to accept what God gave you because it didn't come the way you wanted."

"But..."

"But nothing," Terry says as calmly as she would if she were asking Bernadette to pass the sugar. "Every time we ask God to forgive us, He does. You think you're better than God? You think you can pick and choose who to forgive? Keep holding on to unforgiveness and keep being miserable."

Terry selects two sweaters. One is for Bernadette to wear, the other is to somehow make its way back to California with her.

"I'm not miserable."

"Yes you are. You're miserable because you've always longed for her love. Bunky flying here last summer was the bold step she took toward righting her wrong. At Thanksgiving she apologized to you, but you wouldn't accept it. It's on you now. Whether it hurts you and/or Bunky, you need to tell her what her actions did to you. You can't heal until you do that."

Terry takes a sterling and turquoise bracelet from Bernadette's dressing table. Instead of offering it as an accessory, she places it upon her wrist. "May I have this?"

"No. You have a husband to buy you jewelry. I worked hard for that."

The negative response is ignored as Terry places the matching drop earrings in the second holes in her ears. "These look good. I'll take them too."

"Do I need to run you and your husband down to the jewelry store before you relieve me of anything else?"

Bernadette's vivid dream keeps her body moving about her bed. Within that dream she finds herself before three doors. Eleanor is standing inside the first door calling out to her. She ignores her. She moves to the third door where Hayes' open arms invite her inside. After a period of time she is gently pushed out.

She goes to the center door. It is locked. Each attempt to get it open causes the foundation beneath her feet to quake.

Tears flow from her eyes. In the midst of her sobs she hears, *"When you forgive and confess I will give you your hearts desire. Your forgiveness will bring you closer to Me. Your confession will bring others to Me. Do not be afraid. I Am with you."*

Bernadette's perspiration soaked body comes to an upright position. At the side of her bed she kneels to pray. "Father I thank You for caring enough about me to grant me Your grace and mercy. I ask Your forgiveness for refusing to obey You in forgiving Bunky. Help me to show her the love she deserves as You help me to forgive the past."

Bernadette makes her way to Eleanor's room. She does not knock before entering. Hampered by darkness she stumbles about searching for her grandmother's bedside.

The sudden light from the bedside lamp startles her.

Illuminated by the soft glow Eleanor does not look as formidable as she has always seemed in Bernadette's eyes. Against the richness of her navy blue encased pillows she actually appears somewhat fragile.

Bernadette sees the face of her mother, aunt and sisters inside the grandmother she knows more by the multiple clippings carefully pasted inside a secret scrapbook buried beneath precious memorabilia in her hope chest.

Before her lies a woman loved by masses of people who have only seen her on a movie screen, theatre stage or in a trade magazine.

Respect for who she is and what she has accomplished has been woven into the family tapestry. Her relationship with powerful people has enshrined the family's social status into the "Who's Who Hall of Fame".

Before she looses her nerve words held inside for years tumble out like contents of an overturned basket. "Why did you hate me so much? Why couldn't you love me the way you loved Terry and Zavonne? I know I need to forgive you but it's so hard. I've hated you so long it's hard not to."

Eleanor pulls back her bedding.

Bernadette's look is tentative.

Eleanor's hand reaches outward. Sincere words break through the barricade of silence between them. "I'm sorry, baby. I'm sorry for the years of happiness I stole from you."

Bernadette remains rigid inside familiar yet foreign arms.

Eleanor begins to sing one of the lullabies Addie used to sing to Bernadette when she was a fretful infant.

Bernadette remains stiff.

Eleanor continues to sing. Eventually, her singing gives way to speech. "I came from a time where our color determined a good or hard life. I love you, Twinkle. What I did was wrong, and I'm sorry I hurt you. I'm sorry for the good memories we never had. If you let us we can make the best of what we have now."

Bernadette attempts to leave the bed. Eleanor tightens her grip as she begins to pray. Her forceful words speak to the spirits battling to retain Bernadette as their own. Over and over Eleanor commands the spirits of ungodliness to flee.

Feelings of distrust and anger rival Bernadette's desire to surrender in an effort to maintain residence inside her.

On and on Eleanor declares and decrees Bernadette's deliverance.

"Jesus. Jesus. Jesus. Jesus forgive me for my sin…forgive me Lord…"

Those words from Bernadette's mouth assist two generations in bridging the gap of separation. For the first time in her life, Bernadette spends the night resting in Eleanor's embrace.

CHAPTER 20

In a split second the expression on Hayes' face turns from happy to one of loathing. Bernadette follows his gaze.

"Is she stalking us, Hayes?" Bernadette inquires when she spies Renata headed their way.

Her provocative swagger draws the attention of others.

"What do you want?" Hayes growls when she stops at his table. They discharge looks of hatred toward one another like ammunition from a semi-automatic weapon.

Renata eyes Bernadette, then chuckles.

Hayes abruptly stands, overturning his chair in the process. "You will not cross the line by disrespecting my lady with your foolishness."

Renata boldly draws an imaginary line with the tip of her Italian boot then crosses it with an exaggerated step.

Bernadette moves to the edge of her seat.

Another step brings Renata within a millimeter of Hayes. She tilts her head upward to look Hayes directly in the eyes. "You can play the protective man in front of your new fool if you want," she shouts drawing more attention. "You and I know what you really are, don't we? You're a no good dog who impregnates women then leaves them to fend for themselves." Renata turns to Bernadette. "I suggest you give that dog back to the pound before he turns on you the way he has every woman who thought he could become a human."

Bernadette leaps to her feet. Hayes moves between the two of them. He makes eye contact with the manager headed in their direction. Cold words deliver his opinion, "It is clear who the *lady* is here. Depart from *her* presence."

The manager takes Renata's arm. She shakes free. With head held high she saunters toward the exit.

The drive to Bernadette's house is a silent one. Within that silence every red flag attached to Hayes' displays of questionable behavior wave before Bernadette's eyes.

"I cannot come in like I planned," Hayes says facing Bernadette when he parks in front of her house.

"I only invite people I know into my home. I don't know who you are."

He grasps her hands. "Do not judge me by what may or may not be true. You know I slept with her. If her words are true, today is the first I know of this."

It does not take a high IQ to know Hayes' next destination. Despite what has transpired Bernadette speaks with concern. "You shouldn't go to Renata until you're thinking rationally."

Hayes disagrees. Their heated exchange escalates with neither hearing the other. Bernadette leaves the car in anger. Hayes speeds away in the same state.

Five minutes later Hayes dials Bernadette from his cell phone. "Forgive me. I did not mean to be brisk with you. Are we one?"

No response.

"Pray with me, Twinkle."

Bernadette hangs up.

The phone immediately rings after she disconnects from Hayes. Recognizing Treva's number she picks up. "What's up, sis?"

A synopsis of her dinner with Falimah minus the physical abuse is relayed. Bernadette shares Renata's public performance minus the possible pregnancy.

Treva prays for both their eyes to be opened and for guidance on how to proceed with the adversity before them. Most of all she prays that regardless of how they feel they will yield to God's direction.

Hayes' journey from his car to Renata's front door seems eternal. The slow walk is interrupted when Renata's nosey neighbor cuddling her toy poodle calls out to him. He hopes his nod of acknowledgement will send her away. It does not.

"Hayes." she shouts making her way toward him. "I haven't seen you around for a long time."

Hayes wisely does not offer an explanation.

"Look at you walking around looking like a fashion plate." She shifts the dog to her hip allowing her free hand to roam the lapel Hayes' mint green suit woven with silver threads. Inwardly he groans knowing her hands have touched every inch of her dog.

Compliments for the labyrinth design of his freshly braided hair are given as she scratches the underside of the spoiled canine. He is grateful she is not tall enough to reach his head.

"Lean down so I can get a closer look."

"I am in a hurry ma'am," he says moving up the walkway.

Hayes looks over his shoulder as he rings the bell. The neighbor is still standing there.

Crisp steps upon a parquet floor become louder and louder. Anxiously, he waits. There is no response after several more pushes of the bell.

"I know you can hear me Renata. May I come in please?"

"No!"

Hayes has come too far to leave now.

His persistence pays off. Renata opens the door. She steps onto the porch, then stoically commands him to speak.

For the second time in recent history Hayes is at a loss for words. Renata does not ease his discomfort with her ferocious glower.

"Were your words today true or just a ploy to place a wedge between me and Bernadette?"

"Both," she snarls.

He inwardly processes. *It has been at least eight months since we parted company, nine since we last slept together. Full term should be her current state if she became pregnant at our last encounter.*

"What happened to the baby, Renata?" Hayes demands.

With no detectable trace of emotion, Renata tells Hayes there is no need to inform him about her personal business.

"I have the right!" he shouts with every intension of getting the information he seeks.

Words sharp enough to penetrate titanium assault Hayes. "You gave up your rights when every effort I made to contact you turned into an opportunity to show your disgust for me."

He wrestles with himself to sequester words that, if verbalized, could well spur the often unpredictable Renata Taylor into physical combat. Shoving a hand deep into his pants pockets, he grips the two one hundred dollars bill inside the money clip he habitually carries. Hayes stomps halfway down the stairs only to return to the landing where the battle for control ends.

On and on he rants about her not giving him the consideration he deserved in the matter. The tirade ceases when he sees who Renata has become – a woman who no longer cares about what is best for him at the cost of her integrity.

"Your act is old and your spell over me has been forever broken. I ended up pregnant and rejected by a man who never really cared about me. Your cruelty shed light on what I blinded myself to."

Renata moves close to Hayes. Her whisper screams loudly in his ears. "Once I hang up you are to expunge the memory of my existence from your mind. Do you remember those words?"

Hayes blinks remembering them all too well, but refrains from responding.

"You're a cold-hearted *dog* for saying that to me. I tried everything I could to get those words out of my head, but I couldn't. Despite every effort those words would not leave me. They haunted me day and night until I gave in and did what you asked."

Her tears fall like torrential rains.

For the first time in months, concern for Renata's well being pluck at Hayes' heart strings.

"I was carrying your child, but you were so wrapped up in yourself I was never able to tell you. To grant your wish, I had an abortion. I thought that would *expunge* you and the existence of your child from my mind, body and soul."

Temporary insanity succinctly describes Hayes' state as his very soul seems to leave his body. Visions of his hands around her throat loom before him. Deep within he hears, *be angry and sin not*. Those repetitive words become the eraser causing thoughts of violence to dissipate. When sanity returns Hayes growls, "How could you?"

"It wasn't hard after the way you treated me. I could do what I did because I learned how to be an uncaring dog from the master – you. You are a *dog and a half* and I caught your fleas when I laid down with you."

Powerful words open a gaping wound in Hayes' ego. Pain shows on the face of a man used to controlling women in current and post-relational encounters.

"Let me ask you something, Hayes. Am I messing with your mind because I didn't want to walk around town with my belly stuck out a country mile with your baby while you lay up with your new woman?"

Intentionally cruel words aimed at Hayes' pride hit their mark. His wound is now weeping.

"Do you hate me, Renata?"

A gasp catches in her throat. Hayes is pushed backwards. "Listen you arrogant *canine*. I just told you I aborted our child. As usual your only concern is you. The answer to your question is that I can't hate you. Once I saw you for the dog you really are, I couldn't hate you for acting out on your natural tendencies."

"I am not a *dog!*" Hayes declares in an effort to assuage guilt mounting by the moment.

Renata moves in for the kill. "I don't believe in Darwinism. If you're born a *dog*, you'll die a *dog*. Within your species there are many breeds. You may have put away your Pit Bull demeanor to pick up your current Lap Dog look, but a *dog* is still a *dog*. You just have a new owner and yard to play in."

Hayes takes a step forward. Renata takes a step backwards clenching her fists.

Hayes moves backwards with his hands upraised. "I did not mean to do that."

"*I* am the *lady* of this property. Depart from *my* presence," Renata spits out before disappearing inside her home.

Hayes returns to his car embracing his anger. In doing so it becomes the deterrent that keeps him from addressing what his callous actions have done to a woman who only sought to love him.

CHAPTER 21

Cosmetology skills assist Treva's quest to cover the circles under her eyes, but do not conceal emotions that question her current state.

For the first time in her walk towards the Cross, prayer has not yielded the answer she seeks as to why she should not rid herself of Falimah.

Falimah Meyer, her alleged friend and sister sank to an all time low in the realm of evil by leaving a message on Treva's home recorder the night before. A message that left her sleepless and revisiting pain she has sought to overcome.

Throughout the night Treva replayed recorded words from her once cherished friend stating she forgave Treva's ignorance. Falimah's Saccharin coated venom told Treva she understood her lack of understanding regarding what a *real* woman does to keep her man satisfied. After all, Treva's inability stemmed from not having a *mother* of her own to teach her what a *real* woman should know about men.

In the midst of her vow to totally cut the cord came a still small voice – *"forgive her for she knows not what she does."*

From behind the wheel of his car, Hayes peers at people rushing toward the church.

The young and old are dressed in their finest carrying bibles, tablets and other assorted paraphernalia that will assist their needs for the evening. A handful of men escort their wives. Others walk briskly without so much as offering help to those in need.

From the corner of his eye, Hayes spies a young couple moving away from the crowd toward the shadows of the youth building. He sucks until his cheeks draw inward and his lips become fish-like. How many times as a youth had he used the influx of people coming to a church event as a cover for his personal agenda?

Unconsciously, he rubs his chin with his thumb and index finger. How could he, without any conscience, take the virtue of his sister in Christ behind the very building where they swore to uphold their honor.

Hayes' sense of right and wrong forces him into action. He makes his way to the alcove he so thoughtlessly used for a secret rendezvous. The discovered youth freeze when he calls out to them. Rather than scold, Hayes solicits their help in the sanctuary.

Considerable time spent in prayer helps to calm Bernadette's anger. It also helps to prepare her and her sisters for service.

Anointing flows through each woman as their sincere praise fills the sanctuary. Evidence of total surrender to worship is so prevalent among the majority of the congregation, the pastor comments that if he just gave the benediction, the service would be complete.

After a few acknowledgements, Elder Joseph and Evangelist Addie Lewis are introduced.

Addie walks proudly on Joseph's arm to the dais. He helps her to a chair, and then takes a moment to arrange his notes before speaking.

"This evening has been ordained for the singles. Because we're servants under orders I need you all to understand my wife and I will deliver the message placed in our mouths. Whether you like it or not is on you."

Expressions running the gamut from amusement to offense stare at Joseph.

From her front row seat in the balcony, Treva allows a slight laugh to escape through her coral covered lips. It abruptly halts when she catches sight of Falimah being escorted to a seat on the floor.

The split in her dress, that is just a bit above necessary opens as Falimah puts extra sway in her stride. Her lingering smile that acknowledges Roosevelt before taking her seat brings a frown to Treva's face. That frown deepens when the recently married man Falimah is seated beside fawns all over her while giving her his extra program.

"Go with me to Joshua 24:15. Joseph instructs. He allows them time to find the text before his rich voice delivers the passage long ago committed to memory. *"And if it seem evil unto you to serve the LORD, choose you this day whom ye will serve; whether the gods which your fathers served that were on the other side of the flood, or the gods of the Amorites, in whose land ye dwell: but as for me and my house, we will serve the LORD."*

Joseph looks out at the many faces before him. His bottom teeth rake lightly over his top lip as he taps the lectern. "For those of you who do not speak the Kings' English I'll break it down. Joshua was telling the people he had charge over that they had a choice. They could turn from God and do as they did before, but," his right hand springs outward, "as far as his household was concerned, they were going to serve God."

A few murmurs punctuate the air as Joseph scans his prepared notes. He sips from his glass of water, then presses a lightly starched handkerchief to his lips before stepping around the lectern in order to be closer to the audience.

Joseph looks at his host. "Do I have your permission to get down to it?"

Permission is granted.

"I'm neither a long-winded nor beat around the bush man. Tonight we're going to talk very plain about family responsibility for raising godly offspring."

A few hand claps follow his words.

"We're also going to talk about sex and your choices about it."

Gasps escape into the air.

"Don't y'all take offense. Some of you weren't offended the last time you crawled into bed with someone you weren't married to."

Roosevelt drops his pen. "Big Daddy goin' straight for the throat," he whispers to Nee Nee.

Joseph forges ahead with his oratory.

"Joshua made a choice that his household would serve the Lord. He understood that godliness wasn't something that haphazardly happened. It is something purposely lived. Joshua lived a life of godliness with boldness. So did my daddy. In our house you had two choices. You could live holy or die early."

A hearty amen comes from Will.

Moving closer to those assembled Joseph's expression becomes very serious. "Fathers, it's your responsibility to introduce God and His holiness to your children."

Allen Davis readjusts his reading glasses as Joseph connects biblical truths of the responsibilities of fathers with examples set for him by his own father and other male family members.

Joseph presses forth blending scripture with the good, not so good and just plain wrong choices he has made. He even shares the pain of his manhood being questioned because of stances he took.

Taking a step closer to his audience his frank words speak of how he struggled to keep his physical yearning for Addie under control during their courtship. Surprisingly, he confesses that he almost lost the battle.

Smugness crosses many faces in the sanctuary.

Bernadette and her sisters shake their fingers at their mother, who points at their father then winks at them. Commitment to service inspires Joseph to share the pain of the ridicule he endured because of his determination to come to the altar a virgin.

Hayes leans forward as Joseph speaks clearly of how he struggled to the point that even the ring he accepted from his father as an outward token of celibacy was no longer a deterrent.

Without reserve, he tells that the battle of the flesh raged within him to the point that he considered paying for physical relief.

The hum of the air conditioning is the only sound during Joseph's pause. He stands more erect than normal, turns to his father and bows. "I am thankful for having a father who taught me what is expected of me as a man of God. His words and the way he lives has made me want to be just like him. As open as he has always been, there were nights I had to stay on my face to keep my mind and my body in check."

Literally every man in the room leans forward.

"When it got so bad that I couldn't concentrate on prayer, I called my daddy. It didn't matter to him. I was his son. I had a need. He prayed me through."

Joseph leans toward his audience. "I know some of you think I was a punk because I was a grown man calling my daddy for help. Let me tell you all something. The fact that I knew I could call on him is a testimony to the godly man he is and the one he raised."

"Ooh," expelling from the mouths of all, sounds like rushing wind in the sanctuary.

Candid commentary regarding mindsets that train young men to *sow their wild oats*, then run to the church house to seek a reputable wife wipes the neutral expression Allen Davis tries to maintain, from his face.

"Fathers want their daughters to come to the altar as virgins, but teach their sons it's okay to lift as many skirts as they can. Why? Because their house doesn't serve the Lord. Do you see how devalued our men have become in the enemy's plan?" Joseph shouts.

Amen's rise in the air like hairs full of static electricity. Hayes looks over his shoulder to find Roosevelt staring at him.

Snide remarks, punctuated by feminine self-righteousness, respond to Joseph's words. Joseph is not amused. "Jump off the high horse, ladies," he instructs. "Some of you are not as innocent as you would have us believe."

Silence falls like cement boots to the bottom of a lake.

"Choose," he says barely above a whisper. "I chose to know by the spirit who Addie was."

Terry and Zavonne sitting on either side of Bernadette tap her hands.

"When I wanted to ask her to be my wife I fasted and prayed. I needed to know if she was the one. The one, who, if I went crazy on the honeymoon she wouldn't rest till she prayed my mind back to sanity."

Hayes turns and makes eye contact with Roosevelt.

"Go on with your bad self," Roosevelt shouts as he wraps his arm around Nee Nee.

Joseph's onyx colored hand stretches toward his wife. She stands. "Blessed. Bringing happiness, pleasure, or contentment, to invoke Divine favor upon. Take a long look at my blessing. The Word says, "Whoso findeth a wife findeth a good thing, and obtaineth favour of the LORD. His favor has covered our marriage."

Joseph goes to his wife. Only they understand the expressions they exchange. Taking Addie's arm, Joseph escorts her to the landing.

Addie moves down the center aisle. Anointed gray eyes see beneath the surface of expressions worn to give an artificial aura of perfection.

"She's gonna get us," Nee Nee writes upon Roosevelt's tablet.

"Yes I am," Addie responds to the unseen words. Nee Nee drops her pen.

Wide-eyed stares of a majority of the attendees are trained upon the speaker of the moment.

"Yes, this night has been set aside for the singles, but in order for our children to get to the level of God's expectancy we have to deal with parents because we're their teachers."

With eyes closed she recites I Corinthians 6:19. *"Know ye not that your body is the temple of the Holy Ghost which is in you, which ye have of God, and ye are not your own?"*

Addie can literally feel tension creeping into the room.

"Let me make that scripture plain. Your body is the temple where the Holy Spirit, who comes from *God* and who is *God*, resides. You are not your own. You belong to *God*."

Despair settles upon some faces that look neither left nor right.

Attempts to look unscathed by words reaching beneath the surface to upset previously comfortable mindsets are chuckled at.

Cloaked in heavenly authority, Addie walks to and fro before those her particular words are prescribed. "My husband received generational wisdom from his daddy that came from his daddy. Wisdom orchestrated his being the head of his wife, children and a household that serves the Lord."

Roosevelt pulls Nee Nee close.

"Joe wanted a godly wife. I wanted a godly husband as close to being the man my father was as I could possible have."

Laughter from some is not successfully muffled.

"You all can laugh if you want, but I know what I know. My father set my sister and me up for success by infusing the values of godliness into us. Because he did, I refused to accept any less in the man I'd marry."

"I know that's right!" Terry shouts.

"If you haven't been blessed with parents looking out for you, bring the young man or woman you say you're in love with to the church so we can see them. They need to know that you're joined to people of standard who come from somebody," Addie shouts lifting her free hand heavenward. "The fact that we're checking them out tells them you are valuable to us and we're watching out to see what you may not."

Hayes unconsciously rocks in his seat.

Walking around the sanctuary with her eyes closed, but with the vision of a sighted woman she stops a few feet from Falimah. "You're so valuable to God."

Addie moves on. "We often forget our value as we are exposed to promotions that demonstrate a variety of ways to give ourselves away. With that come options of how to avoid disease and pregnancies. The bombardment of needing to have a man or a woman in our lives is so constant that we will allow ourselves to be degraded for the sake of fulfilling what we consider a valid need. We even answer the mating call in songs penned for no other reason than igniting sexual flames."

Addie pauses to allow her words to sink in before singing a stanza from one of the most sexually suggestive songs in the country. When she sings, *"I'm gonna get it first, I got a virgin thirst"* her voice becomes more sensual than the original artist. Men and women twist and turn in their seats.

"My daddy made it clear to Joe that I was a temple undefiled, a virgin, and would remain so until I became a wife."

"A virgin." Addie places her hand over her mouth. The expression upon her face is that of her possibly having slipped and said a profane word. Removing her hand she says it a little louder, *"Virgin."* She repeats the word several more times. "You saved yourself for me, didn't you baby?" she says over her shoulder to Joseph.

"Yes ma'am!"

"I appreciated the fact that neither my husband nor I had prior experience. When Joe proposed, I knew he was pure. We have grown together and it has been a marvelous journey."

Roosevelt tenderly strokes Nee Nee's hand.

"Being a virgin on your wedding night is literally unheard of among you men, isn't it?"

Many concede rather sheepishly. A single tear spills from her eye. Total silence blankets the room.

As frankly as her husband, Addie speaks of the strong physical attraction the two had toward one another prior and during their engagement. The look of shock on some the faces make her laugh. "I am a woman of God, but I'm also a woman. Joe's been fine from the womb."

Nee Nee shakes her head up and down. "She's right about that. If he looks this good now, I can't imagine what he looked like thirty years ago."

"Isn't your name Mrs. Roosevelt Hillis?" Roosevelt whispers.

"Yes it is, but that hasn't blurred my vision. Twinkle's daddy is fine as can be!"

Roosevelt blows her a kiss.

"More than his good looks, it was Joe's intellect and love of God that kept me percolating. Be that as it may, I knew premarital sex and other activities that include what you all pretend is not sex so you indulge in it, could not take place."

Conviction spreads through the sanctuary like a flash fire inside a paper factory.

"The outcome of your situation boils down to a choice. *Know ye not that ye are the temple of God, and that the Spirit of God dwelleth in you...for the temple of God is holy.* Are you listening to me, Israel?"

Falimah is not listening. Her focus is upon the man beside her. Every smile she gives him is reciprocated with a silly grin. After his third display of foolishness, his wife places his arm in a tight grip.

Falimah crosses her legs giving, a generous view of her thigh. The lips of her male neighbor part like the Red Sea as Falimah feigns interest in Addie's words.

"How many in here can honestly say you're striving to keep your temple holy?"

Light, dark, toffee, bejeweled and unadorned hands move upward.

"Some of you are lying. In fact, some of you have been roaming around like heat seeking missiles. You're so hot that if a man or woman of interest sat down beside you right now you'd spontaneously combust. I won't point you out."

Addie's eyes close again.

"Some of you have the nerve to come into the house of God and flaunt yourself before godly men in an attempt to sway him from God for self satisfaction."

The church member's wife leans across her husband to glare at Falimah.

"Oh I know you all don't want to listen to this woman tonight, but I pray you hear me. Your body is the temple of the Holy Spirit. You don't have to defile it to please others. Stop listening to the devil picking at you because you choose to live holy."

Treva writes furiously in an effort to capture the moment – *My house will serve the Lord. My body is the temple of the Holy Spirit.*

"Ladies!" Addie shouts, "When you lower your standards to get something, you don't get what you deserve. Far too many of you miss your blessings because you're spreading yourself around like, excuse my English, *a temple whore.*"

"Preach mother, preach!" Nee Nee shouts.

Addie's blunt words disarm the appearance of propriety as seemingly staunch-minded men reveal true traits as they snicker and not so covertly point in the general direction of a past conquest.

Joseph quickly approaches the people with a microphone of his own. "Excuse me brothas, but while you're shouting and acting so pious, remember this, a temple whore can't be successful without a *whore monger.*

Large helpings of self-righteousness lodge in throats and choke egotistical men like a fish bone.

"Despite your past, which may be as recent as a few hours ago you can choose this day to serve the Lord," Joseph adds.

Addie moves about the sanctuary. She can see opposition to the message she and Joseph have been sent to deliver, on many faces. The resistant looks do not make her tentative.

"Some of you have been sleeping from woman to woman or man to man. You thought it was okay because it was your right. You forgot you were playing with the emotions of an eternal soul. You casually got out of that bed looking for another conquest, not knowing if your actions created a life. You're called to be men and women of standard. You're not to run hither and yon like mongrel dogs whenever it suits your desire. *You* can *choose* to change."

Indescribable heat surges through Hayes.

"Someone in here is angry. You're so angry you're on a mission to destroy the happiness of everyone around you. *You* can *choose* to let go of the anger. When you let go of it, you can get to the root of your fears."

Walking up the center aisle Addie senses something very strong. "Pride goeth before the fall. You need to confess even your secret sin before you can go to the next level. God wants you whole. He wants you to be free of anything that will separate you from Him. *Choose* you this day whom you will serve."

Bernadette stares intently as she processes words that from birth were seemingly mixed with the milk from her mother's breast. She is so submerged in her own thoughts, that she does not hear her parents extend the altar call. What she clearly hears comes from within. *"Don't be afraid, I AM with you."*

Sturdy legs that can easily hurdle a four-foot hedge seem unstable. *"I AM with you."* She scoots to the edge of her seat. *"I AM with you."* Hands that do not seem to be her own lift her upward.

Bernadette hurries to the altar. Joseph extends his microphone to her. Her eyes meet those of Hayes. Vertical nodding of his head extends his support.

"If you want to be free, it begins with your decision. We lived holy in our home because there were no other options. With all I've been taught I chose to disregard what I know to be right because the man I love is leaving me."

Those who know of the blossoming romance between Hayes and Bernadette lean forward.

"When I offered myself to him in an effort to keep him here, he chose to serve the Lord by turning me away."

Looks of shock, disbelief and self-righteousness stare at her. Addie takes her hand.

"A lot of you are wondering why I would choose to disclose my madness before you and my parents. The greater question is why not? If Christ can publicly give His life for my sins, the very least I can do is to publicly lay that sin at His feet."

Tears fall from Roosevelt's eyes.

"I have repented and I know I have been forgiven, but keeping this to myself would cause me to live a lie. A lie because keeping the secret would taint every word I would try to minister to the youth who look up to me. It would be a lie because the truth of my words would not reach someone God is calling at this very moment. And what is that truth? The truth is that God knows our sins and He still loves us and is waiting for us to confess and repent so we can step out of darkness."

Hayes boldly marches up the center aisle to stand beside Addie. She hands him her microphone.

"I am faced with the reality of having been a Christian of convenience. I was that man slipping in and out of the beds while professing to love God. My choice to surrender everything to God opened the door of right knowledge. Lack of full understanding led me to believe myself exonerated from the sins of my past. Though I am forgiven, there is much required of me in order to grow into the disciple God is calling me to be."

Hayes steps forward. Strong words thunder from his mouth. "It is about choosing obedience. Do not allow your position, the moment of embarrassment your confession might bring, guilt or shame to keep you bound. God is standing waiting for you. There is nothing you have done, *He* will not *forgive. You* have to *choose* to surrender to Him. When you do, I guarantee you God will meet your needs."

Hayes returns the microphone to Addie, then falls upon the altar. With no care of who is watching, he openly sobs and asks for forgiveness.

Roosevelt makes his way to Hayes' side.

CHAPTER 22

Bernadette feels like a thoroughbred awaiting the opening of the racing gates. Her breathing is shallow and her thoughts are charged with strategy as to how to broach the subject of her public disclosure to her mother.

Her peripheral view of Addie behind the wheel of Will's Cadillac yields no detectable sign of what her mood may be.

Their ride is a silent one as Addie maneuvers through streets made familiar by her frequent visits to the city.

In the moment of uncertainty Bernadette turns her attention to the foot traffic.

Men and women on their way to or from a variety of destinations, leisurely stroll arm in arm or singularly.

Girls barely into their teens push strollers with one or two wide-eyed or sleeping babies as if it were high noon. Her heart aches for the walking and wheeled children on the way to their destinations. The pain intensifies as she speculates many of them have no idea of what their preordained destination is.

Bernadette's head feels as if it weighs a ton. She looks at Addie. Throughout years of searching for her place in the world, her mother has always been her confidante. At this moment, she feels as lost as she presumes some of the unknown teens strolling down Rainier Avenue may be.

Slowly she raises her head from the support of the padded headrest. Addie places her right hand upon Bernadette's clasped ones. Despite her current state the soothing touch of her mother is a comfort.

Without taking her eyes from the curving road, Addie opens the door to conversation. "Bernadette, what you did tonight took a lot of courage, especially in front of your father and me."

Visions of her wrestling with Hayes across the floor loom before her. "I'm sorry, Mama."

Addie pats her hand, glances over, then returns her focus to the road. "Hayes turning you away is a sign of his growth, especially given his reputation."

Direct words express Addie's concern. Tension again seizes Bernadette.

"Keep talking to me, baby," she gently prods.

Bernadette's attempt to explain her actions are spoken just above a whisper.

"There's no need in you soft-peddling now. Speak up."

Bernadette hurriedly tells every detail of what she tried to do and how Hayes handled the situation.

Addie's hands grip the steering wheel.

"Do you forgive me, Mama?"

The car comes to a slow roll as they approach the security gate of the Plantation. No response is given until Addie brings the car to a halt at Bernadette's front door. "A month ago you were willing to give yourself to Hayes because he is leaving. What will you do in the next week?"

Bernadette is not surprised to see the lights on in her home. She lets herself in, then makes her way to the kitchen where she knows Joseph is waiting for her.

The medium starched cuffs of Joseph's professionally laundered shirt are rolled up, exposing his strong forearms. Without turning from the stenciled scripture wall, he says, "As for me and my house, *we will* serve the Lord."

She goes to his side. Instinctively, she wraps his around her the same way she did when she sought his protection as a child.

The simple question asked by Addie, is the same one Joseph poses. "Hayes is leaving soon. How do you plan to handle yourself?"

For the first time in her life, Bernadette senses vulnerability in the man who has always been her earthly source of strength.

"Do you forgive me, Daddy?"

"Yes I do. Now tell me how you plan to handle things from here on out."

Desperate to erase the pain her actions have brought, Bernadette relays what happened the night she went to Hayes. Her valiant attempt to shine Hayes' reputation falls upon deaf ears of a man making his way to her sleeping quarters. She follows and finds him before an aged oak encased mirror. His outstretched arms invite her to him.

Joseph gazes thoughtfully at his daughter before asking her to describe herself to him. Adamant words says she believes them to share many of the same traits.

Bernadette allows him to seat her on the edge of the bed.

He kneels before her. "I've done my best to bring you up to value yourself."

"But?" she whispers.

"I can't be with you everywhere you go, but God is always with you. When His gaze is upon you, it's important that the reflection He sees is His. Be His daughter."

Bernadette slides to the floor. Joseph embraces her the way he always has when she has come to him in need or just to be close.

"You love this boy, Bernadette?"

"Yes, Daddy."

"Do you know him, Bernadette?"

Silence.

"Have you prayed to know who he really is? Do you know him by the spirit?"

Bernadette is unable to sleep.

Lying in darkness her inner thoughts whirl like debris in a funnel cloud.

Lilac sheets softly rustle as Bernadette's right hand seeks the bible next to her. She turns on the bedside lamp with her free hand. Thumbing through pages she is not sure what she should read. The book of Joshua catches her eye. Gently pages are turned. Chapter 9. *And they went to Joshua...We be come from a far country...And the men made victuals, and asked not counsel at the mouth of the Lord...And Joshua made peace with them, and made a league with them...And Joshua called for them, and he spake unto them, saying, Wherefore have ye beguiled us, saying...*

Revelation floods her head like overflowing river banks. Joshua entered into a covenant with an unknown tribe because he had not sought counsel of the Lord to know their true spirit.

Throughout her life, Bernadette has always prayed to know who people around her are – until now. This time she has not prayed and blindly attached herself to Hayes for purely intellectual and physical reasons.

Bernadette goes to her knees to pray. "Father forgive me. I have entered into a relationship with a man I did not ask You about. I pray that by Your Spirit what I should know about Hayes, You will reveal."

Bernadette's eyes pop wide open. The remnant of her dream is so vivid that distinguishing between reality and fantasy takes a concerted effort.

She is standing before three doors. Although she wants to enter the first door, something keeps her from doing so.

Inside the third door she relishes the love and attention lavished upon her, but all too soon she is escorted back to the porch. She runs to the middle door. It is locked. Pushing and kicking loosens it slightly. As she continues the foundation beneath her begins to quake.

A voice from above advises her to leave. The warning is ignored. Using her own power she is able to get the door open. When she crosses the threshold, she plummets downward into an abyss of darkness.

Bernadette awakens clawing at the air. Flaying hands send her bible flying. Slowly she gains her bearings. When she is calm enough she turns on the light and then picks up her bible. Crinkled pages of the open text are carefully smoothed. Two lavender highlighted passages attract her attention. *Trust in the Lord with all your heart; and lean not unto thine own understanding. In all thy ways acknowledge Him and He shall direct thy paths.*

***

Falimah's apology does not receive the response she expected.

Instead of accepting the empty words, Treva scrutinizes Falimah standing in the doorway as if she were attempting to sell her snake oil.

Treva walks away without closing the door.

Falimah enters a house as familiar to her as her own. She finds Treva sitting in the midst of the couch in her sunken entertainment room.

Without speaking, Falimah sits opposite her. She removes leather boots not yet broken in, then picks up a nearby magazine and thumbs through it.

Treva walks over snatches the magazine, throws it to the floor then returns to the couch.

Falimah's hard stare does not unnerve her. "You're supposed to be my friend and my sister, but when push comes to shove you turn on me."

Falimah's expression does not change.

"Your act is old. You came over here to apologize, but you don't really mean it. It's just what you do to keep a bit of peace in the family."

Treva leans back. For the first time in years, she really sees the woman she gave control to. Today her newfound strength is reclaiming it.

"You've been dogging me for years with my permission, but that stops today. Once upon a time you had my unconditional love. From here on out, whatever you get from me you'll have to earn. I accept your apology because you were woman enough to extend it, but I'll be watching my back."

This unexpected introduction to who Treva has become snatches the evil from Falimah's double-edged tongue before she has opportunity to speak.

Tender feet are shoved back into boots that should be carried. The matching purse and Treva's magazine are snatched from the floor before Falimah stomps toward the exit like an insolent child being sent to their room.

"Falimah!" Treva calls out.

Falimah pauses, and then turns with a wry smile.

"You don't want to try fooling with me on the job. And you don't want to be fool enough to make another move on Brian. Doing either one will get you hurt."

CHAPTER 23

"And the LORD said unto Moses, Yet will I bring one plague more upon Pharaoh...afterwards he will...And it came to pass, that at midnight the LORD smote all the firstborn..."

Hayes feels as though the ache coursing through him will never subside. Its steady course, from one end of his body to the other, is destroying the image of the honorable man he believed himself to be.

Tension pounds at his temples. Tears splatter the pages of his bible. Closing his eyes does not stop the flow. He embraces himself as his body rocks to and fro, mourning the loss of his aborted child.

Moans turn to wails that he tries to muffle beneath layers of bedding. Tears and mucus saturate the rumpled linens. From his prone position he cries out. "Father forgive me for being a blind man. Everything Renata said about me is true. It is my cruelty that killed my baby. My heart was as hard as Pharaoh's and I would not hear you."

The need to mend what now separates him from Bernadette fuels Hayes' longing to be in her presence. He makes the fifteen minute drive from his house to hers, in ten.

He sits outside the gate for some time before setting fear aside and pressing the button that will alert Bernadette to his presence. Relief replaces anxiety when the gates recess, allowing his entry.

To his chagrin, he is eyed like a stranger when Bernadette answers his knock.

"Please allow me to speak."

Bernadette's slight nod is his permission to continue.

"Renata's words were half true. She was pregnant and left to fend for herself. She, she, she aborted our child," he manages to blurt out. His determination to remain strong is lost when a tear makes a downward trek from his right eye.

"I did not know." He pauses. "Had I been more considerate, she would have had the opportunity to tell me."

Bernadette leans against the door.

"It is one thing to ask to be shown who you are. It is humbling when the vision you are shown is indeed that of filthy rags." Hayes' hand goes to his midsection, then moves slowly upward stopping at his breastbone. "I have learned I cannot begin my journey toward wholeness until I acknowledge and confess all my sins."

His eyes close. "Wash me thoroughly from mine iniquity, and cleanse me from my sin...create in me a clean heart, O God; and renew a right spirit within me...The sacrifices of God are a broken spirit: a broken and a contrite heart..."

"Why are you telling me this?"

Sooty eyes open. Hayes' stare implores her to ingest the sincerity of his words. "Two reasons. My determination is to never again be the man I was."

Bernadette grasps the solid brass doorknob. "Your second reason?"

"Intimacy. I need you to always be able to see into me. There can be no secrets between us. I want us to be so close that at times we are literally one." He touches her hand still upon the doorknob. "Be angry and sin not."

Bernadette's nose wrinkles as she tilts her head. "What?"

"I know those were the words you prayed for me the night I went to Renata. I could hear them clearly. It was your prayers that kept me out of the legal system. That is the love I need. It is what I desire to render to you."

She accepts the yellow rose he extends, then invites him inside.

Hours pass with them sharing what no one else has been privy to. Bit by bit, what were once glimpses of one another become a panoramic views.

Hayes finds Roosevelt and Nee Nee at the dinner table.

He deposits his shoulder bag and coat, washes his hands, then takes a fork from the drawer. Nee Nee's harsh glare halts his forward movement.

"If you were a good wife, my food would be waiting for me," he teases.

"She's a great wife and my food was ready when I sat down at my table. It's good too." Roosevelt interjects before placing a forkful of food into his mouth. "Your problem is that you need to get it together, so you'll be in right position to get you a wife and get outta my house."

Hayes laughs at Roosevelt's rhetoric. "I will remain in this abode with my wife and children forever, my friend."

"Oh, I know you smokin' somethin' 'cause tight as we are I guarantee you, you and your brood will not be movin' up in here."

Nee Nee seconds that.

"Why don't you let me handle my personal business please, Mrs. Hillis?" Hayes responds to Nee Nee's remarks.

"I would if you weren't so slow. Come close to me."

Hayes sits at least an arms length from one who might harm him.

"Bernadette Lewis is the perfect woman for you. She loves and respects you. She's the woman you love, respect and admire. So I will reiterate the words of my husband. Get it together!"

He looks for the backup he does not receive from Roosevelt, who is enjoying every moment of Hayes' discomfort. "Like I said persistent woman, you need to allow me to handle my business. Thank you very much."

"I suggest you do something soon just in case her father ain't as calm as he appeared to be the night she told all your business at the altar," Roosevelt laughs.

"I respect her choice of obedience by testifying about what transpired between us."

"What about you, Hayes? When are you going to obey and quit getting ahead of God?"

Hayes' rapidly tapping fingertips tell on him like a spying baby sister.

"That's what I'm talkin' 'bout." Roosevelt snaps. "You start trippin' when I get too close to the truth. You can run past God if you want, but you won't get what He has for you till He gives it to you. So just wait on Him."

***

Morning prayer has become a pact between Bernadette and Treva. Since Bernadette is out of the office until after the New Year holiday, she calls Treva at the office to pray with her.

Today, they are in sync. Spiritual connections join forces to praise and lift up the needs of others without restraint.

After prayer the two make a little small talk.

"I took that advice you gave me," Treva tells Bernadette as she looks out her office window. "I'm real tired of Falimah right now, but I know I'm not supposed to totally withdraw from her. Want to hear something strange?"

"What?"

"The more I pray about it the more I get a sense that it's not all about her stank attitude. It's more about the growth process we both have to go through. I believe once we both shake loose of whatever is in our way, we'll be able to be friends, the way you and I are now."

Treva looks out the window to see Hayes.

"You're not going to believe this, Bernadette." Treva presses her face against the glass. "Hayes is next door. It looks like he's praying over the dirt. Now, he's putting some into a baggy. Do you want me to have security go over and check on him?"

"Leave him alone. I'm sure he has a reason. He'll tell me if he needs to."

"Are you sure he's not over there conjuring up some kind of spirit?"

Bernadette laughs.

"Alright," Treva teases, "but don't say I didn't warn you if he tries to put a root on ya."

Bernadette hangs up laughing. On impulse, she dials Marabel's. The last pair of shoes has been sold. An online bidder paid four thousand dollars for them.

***

From the drawer of his desk Hayes, pulls out a leather bound journal. Imprinted in gold across the front are the words '*Pathway to Independence*'.

He turns to the section titled '*Projections*' that is divided into three sections. Goals from the previous year are studied. Delaying the expansion of his clothing line until this year allowed him to build capital to be used at a more opportune time. That time presented itself six months earlier. With that in place, his client base has almost tripled.

After tithes and offerings the increase in earnings has allowed him to reinvest a sizeable sum back into the business. A second portion went into a venture promising handsome returns. What remained he split between a deposit into his retirement account and a principle payment on the loan on his bookstore.

In order to minimize gasoline expenses, Hayes sold the Hummer. Rather than purchase a new car for himself he negotiated a lower price of a new Toyota Camry, paid for it in cash, and then asked his pastor to gift it to someone in need. He then took possession of his mother's debt-free Lexus, which had been parked in her garage since his father gifted her with a new BMW for her birthday two months earlier.

Hayes turns to the section where next year's goals are written. A few notations are made beside line items. The outstanding amount due on the Tacoma store is studied. Plans to prepay the loan have moved faster than he anticipated. He makes a note to begin looking for a suitable investment to shelter his disposable income when the building is paid off.

In bold letters, he adds a goal to next year's plan. With care he reads the statement he has rehearsed many times in the seclusion of his home, car and offices. They are words that will forever change his life if acted upon. His hand pauses a mere inch above the page as he considers whether or not to erase the entry.

The decision to move ahead closes the book and sends Hayes out the door to take the next step towards destiny.

Joseph declines Hayes' offer to make him a cup of coffee.

Hayes takes a seat. He chuckles as he studies the back of this unusual man, making tea.

"Are you upset about our confessions?" Hayes asks.

Steamy liquid is stirred, but no response is given.

"If your concern is whether my past habits might be a problem health wise for Twinkle, I can assure you they are not. I have abstained from sexual activity for close to a year. No drug has entered my system in over five years. I would not kiss Twinkle's finger if there were a remote possibility of transmitting anything to her."

"Why are you telling me this?" Joseph asks moving to the seat next to Hayes.

"As her father, you need to know all there is about the man who desires to marry your daughter."

Joseph moves close enough to feel every breath exiting Hayes' mouth. Ever so slightly he nods, giving Hayes permission to continue.

"I do not sit before you seeking to announce my financial holdings. I believe the content of my character is of greater importance to you."

Joseph nods.

"Devotion to God, integrity and dedication to the marriage covenant is what you require of any man seeking Twinkle's hand in matrimony. I have prayed that you and your family would come to know me by the spirit. I believe that this has transpired. You know me to be a man whose life is transforming. I am the one who will love her more than you already do, Mr. Lewis."

"Why do you want to marry my daughter?"

"Because of who she is." Taking a step toward boldness, Hayes does not hold back a single detail of his relationship with Renata, including the argument he and Bernadette had prior to him confronting Renata about the abortion.

Joseph's facial expression remains unchanged.

"When we argued, my words were foolish and prideful. Regardless of my madness, she prayed. I could literally feel Twinkle covering not just me, but also Renata with her prayers."

Joseph sets his cup aside. "You're a pretty confident man aren't you? Down home we call men like you Slick Mouth Johnnies."

"I have been bred to be a confident man. At one time, your definition would concisely define my previous motives. I am no longer that man. Who you see before you today is a man who is confident in his like, love and respect for Twinkle – the woman I want as my wife."

Sitting forward Joseph asks, "What makes you think you're worthy of my daughter?"

Hayes replies without hesitation. "Someone once told me that marriage has more to do with how purposes line up than physical attraction and emotional compatibility. Although the latter two are important, the first is priority. We have shared our known purposes and I know that they are compatible for our marriage and most of all for the Kingdom. I will give her space to grow as I grow with her. Part of that growth includes challenges to who we are. You have been her covering since conception. I am spiritually and intellectually able to assume that position without a lapse in coverage."

Joseph takes a long sip from his mug before asking, "What does my daughter need?"

Hayes' grin is wide. "She needs spontaneity, romance, a bottomless pot of greens and an unlimited source of shoes." He pauses, rubs his chest then continues. "Twinkle is a hard lover. When she gives, she gives her all. So do I. She needs and has my heart, my prayers, friendship and my utmost respect. I will be the husband who leads her without seeking to control her, because she would never succumb to such nonsense."

"What about children?"

"We both want three or four."

Joseph adds a splash of lemon to his tea. "Twinkle's the head of a rising corporation. Would you expect her to give it up for you?"

Hayes squares his shoulders to assert his physical manhood. "I am more than able to care for my wife. More than that, I am able to respect what she has built. What Twinkle is doing is attached to the purpose I have been called to. I plan to purchase the property next door to Covenant Place."

Hayes' words unlock Joseph's businessman door. "For what purpose?"

"When I return from Washington, I will open a school for deaf children." Reaching into his shoulder bag, Hayes pulls out a baggy filled with dirt. "I walked the property lines and prayed. I *will* take possession of the land I have been assured is mine."

Hayes studies Joseph's silence. "What is on your mind?" he finally asks.

"You say you'll give Twinkle room to grow and that you know she won't be controlled. Who will be the head of your house when the two of you don't agree?"

"God."

"Being a husband is serious business. If you were listening to me the other night, you heard me say that before I put the ring on my wife's finger, I went to the Lord. You need to hear Him and not jump ahead of His timing."

Joseph reaches into his pocket. He draws the knife he compulsively carries from it. "You're headed in the right direction, and most men would wrap their daughters up with a bow and place them in your hands. I'm not most men."

"Neither am I," Will says from the doorway. "You doin' whatcha should by comin' to see my son 'bout Twinkle, but he ain't the only man you gonna have ta deal with when it comes to her."

Hayes feels unusually calm for a man being hit with blasts from both barrels of the Lewis' shotgun. He stands and graciously offers a chair to the man of the house.

CHAPTER 24

Sitting in the simply decorated sanctuary Hayes smiles knowing Zavonne is having the wedding she prefers rather than the Hollywood production of her grandmother's dreams.

Zavonne gave her bridesmaids leeway to design their own dresses. Knowing Bernadette's flair for the unusual, Hayes eagerly awaits her entrance.

Bernadette does not disappoint her fashion-conscious beau when she glides down the aisle as Zavonne's maid of honor.

The most touching part of the ceremony is when Zavonne is escorted to her parents seated on the front pew.

Joseph stands.

Hayes leans forward when Zavonne's left hand is lifted.

Ever so gently she removes the smaller of the two diamond rings and then places it into Joseph's outstretched hand. "I honor God and you, my father, by returning this ring as a sign that I have kept my pledge of virtue."

She salutes Joseph with a formal curtsey. When she rises, Joseph embraces her with tears falling from his eyes.

The reception is the extravagant affair more suited for Eleanor's tastes.

Hayes carries his chair from the table he is assigned to, to the one directly in front of Bernadette at the bride's table. The sight of these two lovebirds silently communicating with each other is amusing to many.

Unable to wait any longer, Hayes leads Bernadette away from the festivities.

"Where are you taking me, Hayes?"

"Some place where we can talk."

He leads her to a suite. His shaking hands struggle to insert the key card. She takes the seat upon the couch. Hayes sits at her feet with his back to her.

Amber oil he applied hours earlier waft upwards. He tells her of his plan to purchase the property next to Covenant Place.

"What?"

He moves to her side. His face is close enough that his lips brush hers as he speaks. "Purpose dictates the property be in our legal possession when we return from Washington, after I graduate."

"When *we* return?"

Hayes goes to his knees before Bernadette. "The first day I met your Grandmother Burton I was warned that if my intensions toward you were not honorable, I was to remove myself from your presence."

Lifting Bernadette's left foot he removes her shoe. With extreme tenderness her foot is massaged.

"What are you doing?

"Shhh…"

Bernadette leans back and closes her eyes.

"I have a present for you," Hayes softly whispers.

Her eyes spring open. Before her is an elaborately wrapped purple and gold package. Hayes' nod encourages her to open it. What is revealed leaves her momentarily speechless.

With the care of a mother picking up her infant, Bernadette removes her gift from the box.

"How did you know?"

"It is my business to know your heart's desire."

Firm, warm hands place her gift – the diamond encrusted shoe from Marabel's upon Bernadette's foot.

"Hayes," she croons. "They feel like they were made just for me. They look just the way I imagined they would."

"But Hayes…"

She tries to express why she cannot accept such an extravagant gift.

Hayes interrupts. "Did you not say that you would marry someone to get these?"

"How did you know that? I never verbalized that to anyone."

"It is about intimacy. What would be the point of allowing you to see into me if I did not care enough to pray so that I might see into you?"

"Hayes?"

"Shhh..."

From the breast pocket of his custom-made suit Hayes removes the ring he designed and had made four months earlier – the first time he entered the words 'propose to Bernadette' inside his life strategy journal.

Upon bended knee, he speaks. "The night we met, my goal was to conquer you physically. As time passed, I came to love you. Since I have met Jesus, I have learned what friendship really means. As we have grown together, love has turned to like."

Her eyes widen.

Hayes clarifies his words. "You can love someone, but not like them. I like you, Bernadette Lewis. I know the changes that have taken place in me because of God and you. I know your time has not been wasted. I found you. I am the best there is for you. Will you marry me?"

Bernadette looks at the shoe on her foot. A single tear makes its way down her face. Words of wisdom flood her head. *Let him get good and saved. Just because a good man finds you doesn't mean you have to bless him with the honor of being his wife. Do you know him? Do you know him by the spirit? You don't have to settle. You have choices.*

"Bernadette, will you marry me?"

No response.

"Will you marry me?"

Bernadette's lips move, but no words come forth.

Hayes' heavy breathing is all that can be heard in the room.

"Bernadette, will you marry me?"

Gently, Bernadette's manicured fingertip outlines Hayes' face. "Please listen carefully to what I have to say."

She pauses, takes a deep breath, then continues.

"As much as I like, love, respect and desire you, I can't accept your proposal."

Hayes is unable to conceal his disappointment.

"Why?" he softly asks.

"When I marry, it will be to a man rooted in and walking with God because it takes more than human love to sustain a marriage. What I have now is good. I won't give it up for the sake of carrying your name. More than that I won't go against what God has told me."

Her finger pressed to his lips halt Hayes' response.

"I've prayed to know you by the spirit. I've been shown a glimpse of who you've been called to be. Because I have, what I cannot do at this time has been revealed."

Hayes looks down at the ring still in his hand. Bernadette continues.

"You've accepted the call upon your life, a call that requires more time alone with God than you would have if we married right now. Accepting this proposal would stunt your spiritual walk. Stop trying to get ahead of God. Slow down and concentrate on being the man you were birthed to be."

Internal fireworks explode filling Hayes' ears with words of wisdom spoken to him in love. *Just 'cause Twinkle's a full package don't mean she's the one you supposed ta have. You have a purpose and a vision and so does she. How do they connect?" It's not about the emotion man, it's 'bout how you guys gonna work together for the Kingdom. You can be a fool and yoke up with pretty, but I'm tellin' ya now, that yoke's gonna bring ya to ya knees if it wasn't supposed ta be on ya in the first place. You can run past God if you want but you won't get what He has for you till He gives it to you. Wait on God.*

"I believe we are right for one another. It's just that now is not the time."

The brilliant platinum and diamond setting with a three-carat center-stone is returned to Hayes' pocket.

"Are we still friends, Hayes?"

The depth of Hayes' dimple does nothing but enhance his physical appeal as he grins up at Bernadette. As tenderly as the shoe was placed on her foot, it is removed.

"Hayes?"

"These shoes will only be worn by my wife."

Bernadette's knees meet the carpet. "Pray with me Hayes," she whispers.

Dear Reader,

     I take this opportunity to thank you for reading Business Unusual. This story was placed in my heart for the specific purpose of (re)focusing our vision upon God, and what He desires for and from our lives. Business Unusual encourages us to take hold of that which can be had for the asking – eternal salvation through relationship with and obedience to God.

     God is a forgiving God who accepts you as you are. Despite the mistakes you have made, the trials you seem unable to overcome, or even the thought that you cannot come to God until you get straight – He still loves you and welcomes you with open arms.

     If you have chosen to accept Christ as your Savior, I congratulate you. I also encourage you to seek a church home in order that your walk with the Lord grows and that you develop into a disciple.

     No life is a mistake or any mistake too great. You were placed on this earth for a specific reason, therefore I say, take hold of that which is yours and walk boldly in **YOUR ASSIGNMENT FOR THE LORD.**

Linda!

On Assignment
Linda F. Beed, D.R.Ed.
Email: lindaonassignment@yahool.com
www.lindabeed.com
ww.lindabeed.blogspot.com
www.myspace.com/lindabeed

1. How would you describe Bernadette to a friend?

2. How does her handling of Falimah's insubordination speak to her walk with Christ?

3. Out of the abundance of the heart the mouth speaketh. Do you believe Bernadette handled the signs of Hayes' questionable character appropriately?

4. Bernadette's dreams spoke to her situation. Why did she choose to ignore them?

5. Many would call members of the Lewis/Burton family interfering. How would you describe them?

6. Hayes began to change as he spent more time with Bernadette. Why do you believe the change did not come during the years spent with Roosevelt and Nee Nee?

7. Does Hayes' friendship with Roosevelt and Nee Nee seem unnatural?

8. Although he professes a desire for change, what do you see as Hayes' major obstacle?

9. Treva is a strong woman in her own right. Do you believe someone like Falimah could use her the way she did?

10. What is the danger of not knowing your value?

11. Are we really responsible for the next generation?

12. Is there danger in disobeying God?

13. Do you know the difference between church attendance and having a relationship with God?

14. Does your house, the temple of the Holy Spirit, serve the Lord?

MORE ACKNOWLEDGEMENTS

Allen, Andrea, Asa, Atise, Bali, Bria, Charles Addison, Charles Ray, Chanel, Chris, Cynthia, Dante', D'Juan, DeAndra, James, Kendall, Khalya, Malika, Marcellous, Montana, Peyton, Ravyn, Raymond, Roger, Shakila, Shayla, Stacy, Quiana, Terra, Terry, Thalia, Tony, Tonya and Treva, – Nana, Auntie/Cousin. Linda has been praying for all of you. Many thanks to: Stacy Hawkins-Adams, Senoria Allen, Gloria Thomas Anderson, Dr. Helane Adams-Androne, Eboni Anglin, Charlotte Antoine, Madelon Beverly-Banks, Kathryn Baker, Monique Baldwin, Leona Beckton, Fauzia Belcher, Sheryl Bell, Kendra Norman-Bellamy, Andre Benjamin, Barbara Benjamin, Ellen Benson, Dr. Gabriel Brooks, Carol Brown, Carolyn Bledsoe, Tarsha Burton, Coni Campbell, Stuart Campbell, Jake & Sharon Corner, Antoinette Daniel, Valerie Davis, Lawrence & Terris Dennis, Kay Ditzenberger, Dr. Ollie Dixon, Dean & Judy Elders, Mother Edyth Gandy, Choclit' Handley, Dottie Hepzibah, LaShaunda Hoffman, Carol Houston, Pastor George Houston, Kellie Howell, Melinda Hughes, Carmen Jones, Harry Johnson, LeAnne Jones, Lisa Kelly, Robin Kelly, Mother Evilena King, Katrishka King, Angela LaBow, Virginia Laird, Meko Lawson, Shunda Leigh, Shawn Lynch, Lucy Marshall, Kevin McAfee, Michelle McGriff, Marvin McWilliams, Gloria Mitchell, Minnie Miller, Gwen Mills, Caroline Mitchell, Mother Charlene Mitchell, Minister Jill Morris, Pastor Neshella Mitchell, Jamila Page, Vivian Phillips, Melissa Reese, Curtis & Cheryl Retic, D. Rodriguez, Seattle Chapter Glory Girls Book Club, Pat L. Simmons, Gina Softley-Singleton, Joanqua Smith, Minnie Smith, Carol Solomon, Chad & Ericka Stewart, Val Taylor, Nefertiti Thomas, Tiffanie Toms, ElDoris Turner, Nekea Valentine, Pat G'Orge-Walker, Gevelle Wagner, Linda Walters, Beverly Wardlow, Audrey Washington, Barbara Washington, Willie Wasson, Dr. Tawnya Pettiford-Wates, Carolyn Williams, GG Williams, Cherri Willingham, Ciji Wilson, Jessie Wornum, Eve Worrell, and Roberta Byrd-Wright. A very special thank you to **Gwendolyn Chambliss** and **Vershean Mobley** of GP Institute of Cosmetology. **Ben Singleton** and **Keith Williams** – thanks for helping me out with the pictures. You are a true blessing.

If there is anyone who has not been mentioned here, please do not take offense. I love each of you who have contributed to bringing this project to fruition.

LOCAL BUSINESS AND ARTISTS

Blu Water Leschi Café: 102 Lakeside Ave. Seattle, WA 98122
(206) 328-2233

Carol's Essentials: 1106 – 23rd Ave. S. Seattle, WA 98122 (206) 322-9390

Casuelitas Island Soul: 2608 S. Judkins, Seattle, WA 98144, (206) 329-1202

Elliott Bay Book Company: 101 S. Main St., Seattle, WA 98104
(206) 624-6600
Flyright Productions – 2304 E Madison, Seattle, WA 98112 206 860-9813

Jones Barbeque: 3810 S. Ferdinand Suite F1 Seattle, WA 98118
(206) 722-4414

Joy Unlimited: 2301 S. Jackson Seattle, WA 98144 (206) 860-9442

Kallaloo: 7820 S. Ferdinand, Seattle, WA 98118 (206) 760-7766

Nubia's: 1117 – 1st Ave. Seattle, WA 98101 (206) 622-0297

That Brown Girl Catering: 801 -26th Ave. E., Seattle, WA 98112
(206) 328-7654 www.thatbrowngirlcatering.com

The Wellington: 4869 Rainier Ave. S. Seattle, WA 98118 (206) 722-8571

Willie's Taste of Soul: 6305 Beacon Ave. S. Seattle, WA 98108
(206) 722-3229

GP Institute of Cosmetology – 3401 Rainier Ave. S. Seattle, WA 98144
(206) 760-3333

Michelle Lang and Still Water: www.michellelang-stillwater.com
www.cdbaby.com/mlsw2
www.myspace.com/michellelangnstillwater

Val Taylor: valseven2003@yahoo.com

Vanessa Love-Davis: rravan_love@hotmail.com

Walter Finch – http://www.myspace.com/walterfinch

ABOUT THE AUTHOR

Dr. Linda Beed earned her Master of Theology (Magna Cum Laude) and Doctorate of Religious Education from A. L. Hardy Academy of Theology. The student writing handbook she developed is a valuable tool that continues to be used by the Academy students. Following six years of teaching Dr. Beed retired from the Academy.

Dr. Beed and her husband reside in Seattle, Washington. They are long-time members of New Covenant Christian Center under the headship of Apostle Tony and Pastor Renee Morris. She is also a nineteen year Youth Minister and currently serves as instructor/administrator of New Covenant's elementary Children's Church.

Overcoming obstacles that told her what she could not achieve, is the inspiration that drives her to help others. Her passion for teaching and writing the Word is what led to the development of On Assignment. Business Unusual is the first installment from the Covenant Series to be published through the company. The primary focus of written, audio, spoken and dramatic presentations from On Assignment, will always be placed on the value God has for us and the fact that regardless our stumbles/circumstances, His love and plans for us does not change.

Dr. Beed serves as co-chair of the Faith Based Arts Conference and co-coordinator for the AA panels of the Romantic Times Convention. She is also a member of the Seattle chapter of the Professional Women of Color Network, and American Christian Fiction Writers.

As a workshop developer and facilitator she has traveled across the country to lend her special blend of teaching and motivation to help inspire and encourage others to walk in their God-ordained purpose.

ALL THINGS WORK TOGETHER

Fred Bennett was a world-class womanizer before giving his life to Christ, and now he struggles to abstain from further sex until marriage. As he transitions from player to prayer, his heart leans towards his friend Yolanda Mason.

Yolanda returns Fred's feelings, but she also likes Raoul Carizales, a private investigator who specializes in finding missing children. When one of her fifth grade students is kidnapped, Raoul is hired to find him. Fred unexpectedly finds himself forced to work with Raoul to solve the case.

As Fred's best friend Max Carson and his wife Donna deal with their new marriage and their increasing role in the ministry of their church, Fred struggles with celibacy, his feelings for Yolanda, temptation from an old girlfriend and the desire to punch Raoul in the nose. His friendships with Max and with Dr. Randy Errell sustain him as he endures.

Fred, Yolanda, Max, Donna, Raoul and Randy are confronted with trials that seem beyond their ability to cope. God's presence in their lives or the lack thereof will make or break their situations.

Maurice Gray is the author of *To Whom Much Is Given* and the sequel *All Things Work Together*. He also wrote *"Traveling Mercies,"* a short story in the Essence best selling anthology *Blessed Assurance* (by Literally Speaking Publishing). Through his publishing company **Write The Vision**, he has published two nonfiction books, *I Really Didn't Mean To Get HIV* by Livingston Lee and *Ocean View* by Fred Gaines. He currently serves on the faculties of the Sandy Cove Christian Writers Conference, the Greater Philadelphia Christian Writers conference and the Faith Based Arts Conference.

Maurice works as an HIV/AIDS counselor/tester at the Beautiful Gate Outreach Center in Wilmington, DE. He belongs to the Wilmington Alumni Chapter of Kappa Alpha Psi Fraternity, Inc. and the Greater Newark Area Toastmasters club. He lives in New Castle, Delaware.

All books available at Amazon.com, Barnes & Nobles.com and on author website: www.writethevision.biz

CPSIA information can be obtained at www.ICGtesting.com
Printed in the USA
BVOW08s1645071113

335548BV00001B/40/A